THE
BROTHERHOOD

Deborah Rae Cota

Other Books by Deborah Rae Cota

The Dante Chronicles:
The Kindred

ISBN/EAN-13: 978-1456380779 / 1456380779

For all those we have lost,
but will forever live on
in our hearts, minds, and souls...

Yesterday...

The Teacher

Every morning, it's the same thing: get up, go to work, pin on my nametag du jour, read the letter before starting my shift.

My friend,

I've asked my sister-in-law, Liz, to send this letter to you in the event of my death; therefore, if you are reading this, I failed.

The Erudite tried to prepare me but their cryptic information, even after you helped decipher it, was insufficient and there was no turning back for me. There are still pieces of the puzzle that we can't place. I don't think the Erudite expected Lilith's plan to be so intricate and wide-spread or knew the depth of devotion of her followers...or perhaps they did and were just as blindsided. You were right. They are many and they are strong.

Enclosed is the key to the Royal vault. Bring the project and my journals; lock them up there. Ask Liz for help past the guards.

Please, I beg of you, do not lose the Master Watch. It must go to the Sentry. The Sentry is the only one with the strength and ability to use it. When the Sentry is appointed, you will know. The key will tell you. You must do whatever is necessary to get the Watch to the Sentry. Our families and our friends' lives depend on it. You know what will happen if the Brotherhood gets the Watch.

I tried so hard to protect you from the horrors that consumed my days and nights. I fear they are yours now to conquer.

It isn't safe for you. Hide: quickly, quietly, carefully. The Brotherhood knows. They will stop at nothing to find you and the watch.

Please...tell my brother I love him very much; I'm sorry to leave him with such a divided nation and so much danger ahead.

It has been my honor and privilege to call you friend.

Stolas Dante

"Professor? Hey! Professor!"

"Oh, good morning, Ignatius!" I answer with enthusiasm, as I fold my letter and put it back in my pocket.

"Good morning, Professor. Looks like you were far away there. What's *her* name?" Ignatius laughs, elbowing me in the ribs; his mousy brown hair still shaped like the pillow he slept on.

I smile, "No, Ignatius, nothing like that." My young co-worker smiles and winks at me, teasingly trying to make something clandestine of a long-existent, tragic secret I keep; I laugh in defense at his good-natured ribbing.

"I read that book, Professor. Took me a while, what with all the extra holiday hours I picked up."

"And what did you think, Ignatius?"

"Well...it was *nothing* like the movie, that's for sure. I mean, I always knew that the doctor had a God complex by his obsession for perfecting the creature; but I never gave any real thought to the loneliness."

"Loneliness?" I ask my young friend as I see a puzzled, yet thoughtful, expression come over not only his face but also the whole of his body.

"Yeah...everyone was so lonely and found it so hard to be alone with themselves. I got the feeling that the doctor not only made his creature for the notoriety and attention but also for a friend. He had no one, really. He married, but he was so obsessed with his creation that even she was lonely. She married, as did most women of that time, to gain identity. The only one who really knew themselves well was the creature."

"Interesting. So, did you enjoy it?" I ask, watching Ignatius' eyes grow large.

"Yeah, Professor...I loved it...but it got me thinking."

"About what?"

"Do you think God is lonely? Is that why people die? So He isn't alone?"

My young friend's observations bring to mind the many people I've lost over the years struggling to keep my promise to Stolas; innocent lives and lost rogue Demons who were lead blindly to ruin. I was just about to answer him and try desperately not to roll into a theological dissertation or reveal my secret by discussing the Dominion and their ways and beliefs when our supervisor's voice bellows over the loud speaker calling for assistance.Taking out my pocket watch, I check the time. "Well, my friend, duty calls," I say with a heavy sigh, taking my time card and lining it up with the arrow to allow the correct time to print.

"I'm re-stocking the Garden Center today; if you need any help with the heavier stuff, you know…mulch, soil, rocks and stuff; come get me. I don't want you lifting anything heavy, Professor."

"Well, thank you, Ignatius. I'll do that," I say, laughing to myself at the nickname he insists on calling me after watching me complete a crossword puzzle in ink during our lunch break. "I have several more book suggestions for you if you're interested?"

"Sure, Professor," Ignatius says, following suit with his own time card. "But I think I'm ready for something light this time. Got anything funny on that list?"

Nodding in agreement, Ignatius and I walk silently towards the Garden Center as our Supervisor, Curtis, is walking out.

"Boy have I got a live one for you, Professor. Lady wants to know something about a Deefer? Um, a Dorffin? No, no, a Bacadoon? A fendahui?"

"A Dieffenbachia?" I correct. "Member of the *Araceae* family and native to the Central and South American rain forest."

"Yeah, that's it," Curtis answers with a wrinkled brow. Taking a stick of Juicy Fruit from his pocket, he unwraps it, tosses the wrapper at Ignatius' feet, and slurs, "Can you help?"

"Certainly. Where is the fair maid now?"

"Look for blue hair, support hose, and be sure to speak loud. Her name's Wendy," Curtis laughs. "What the hell'r you doing just standing around, *Icky*? Get your ass to work!"

Nodding to Ignatius, as he rolls his eyes at the rude moniker and attitude Curtis dispensed, we head out to our assigned area.

Rounding the corner of the citrus tree and succulent display, I find the elderly patron of which Curtis spoke. Smoothing my apron and tugging on my collar to a more comfortable and becoming position, I clear my throat and address the matronly customer, "Madame, I hope you do not have any pets for I fear the Dieffenbachia may be hazardous."

She giggles, "Well, well, well, aren't you just a handsome sight?" She fans her blush and takes a small sheet of blue paper out of her black, patent-leather purse with her white-gloved hand.

"Here," she says, handing me the paper. "This is what I'm looking for. Oh, my, I'm so sorry," the elderly woman says, as she drops the paper.

"No, no, that's quite all right, Madame," I say, stooping to retrieve the blue note that appears to be blank. Flipping the paper over, I feel the grain of the small sheet grab at my fingertips like strong adhesive tape. Tending to my digits I see no mark, sign of peel, or remnant of adhesive; but when I look back at the paper, I notice an interesting development: my fingerprints are starting to appear on the surface like an old Polaroid photo, simple black lines and semi-circles at first until the unique patterns turn to a bright and glowing gold.

"Well, if it isn't *the Teacher*. So good to finally make your acquaintance," the elderly woman says, with a fiery youth in her eyes.

Stepping away from her, "I'm sorry, Madame, you're mistaken...I..."

"The tape never lies," she says quietly, stepping towards me as I try repeatedly to remove the gummy litmus from my hand. "Teacher," the woman says kindly, "you know why I'm here. Give it to me."

"Madame, I'm sorry. My name is not *Teacher* and I don't know what..."

"TEACHER!" the woman barks. "Don't make me do something we'll both regret."

"Regret?" I laugh. "You don't know the meaning of the word. My home was destroyed while my *father lay sleeping in it*. I've had to move, change jobs and my name twelve times because of the path of destruction *your kind* have left behind. My best friend was murdered and numerous innocent lives lost. What *more* do I have to regret?"

"Oh, I'm sure we can find something," the Demon says, her blue hair fading to white to match her pasty skin. Cloudy, pale-blue eyes give way to the more familiar red and sunken orbs, fixed on mine with a steady gaze that I don't dare break; but break I do at a familiar voice crying for my help, and the sound of a motor revving from the rear, delivery-dock area.

"Ignatius?" I whisper to myself, moving away from Wendy. I give a good hard yank on a stray garden hose left behind at closing, tripping her, and causing her to fall face first into a large display of Peruvian Torch cacti.

Running to the receiving area, I grab a seventeen-inch hedge shear from the wall and cautiously turn the corner.

Tied up and lying on the ground behind one of the hydraulic backhoes we rent is Ignatius; the diesel engine grumbles to a halt as Curtis sees me at the roll-up door, and his eyes dart to my right. I can only assume it is Wendy approaching that has caught his attention. Turning just in time to catch her swinging a shovel at my head, I duck as she misses me; and I come up with shears open, snipping off her head with a snap.

"Give us the watch!" the pasty-white Demon yells with Curtis' voice as I watch Wendy's severed head and body render to dust with a shiver. They must have been assisted by a witch or warlock; some sort of glamour spell to make them appear human. Without the Royal-issued heart, there is no other way. Curtis starts up the noisy backhoe and playfully moves it forward and back, making Ignatius scream for help each time he rolls near.

"Such a waste to kill this human for a hunk of metal that means nothing to you. What would Stolas say?" Curtis yells.

Hearing the ticking of my pocket watch and feeling my heart race in counterpoint, my brain fogs with memories of Stolas: coaching me, teaching me all the ways of his people, passing along all the knowledge he'd attained over the years.

"*Teacher*, it doesn't have to be this way. Simply give me the Watch and this will all be…over. You know, Stolas really should have thought twice before healing you that day. We can *smell you* wherever you go."

"LET IGNATIUS GO!"

"GIVE US THE WATCH!"

"You know I can't!"

"Your call, Teacher," Curtis says as he revs the motor

"Professor, help me?" Ignatius cries.

"Here!" I yell, tossing my pocket watch to the demon.

"That wasn't so hard, was it, Teacher?"

"Let Ignatius go!" I demand.

The Demon looks at my terrified friend, then at me. He gives me a look of forlorn and understanding that dissipates quickly into a maniacal grin and laughs, "I don't think so, *Teacher*."

In that instant, I act fast; reaching for the detonator I keep attached to the back of my nametag, I press the button. The decoy watch I've always carried; one of the many failed experiments Stolas and I saved; makes a ticking and popping sound before it explodes in Curtis' hands, rendering his arms to bloody stumps and blowing bits of bone and metal into his face and eyes, blinding him. Grabbing the shovel from beside Wendy's ashes, I throw it like a javelin at Curtis; bursting the windshield and hitting him in his neck, taking his head off with a thud, but it was too late; Curtis had enough time to shift the vehicle into reverse before detonation. His foot turns to ash and the backhoe rolls backward over my young friend, crushing him into the blacktop and bringing his cries of help to an immediate halt. Unable to look at the site, my vision completely drenched in furious tears, I pace, trying to think of what to do. Hearing the voices of other employees and customers coming up quickly behind me, I trust my gut instincts and act.

I run.

Uncertain of where I'm going, I just run; but stop as I reach the end of the parking lot because my stomach has reached my throat, and I can't keep it down any longer. Wiping my face with the skirt of my apron, I disgustedly untie and remove it, crumpling it into a ball and tossing it behind the spider-riddled Japanese Box bush that surrounds the perimeter.

Regaining my senses, I walk to the bus stop as an old AC Transit creaks and belches to the curb. Not knowing where the bus will take me, I board, flash my pass, take an empty seat, and watch for any familiar street close enough to my apartment complex. The bus stops at the Hayward BART station; I exit the back doors and quietly make my way home, reliving the past with every step.

It seems like yesterday when the letter arrived. I was living in Berkeley at the time; a librarian at the public library, voluntarily teaching people to read in my off hours; never feeling a need to look over my shoulder and never fearing for my life or the lives of those around me. Now, another innocent life has been lost because of me. How many more have to die before…? Arriving at the door to my complex, I search for my key to open the glass security door; but I meet my neighbor as she is leaving with her laundry.

"Howdy, Neighbor, are you all right? Those people workin' you too hard over there?" Amelia, my neighbor from across the hall, asks; her brown eyes full of concern.

"No, I'm, I'm not feeling well. Came home early," I reply, holding the door open for her.

"Oh, I thought perhaps it had to do with whatever is glowing there under your shirt."

Looking down, I see what Amelia has noticed. Embarrassed, I turn away and say, "Oh, that. That's just a new children's toy I'm working on. It's…"

"Toy?" Amelia giggles. "That's no toy! What is it...*Teacher*? Does it have anything to do with *the Watch*?"

Trying not to react, I press the elevator button; the lighted indicator arrow doesn't glow in acknowledgement to my request so I move hastily towards the stairs

"Why don't you just give us the Watch, *Teacher?*"

Refusing to acknowledge Amelia, I reach for the door handle; but she beats me there, the lovely brown of her eyes replaced by their actual blood red. She grabs at my shirt where the key lays nestled, but I shove her away; and her laundry flies through the air as she falls. Losing my balance, I stumble to the wall behind me. Feeling the fire alarm, I pull the white tab firmly. The apartment building lobby fills with the deafening screech; Amelia covers her ears and glares as I look back before escaping through the stairwell door and race up the stairs to my apartment.

Arriving on the third floor and without looking back, I run to my door while neighboring tenants stampede in the opposite direction. Opening the door, I step inside my barren abode and breathe. Turning the deadbolt, I realize a warm pulsation on my chest. I reach inside my shirt and withdraw the key that hangs there from a burgundy satin ribbon; but as soon as it's freed from the confines of the cloth, it shoots like an arrow straight out in front of me, tugging me urgently in a northerly direction.

Walking along with the pull of the key, I step out through the sliding glass doors to the balcony. Turning to the east, the key continues to point north. Turning to my right again and facing west, the ribbon starts to choke me. I realize I will need to be careful with my little brass divining rod; the pull is strong now; but I fear the closer I get to my pre-ordained destination, the pull will be uncontrollable. Death by skeleton key is not how I envision going.

Still happily toying with my compass, a single explosive sound echoes from my front door, rattling the walls of the empty rooms. I tuck the key back under my shirt, tiptoe across the floor, and quietly open the hallway closet. The distant blast of a horn tells me that fire trucks will be arriving soon when another violent sound shakes the room around me, and a familiar voice calls to me from outside the door.

"Teacher! Teacher! Give us the Watch, and we'll leave you alone...we promise!" Maniacal laughter follows, confirming my belief of who it is.

"You were right. They are strong."

Stolas' affirmation clouds my heart and mind; but the fire alarm's abrupt halt brings me back, as well as the thunderous pounding on my door that splinters it from top to bottom. Stepping inside the walk-in closet, I grab the ready and waiting backpack and quickly make my way from room to room grabbing my daily necessities. Changing out of my work shoes and into my hiking boots, I make my way to the kitchen and take a gallon-size, zip-lock bag full of dried fruits and jerky and four frozen bottles of water. I toss them in my backpack and grab my fleece-lined denim jacket from the coat hooks in the hallway facing the front door. Another resounding thud makes the crack larger. A giant, red eyeball peers in at me through the jagged shards.

"Peekie-boo!" Amelia giggles.

"Here we go again," I think aloud, as I feel the warmth of the key wriggling to be free. *Hang on, little guy, I'll get you home.*

Taking the grey, wool muffler that waited patiently beneath my jacket on the hook, I wrap it around my neck and tie a loose knot to protect the key from spying eyes as I head back to the balcony. Peering over the edge, I see the firefighters climbing back into their rig and readying to leave the false alarm as I step up on the ledge. Three running leaps across my neighbors' balconies and another off the building down into San Lorenzo Creek, and I'm free; one of the benefits of Demon blood in one of the fastest wide receivers ever to wear the blue and gold and grace the field of battle at Memorial Stadium with the Cal Bears. That was about the time I met Stolas. It was summer, and I was just about to start attending UC Berkeley on a football scholarship.

I was born in Birmingham, Alabama; don't remember my mom much, but she decided for me at a very young age that I would be better off with my dad in California. She packed me up with my Aunt Penelope and asked her to drop me off in Piedmont on her way to Hollywood where she was going to be a movie star. After I arrived here, Dad really didn't know what to do with me. I was always bored and had a knack for getting into trouble, which is also how and where I learned to run…fast. So, he got me a library card and hoped my love of reading would keep me busy there.

I'd run there after school every day, then run home and read whatever I borrowed; after I'd read all the books in my grade level there and the librarians caught me reading books they felt were too mature for me, I was only allowed in if Dad accompanied me. So from then on when I wasn't in school, I would spend the day in Dad's shop watching and learning his craft.

Raleigh's Novelty Clocks was a popular place. Not only because Dad could fix any clock or watch ever made; which he could; but also because of Dad's special creations: alarm clocks for children that allowed them to wake up to their mother's voice, a whimsical cuckoo clock that had a mailman being chased by a bad dog at the strike of the hour, and everyone's favorite: a giant globe with a small time piece for every time zone which housed a hidden, built-in day counter so that on New Year's Eve each zone that passed in the new year would be welcomed in with *Auld Lang Syne*.

Customers and local shop keepers from all walks of life would come in, and I talked to all of them. They found me personable and a quick study, and many of them would ask Dad if I could work for them sometime. Dad left it up to me. I saw it as a chance to learn. Basically speaking, I've been working all my life and learning every minute.

I started with Mr. Lee, selling fresh meat and vegetables off his truck; and then run home smelling of bacon and bringing bags of fresh fruits and vegetables to Dad. Then, Mr. Fernandes asked me to help at his gas station where I learned the finer points of automobile repair and maintenance. Every evening after work, I'd run home and work on Dad's old blue Plymouth Valiant. Upon learning what an industrious worker I was, while still able to keep up with my studies, my eighth-grade algebra teacher, Mrs. Thrower, recommended me as a student tutor through a program started by UC Berkeley when I entered high school. This was my first taste of teaching, and I loved it. I gave grades to the students that were averaged with their own; I was paid fifty dollars a month; and earned an 'A' on my report card for a job well done.

Finding what I really wanted to do with my life was exhilarating but posed a problem. There was no way Dad was going to be able to put me through college on what he made at the shop. I was on the track team then; and during a competition, the football coach, Mr. Pacheco, who was also my American History teacher, came up to me and asked if I'd ever considered playing.

"Lot's of scholarships available to the right person," he told me. I knew it was the only way.

From that day, I ran: to school, from school, to practice, from practice, to work, and then all the way home to eat dinner with Dad and swap stories about each other's day. My speed caught the eye of a local scout, and I earned the full-ride I'd hoped for college.

During the summer before my Freshman year at Cal, I promised Dad I'd spend it with him and help at the store. It was an old shop in Piedmont when I first moved here, and it was getting older. The cathedral ceiling was in good shape, but the oak floors needed a good spit and polish, and the bathroom had a leaky sink. Finally having the time to devote to it, I told Dad I'd be right back and took a quick run to downtown Oakland.

When I arrived at Four-Star Hardware, the owner, Mr. Kim, said he didn't have what I needed but was sure that Buckman's up the street did. He told me to be careful because they'd had some trouble with muggings in the area. I thanked him and headed out. I'd only gone a few blocks when I heard footsteps coming up fast behind me and someone yell, "Your kind don't belong here!"

Two kids my age, with dirty, greasy hair and clothes to match, tackled me from behind. The older of the two was pounding at my midsection with his fists, while the other danced and howled waiting for his turn, spewing obscenities and derogatory expressions about the color of my skin. I'd had minor incidents before because I'm black, but never anything this blatant or this violent.

Getting my wind back, I constricted my body and flipped the assailant off of me; but when I tried to stand, I felt something snap at the back of my head and then everything went black.

When I woke, I was laying on a burgundy-velvet couch in front of a stone fireplace, alight with a blazing fire. The lavish room was striking, and the fire's light danced off the curio cabinets and chandeliers. Sitting up, I felt light-headed and immediately reached for the back of my head fully expecting to feel my brain hanging out but there was nothing; I looked down at my clothes and found the signatures of my cowardly attackers. It was the only reason I could come up with to explain the five bloody and burned holes in my white, button-down shirt; they had a concealed weapon. Peeking inside the round, open spaces, afraid of what I'd see, I found no wound or blood.

Was it a nightmare? Did I die? Is this heaven?

"No, it isn't a nightmare; and you didn't die…and believe me…you're not in heaven," the silver-haired man said, walking in with a white, long-sleeved button-down shirt over his arm. "Here, I think this should fit," he said, handing me the shirt. Looking at him incredulously, the man laughed and stepped back. "Please, forgive my manners. My name is Stolas. Stolas Dante. You'd been mortally wounded by those two human *rogues*. I rescued you, made sure your attackers were properly taken care of, and brought you here to my father's home until you are ready to return. Our physicians saw to your wounds. You lost a lot of blood, and I had to give you some of mine. I'm afraid that shirt is a lost cause."

The man, Stolas, stood with his hand extended to me; and I didn't know what to do. I was in such a state of shock that I was rendered speechless. Finally coming to terms with all that had happened, I slowly raised my hand and shook his; there was a twinkle in his eyes and a warmth in his voice that reminded me of Dad when he would get an idea in his head; and then, somehow, I wasn't scared anymore.

Stolas and I talked: about The Dominion, Earth, who I was, who he was, how he was told to look for me. Incredible stories to believe; but believe

I did and still do. We talked for what seemed like hours; yet, when he returned me to my home through the mirrored portal, it had only been half the time.

"Stolas, I...I have so many questions, there's so much I need to know. This mirror for instance, how...?"

"My friend, you know how the mirror works; I explained to you that I gave you my blood. You know what I know. Take a deep breath, relax, and then ask yourself what you need to know."

Doing as I was told, the information just came to me; I understood clearly the physics of the portal and watched as a huge smile came to Stolas' face. He patted me on the back, told me we would meet again, and promised that all my questions would be answered as they came.

And so began my years of study with the man whom I called friend.

Upon returning to Dad's shop, I fixed the leaky sink in record time because I instinctively knew exactly what to do. Never bought the parts I needed, just used the same old ones; fixing them with spare copper coil from Dad's equipment; coercing the parts to do exactly what was needed. It was like magic. Dad couldn't figure out how I did it, and I couldn't find the words to tell him.

Standing in the middle of the creek bed, I turn in a complete circle making certain I'm alone. Freeing the key from its safe confines, it points north as before. Returning it to safety, I feel the soft, silkiness of the ribbon and remember the girl that left it behind and then wonder if she made it to safety. Putting the memory away for another time, I take a deep breath and start walking.

Cities look so different from the watersheds. The wildlife gaze at me like they, too, think I'm crazy for being here. Homeless people, who have set up camp in the shadier places, call to me for cash or something to share. Feeling sorry for them and the position they are in, I long for the time I spent in The Dominion. No homeless there: all are cared for, protected and well, with food on their table, a roof over their head, work to give them purpose. The Demon are not human, yet most of them show more humanity than my own kind.

So many years have passed since then; not a day goes by that I don't think of Stolas, smile and thank him for all he did for me. Not only did he save my life, but he also brought to me an education and a level of understanding and breadth that I never believed possible.

Having always been a bright kid, I learned quickly with Stolas' influence; not to mention his blood. There is nothing I can't learn. Read a book once; I know the subject backwards and forwards. Listen to a recorded language lesson; I can speak it fluently by the end. Show me something new; anything new; I'm a master within hours.

Except for snake wrangling...

Don't know why? Just don't like the things. *They give me the creeps!* The way they slither, sway and wiggle around...Big ones, little ones, all the colors of the rainbow. Some with fangs filled with deadly venom; others that quietly strike out and drain the life out of their prey, squeezing until there is nothing left with every contraction.

Kind of reminds me of Lilith.

I wonder if that's why I don't like them? Because they remind me of her? But Lilith didn't just give me the creeps, she gave me nightmares. Always said she'd be the death of my friend. *I hate being right sometimes.*

Stolas knew that kid of hers wasn't his; broke his heart to confess that to me. He wanted so much for Corson to be his son; raised him as his own none the less. But Lilith got her dirty claws in him early, and he was ruined. All of his childlike innocence shattered before he ever had a chance at a good life.

I wonder what kind of man he grew up to be?

Walking along the San Lorenzo Creek bed, I find myself at a fork in the path. Checking in with my little brass friend, he directs me to the path on the left and on to Chabot Creek. A few steps in, I find a pathway that leads up and out to the street. Looking around to confirm I'm alone, I take the path and find myself at a familiar picnic area. Walking past the small empty parking lot of Carlos Bee Park, I find a lone picnic table to rest; reach in my backpack and grab a bottle of water, drink the melt off, and then exchange it in the pack for my journal.

After receiving Stolas' letter, I started keeping a journal: collecting maps of every city I lived in, record of every fake name I used, notes of all the jobs I held; storing it in the backpack along with a few hundred-dollar gift cards, socks, underwear, first-aid kit, Mylar blanket, sunscreen, bug repellant, and anything else I could think of that I'd need while on the road; any road; waiting and watching for the future Sentry of The Dominion to be appointed.

Opening the journal to a blank page, I sort through the maps for the one that shows Castro Valley and the surrounding areas; including the waterways and their local footpaths and bike trails. Recalling the direction I was standing when the key first reacted, I run my finger along the veiny lines; waiting for a reaction from my little, brass, traveling companion. Drawing my hand north and tracing over Danville and Walnut Creek nets nothing; when I start drifting my hand a little to the left, I feel the key grow warm. Searching further, I veer my touch a little to the right over Dublin and San Ramon but the key grows cold; as well as when I drift far left over Daly City. Returning to my initial direction, I feel the warm metal awaken. Continuing in the North-West direction, I feel the key start to vibrate. Casting my hand further and further on, the faster and more pronounced the vibration becomes until suddenly the key's gyrations become so violent that it jumps from the safety of my shirt and muffler and points vehemently to where my hand rests on the map; pulling so hard that my head and shoulders go with it, and I slap myself in the face with my journal.

"Berkeley? The Sentry is in Berkeley? All right, little guy. I'll get you home."

Making some notes in my journal, I replace the maps, close it up and return it to the safety of my backpack. Opening the front pocket, I retrieve a piece of beef jerky from the freezer bag and toss it in my mouth before strapping my pack back on and tucking the key back under my clothes. I take a few steps back towards the path to continue my trek through the waterways but hear a rustle in the trees followed by a subtle clicking sound like castanets. A chill runs over me, and I decide it better to stay on populated streets for a while. Haven't heard anymore about the body parts being found, so things might be a little safer now. Then again…

I wonder if that's why the key awoke? Did the Sentry stop it? Was it Demonic? Lower-level? Mid-Range? From the description of the pieces and the frequency of occurrences, I'd almost say it was Vorax; but it couldn't be; they were outlawed eons ago according to Stolas.

Stolas taught me all about the many dimensions of Demons. From the hierarchy to the gutter slime, they range in variety just like humans, but evil is evil, no matter the size, shape, color, or race for that fact. I learned that first hand long ago.

Midday; the sun is high and the air crisp and clean which means the New Year's Eve revelers will need to wear a sweater or two tonight. Exiting the park, I turn right and head to Redwood Road and a quaint, little town called Castro Valley.

Walking along the cracked, gray sidewalk, lost in my memories of conversations passed, I again hear a rustling from a nearby picket fence, consumed by ivy. The same clicking sounds I heard moments ago but clearer; stronger than before with a response of an even deeper, sharper pop; like knuckles cracking; coming from a twitching evergreen across the driveway of a beige, stucco house. I slow my gait but don't stop. My mind is a blur, roaming the archives of information provided me in a single drop of blood. Pieces fall into place creating an image like an entry in an encyclopedia that instantly speeds my pace as I look both ways and chance jaywalking to the next cross street. Stepping lively, but not running, I keep my head up and eyes open; recalling the maps in my mind's eye. Zeroing in on where I need to be, I pick up the pace. The clicking is near. Not too close; close enough that the hair on the back of my neck stands on end.

Cautiously surveying the area, I check for witnesses; and upon seeing that I am alone on the long, residential stretch of Orange Street, I veer left where it turns into Lake Chabot Road and make a run for the steel overpass to Norbridge Road.

On my way up the ramp to the crossway, I see the congested freeway traffic below; no doubt due to the inconveniently placed fluorescent cones, courtesy of Cal-Trans, bogging-up travelers and commuters alike. Slowing to a gentle jog, I startle again at a grating noise reminiscent of fingernails tapping cheap crystal; stops and starts as if keeping up with me but not wanting to be obvious. Testing my theory, I sprint to the middle of the tube, reach in my pocket for my bottle of water, twist off the top and stop. Listening closely, I turn quickly in the direction of the tapping and flick the open bottle; splashing icy water in the direction of the clickety-clack noise.

The Speculari, no longer able to camouflage himself by appearing to be the concrete or the cyclone fencings, sizzles and screams as the water dissolves its crustaceous, rock-like casing to reveal its soft and slimy, pink under body. Its eight, spindly legs dissolve to mere ooze and slide through the cyclone enclosure, falling onto an unsuspecting motorist below. Tires screech and metal hits metal; poor soul, didn't mean for that to happen.

Spending far too much time watching the Spec die like a slug in salt, I again hear the clicking sound. Looking up, I relax my eyes as if looking at an optical illussion and catch the movement of a bigger beast.

Capping the bottle, I turn and run full speed to the end of the caged tunnel and take the ramp down to the street below. Taking one quick glance left, I see my destination; a look to my right, my reason to flee, as the Spec tries to blend in with the color and texture of the cement floor. He moves along with three smaller companions as they creep about on the metal roof and sides. Looking more like a child's creation from an old erector set, their multi-jointed legs allow them fluidity and speed; yet, something about their gait reminds me of a marionette.

Running out of the tube, I use the cars parked alongside Norbridge Road and take four giant leaps down into the waterway known as Castro Valley Creek. Waiting at the bottom of the waterway beneath a protective concrete overhang, I hear the familiar clicking again. I look up at the railing I sailed over and see the grey, spindly legs of the bigger Spec as it feels the air, trying to sense my presence. Castanets rattle and again are responded to with a deep and scolding pop. They are communicating; tapping their sharp teeth together as if using Morse code: closing, opening, stretching their mouths for emphasis.

Stolas taught me simple phrases: greetings, warnings, how to ask directions when lost (if you're ever lost in the Dominion, ask a Spec, they know all the short cuts and the best places to get cheap food). But Specs are small-minded, heartless, little thieves and won't break a nail if there isn't something in it for them. So, naturally, they're spies for whoever holds the biggest purse; in this case, it's got to be *The Brotherhood.*

The sound of rapid-fire clicks and clacks rises from above as the smaller Specs tap their sharp nails impatiently on the concrete ledge. The repetitive pattern touches my ear and pieces fall into place.

"Rain is coming!"

"Rain is coming!"

"Rain is coming!"

I gaze up at the winter sky and smile at fluffy life preservers floating into place overhead.

A series of stern pops grows, drowning out the annoying clickety-clack, *"Silence, silence, SILENCE!"*

The large, spindly legs disappear from the ledge; and the familiar scratching of the Speculari's nails on the asphalt tells me they're moving away but not far. Stepping out slowly from the wall, I listen carefully and feel a single drop fall on my cheek.

"Thank you," I whisper to the sky.

Draining what's left of my first bottle of water and weapon of choice against my current foe, I stoop down and fill the bottle from the last rainfall collected in the water way; return the cap, put the bottle in my jacket pocket, and start walking to the far end of the creek in the gentle, winter rain.

Once at the end of the fence surrounding the creek, I climb up, out and then over into the backyard of a tan duplex where a young woman is covering her hot tub.

"Get out!" she screams, grabbing a rock from a landscaped fountain area, hurling it at me.

"I'm sorry, please, forgive me…I'm leaving!" I call out, ducking the rock and a rubber dog toy.

"Goddamned homeless," she mutters under her breath. "Get a job, you bum!"

"Have a nice day!" I say, laughing to myself; shaking my head at the woman's reaction. Watching her chase me, all arms and legs, throwing anything and everything she can grab, reminds me more and more of the spidery Speculari chasing me; both chattering away and both moving in all directions; the stream of obscenities now flowing from her lips only proves she is just as heartless and narrow of mind.

Brushing off the remnants of the clods of dirt from my jacket and pants, leaves streaks of mud from the still falling misty rain. I continue walking down Rutledge Road to the highly populated, main thoroughfare of Castro Valley Boulevard. Remembering the map and feeling my little brass buddy stir, I make a left and head for Lake Chabot Road.

Walking the long stretch of road past numerous doctors' offices and then a couple of hospitals, I remember Dad's last days and grow angry. I was living in Berkeley, working at the public library, waiting to hear if I'd been accepted to Cal's Graduate School of Education when I received a call at work from an unknown neighbor of Dad's who must have been outside in the wind because he was shouting. His name was Galen, and he told me Dad had slipped and fallen down the stairs in front of his apartment. Before I could thank him, the phone went dead. I explained the situation to my boss, Neal, and then left to get Dad.

By the time I got there, an ambulance had arrived; and they were readying Dad for transport. I parked my car (I was driving Dad's Plymouth then) and ran to his side.

"Oh, Son! Such nonsense! All this fuss! I fell…that's all. I'm fine. Really! I'm fine," Dad said, with a wince as the paramedics lifted the gurney to extend the legs and roll him to the ambulance doors.

"Are you Galen?" the young, tall, red-headed paramedic asked.

"No," I replied, noticing the multiple band-aids on his hands and face.

"Well, we got a call from Galen to come to this address. Your dad took a bad fall. I think he's fine, but we'll take him in for a good look over."

"Hey, it's okay, kid," the other paramedic says to me, as he pats me on the back and takes my hand in his to shake it. "I'm Raffa. This is Nate. We're gonna take good care of your Pops. Don't you worry. You can follow us there."

Seeing my dad there on the gurney, he looked so small and helpless; not at all like the giant man who welcomed me into the dark and magical clock store so long ago. He looked up at me and winked; smiling and laughing with Raffa and Nate like they were old friends as they retracted the legs of the gurney and lifted him in to the ambulance.

Raffa and Nate were right. Dad was fine; better than fine. He raced me to my car after the doctor released him; not even a sign of arthritis in his hands or the muscle spasms he'd get in his back from hovering over his projects. I brought him home to my place and made him promise to move in with me. He agreed over a grilled two-pound steak, twice-baked potatoes, fresh-steamed asparagus with citrus zest, and one of the finest bottles of Pinot Noir made in Sonoma; all thanks to the week he let me spend with a young sous chef named César from a bistro up the street. Dad was the best roommate I ever had; as a child and as an adult; I couldn't have asked for more. The day the letter arrived, I'd come by Dad's shop to have lunch.

"This came for you, Son," Dad said, handing me the envelope while biting into his chicken-salad sandwich.

Taking the envelope, I noticed the return address was blank but the handwriting familiar. I hadn't heard from Stolas in days; the last time I did, he was tense and short with me; apologizing for his poor attitude constantly. I set the letter aside and enjoyed my lunch with Dad but had a gut feeling of dread over the letter.

"You know…," Dad said, "I got a letter like that once. Scared the hoopty out of me."

"Yeah?"

"Yeah. It told me I had a son and that he was coming to live with me," Dad recalled, looking at me with that ornery twinkle in his eye. "Second best day of my life."

"*Second best?* What was the first?" I asked curiously.

"The day you walked in that door."

When I returned to the library after lunch, my boss was gone; and a new shift manager named Timothy was there. The letter was in my back pocket driving me insane. It was a quiet day so I spent my time in the stacks shelving books. Everywhere I went, Timothy followed.

"Don't I know you from somewhere?"

I shook my head no and smiled.

"Yeah, yeah…sure I do," he said.

Shaking my head no again, I felt something in his presence that was making me edgy.

"Oh, come on…sure I do. You're the *watchmaker's kid.*"

He had my attention.

"Yeah, I knew I knew you," he said, as he started to walk away. "Your picture was in Stolas' crap. He's dead you know. She took care of it. Looks like I won the pool. I found you first."

My mind was racing. Demons, especially the ones on her side, are known for lying; but considering how strange Stolas was acting, and the fact that I'd not heard from him…

"I'm not lying; and yes, I'm on *her* side. And you haven't heard from him because he's …"

"Dead. I know. I heard you the first time."

Timothy feigned amusement at my displeasure and then quickly jumped to his main reason for talking to me, "I've gone through your locker, and the box of reading materials you use to teach with; but *it* isn't there."

Rolling the book cart out of the aisle and back to the check out counter, Timothy followed me as he sucked something out from between his teeth.

"Well, *Teacher*…where is it?"

"Where's what?"

Timothy looked into me; past my eyes, deep into my mind, so hard that the red of his real eyes burned through. The mind reader struggled to see past the mental roadblock Stolas taught me to raise against his kind.

"Envision a brick wall, a mountain or a boulder; anything impenetrable by the naked eye," Stolas would say.

"Well, shit! Aren't you talented?" Timothy mocked. "But not *that* talented. We know where your dad's shop is, and we know where you live. Well...where you *used* to live."

Shoving the cart hard into Timothy's groin, he let out a wail and doubled over in pain as I hurdled the counter, heading for the fire exit by the parking lot.

Passing the children's room, I turned the corner to the reference section and found my boss, Neal, seated at his desk with his head propped upon his closed fist. I called his name quietly as I tiptoed near; once, twice, three times I called until I got close enough to realize why he didn't answer. The desktop blotter was red with blood; the calendar printed on it no longer visible. Cautiously I moved around to the front of the desk and saw his face; fear and surprise frozen in his eyes from when his throat was cut; no doubt by Timothy.

"He died quickly. I don't think there was any pain. Well, there wasn't for *me* anyway," Timothy laughed, from somewhere amongst the shelves.

Remembering Stolas' tutelage, I turned off my human mind and acted strictly from my transfused Demon instincts; the boiling, electrified blood coursing through my veins; I became the primal beast that every mammal is, deep down, incarnate.

Slipping out of my shirt, shoes and socks, I left them in a trail leading to my target of choice; tearing the shirt to pieces to make Timothy's destination exact.

"Oh! Are we playing *a game*? I *love* games!" Timothy said, gleefully skipping about as I watched him from my perch, high above on the rail of the upstairs audio equipment area; moving carefully and quietly about. Timothy moved into range, picking up the pieces as he walked along and impatiently stepped directly on my target. "All right, I'm here. Where's my prize? Come on out and give us a kiss, big boy!"

Silently, I dropped down on him; crashing to the ground, he tried to roll me over to gain the advantage; but I was bigger, stronger, and was acting with pure, blinding, white-hot anger. Pinning him to the ground with my left foot in the middle of his back, I knelt down on my right knee beside him and then wrapped my right arm tightly around his neck; wrenching his upper body up and off the ground. Grabbing my right hand with my left, I pull; Timothy whimpers, then starts to choke out a laugh.

"Killing me won't change anything," he whispered, straining for breath and grabbing onto my right arm when I pulled tighter. "There will always be more to follow me. Thousands!" Stepping harder on Timothy's back, I felt something pop under my bare foot. "Why, even now, as you waste your time here with me, there are others waiting in the wings to work towards the cause. They'll search and hunt and take care of all the loose ends. You know what we want…where do you think we'd look first?"

Momentarily, I allowed my guard down. I'd no idea what he wanted; what *they* wanted.

"You mean to tell me you still haven't read that damned letter? Let's see…I'll just give you the highlights…My friend, blah, blah, blah, in the event of my death, blah, blah, I failed, blah, blah…HIDE. THE. WATCH."

Timothy was speaking clearer. I'd relaxed the pressure I was applying; getting lost in my own head. Stolas dead. Hide the Watch. Where would they look…?

"Oh, he figured it out," Timothy sighed, with more joy than I could stand but grunted when I got back in the game and tightened my grip; decided my next move.

"Well, what will you…?" was all Timothy got out when I snapped his neck. Focusing my energy like Stolas taught me, I gave his head one more, good, hard twist and off it came. Within seconds, he was dust.

Using the fire exit in front of me, I hit the door running, set off the alarm, and headed to my car; turned the engine over and made my way to Piedmont.

I arrived in record time, only to find out Dad closed the shop early. Relieved, but not at all comfortable, my mind started spinning again. Timothy knew about the letter...*the letter*.

Took the letter from my back pocket, opened it and read it for the first time. Unable to believe the contents, I read it again and again and again and...

"Protect you from the horrors..."

Lilith? The Brotherhood? His family...My family.

"Fear, they are yours now to conquer."

I shoved the letter and brass key back in the envelope and back into my pocket; jumped in my car and raced home to Berkeley.

So strange...How remembering the past; so long ago; can all at once seem so recent, like yesterday. Makes time fly, especially while walking in the rain a couple of miles. The hood to my jacket is up, and I don't recall pulling it on. The rain, starting to stop now, leaves me vulnerable to the Specs. Pulling my hood down, I listen carefully for the familiar clickety-clack.

Silence.

Needing to stay close to water, I purposely chose a path keeping me close to it, including Lake Chabot Park, especially since it's New Year's Eve. There should be few, or at least not as many, park goers there.

Entering the gate, I am alongside a couple of runners who, from the looks of them, would be out running no matter the day, temperature, or chance of precipitation. It's late afternoon, the sun is just starting on its regular descent beyond the horizon, and my ears pick up the familiar clicking from before; upon further investigation I find it to be nothing more than a weary, old fisherman having trouble with his reel. I smile at him; he shakes his head.

"Damned old thing!"

"May I?" I ask, putting my hands out to take the antique fly reel.

"Sure...but I think it's hopeless," the old man said sadly. "It's my favorite. My *sister* gave it to me for my birthday."

From his demeanor and the emphasis he placed on the word 'sister', I gather he loves her very much; the uneasiness in him that the reel may be beyond help is more than evident.

Tinkering with the reel, I use a small screwdriver, borrowed from the old fellow's open tackle box. My familiarity with the model and its more than fussy tension wheel comes from years of fixing Dad's on our yearly fishing trips to Truckee. Without fail, we'd settle ourselves down on the shores of the little-known river, ready our lines, cast off…and a stream of the funniest, made-up obscenities (the man never once cursed in front of me) would come flowing from my dad. I'd hold my rig out to him, and he'd hand me his saying, "Fickle little thing. Just like the woman who gave it to me."

It was the only time he'd ever mention my mom.

After adjusting the tension and the alignment, I spun the old man's reel and the line fed smoothly and evenly. Handing his rod back to him, I say the same thing I'd always tell my dad, "There. She just needed a little attention."

The man laughs, "Just like the woman that gave it to me."

Smiling at the déjà vu moment, I suddenly panick. The familiarity and feeling of comfort made me wry; all the other Demons knew stuff about me, too.

"Is there something wrong?" the man asks.

"No, just running late," I say, looking at the sun's position. I hand the screwdriver back to the old fellow, "Happy New Year, Sir!"

Backing away and turning to go, the old man calls out to me, "Thanks! Happy New Year to you, too! Be careful on those paths, there's been some strange things happening there lately."

Turning around, I wave to the old guy as he gets in his boat and paddles away from shore.

Jogging at a steady clip, I head out along the West Shore Trail, staying as close to water's edge as I can, watching for anything that moves and listening for anything out of the ordinary. Even though I'm keeping my body temperature up by jogging, a chill runs down my back. Somewhere near, there is a fire; a nearby home, maybe a campsite; the smell of smoke disturbs me. I pick up my pace to get beyond it, but the faster I run the stronger the smell. My throat burns; eyes tear up and make it hard to see. Still running along the lake's shore, but it looks and feels like then…like *that day*.

I had to park several blocks away; the Fire Department blocked my street; so I parked and ran, dodging police and other firefighters, telling everyone that tried to stop me that my dad was in the house; repeating myself over and over as I tried to get closer. Smoke filled my lungs as I fell to my knees; eyes stinging from tears when I saw my home rendered to nothing more than charred remains, not knowing if my dad was in there or where the Demons were. Flinching as I felt an arm go around my shoulders and an oxygen mask cover my nose and mouth. It was Nate, looking at me with eyes filled with sorrow. Raffa stepped in front of me as a covered gurney rolled by. I moved side to side to see beyond the big man, but he shifted feet and blocked the view.

"I'm sorry. There was nothing we could do," Raffa said, as he knelt down in front of me. "Is there anyone we can call for you?"

Shaking my head, I stared at the ground and watched the feet of Raffa and Nate shuffle around me. Another set of shoes joined them and then a male voice asked, "This the next of kin?"

Nate answered, "Yes."

Raffa touched my arm, "The police need to speak with you. Are you able...?"

"He's my father!" I snapped; feeling as if I was abruptly awakened from a nightmare, when in reality I was awakening in one.

"I'm very sorry for your loss, Son, but..."

Ripping off the oxygen mask I yelled, "Don't call me son! I'm not your son! The only men...the only *man* who had the right to call me that is dead!"

They're both dead, I thought to myself.

"All right, all right, let's just calm down. Now, we just want to ask about your relationship to Timothy? Your neighbors said your father came here with him. He told everyone he was an old college buddy."

"Timothy is *no buddy of mine*! He's the devil! He's evil! You hear me? Evil!"

"Yes, I hear you. Do you know where he ...?"

"He's gone. Disappeared. He did this. HE DID THIS!"

"I see. When was the last time you saw him? Do you know his last name? Last known address? Anything you can tell...?"

"No last name. No address. He's taken everything from me. Everything! And he's, gone."

Reliving the memory of that day, I can feel the heat of anger rising in my body; throat, dry and tired just like that day; and my face, warm and wet from tears. The faint sound of snapping twigs catches my ear, and I stop. A large squirrel is dancing across the path, looking for any snacks it can find. I smile as it scurries away. Continuing on my journey, I look at the long path ahead of me. Tree branches blow in the light breeze coming in from the West, and their movements play tricks with my eyes.

Young, lithe trees reach across the pathway to their larger siblings creating a canopy of winter-barren branches and twigs; moving and swaying with the breeze, but also bucking and twitching to a rhythm all their own. I hear a series of clicks, followed by one loud pop, and then I stop.

The Specs have found me. Disguising themselves amongst the canopy of branches, the trunks of the trees, the toadstools at the base, and the rotting leaves turning to mulch on the ground; hiding in plain sight, nervously unable to stay quiet for long, working together to lay in wait for me to walk beneath their trap.

Taking three steps back, I watch the living canopy twitch and shake with anticipation as it follows me with equal pace. I pull the bottle of rainwater from my jacket, and wield it in front of me like a gun.

Nothing. They don't move. Obviously aware that my one bottle of water is no match for the multitudes of *them*.

In my mind, I toy with an escape; which only really consists of turning around and running for my life; when my peripheral vision picks up another movement to my right. I chance a glance.

As if a giant vacuum took aim at the lake's surface, a wall of water grows straight up in the air then curves itself over, ever so slightly, towards the team of Specs. The critters' canopy trembles with fear, watching every drop of the reverse waterfall.

"Hey! Hey, Mister! Mister! Over here!" the familiar voice of the elderly man says, booming over the sound of the fall.

Stepping closer to the shoreline, I cautiously look behind the aqueous wall with wonder at the little, elderly man who is sitting in his boat; his index finger pointing at the top of the waterfall's edge; playfully bending the top of his finger up and down; bringing the curve closer to the Specs each time.

"How…?"

He hesitates and then smiles and winks at my obvious puzzlement, "Don't ask…think. You already know how. That is…if you *are* who I *think* you are."

The man speaks to me with a familiar tone; like one I'd heard long ago when I woke on the velvet couch. I look at the waterfall, then at the man and nod.

"Who…?"

"Stolas sent me here to shadow the action of the Specs and the other rogues that were after you. Clean up after any mess they left behind. Keep an eye on you, too. Never had a chance to meet you face to face; you always high tail it out before I have a chance to say hello. Hello!" the man says, waving his free hand. "My official title is Royal Cleaner, but you can call me Declan."

"You've been…a shadow?" I think aloud, still unable to form a complete sentence with all the wild thoughts filling my head. Stolas has been gone for years, but my friend is still looking out for me.

"I know there's something important you have to do; somewhere you need to be. Don't know what it is; don't need to know; *don't care to know*; so, this is what you will do. These Specs are going to stay right where they are," he says to the canopy of Specs, "aren't you?"

A series of disgusted clicks and clacks I discern to be an unhappy and somewhat wary agreement are articulated.

"And you, Son," the man says, looking at me, "you are going to run; fast as you can; to the end of the trail and straight on to the golf course. Coming on dusk now, so the sprinklers will be on. Go! Now! I'll be cleaning up this mess. Keep in mind, there'll be more of these; somewhere. These bastards breed like rabbits. Be careful. Go on now."

I nod to the man; the first one I let call me son in years; and then run down the path just as he said. As I run away and round the bend of Bass Cove Trail leading up to the dam, I hear a loud splash and the robust, boisterous laughter of the old man.

Taking a single step on to the greens of Lake Chabot Golf Course, the sprinklers start up. From deep in my gut until my body shakes, I laugh for the first time in a good long while. Totally tickled by all the amazing news I've just learned; not to mention the funny, little dance the escaped, stray Speculari are doing as they dodge the rapid fire, synchronized sputter of the multiple sprinkler heads.

"Woo-hoo! Come and get me, *bug*! Ha! Can't, can you? I'm right here, you ugly, stupid nits!" Jumping and waving wildly at my eight-legged nemesis, I turn and happily walk on through the multi-directional coordinated spray.

Listening to the sprinklers' symphony of point and counter point rhythms, I remember the first time I walked into Dad's shop and listened to the ticking of all the different clocks. Sometimes I found myself thinking, talking and walking in time to the loudest ones, just as I am now with the sprinklers. I arrive at the opposite edge of the golf course in record time and stop to take a short break before going on. It's dark now; the sprinklers have stopped, and I'm soaked through and through. Taking a good long drink from a new bottle of water, I savor a few pieces of beef jerky. Taking off my scarf, I wring the water out and feel my brass companion wriggle with excitement.

"Steady, little guy, steady. We're almost there," I think, shoving the wet scarf into a vinyl-lined pocket of my backpack and taking a clean, dry one from inside, as well as a quick change out of my wet socks and hiking boots. The terrain I will meet now is primarily asphalt, and I expect a need for speed to stay away from the pesty Specs. Grabbing my running shoes from my backpack, I take the warm, dry, tube socks I keep stuffed inside, pull them on, and lace up my shoes. Hearing a faint, familiar click again, I remember something Stolas once told me.

"They're impatient to a fault," he'd say, and then laugh until he was crying.

I remove the damp scarf from the pocket of my pack and keep it in my left hand with the wet socks, hold my hiking boots in my right, and then start walking quickly down Golf Links Road.

As I hear the clicking gain on me, I quicken my pace. Taking a detour through the Oakland Zoo parking lot, I drop the scarf at the ticket gate as I jump the fence; and then stealthily sneak my way around the animal pens. Passing by the African Wildlife yard, I get an idea.

Sneaking quietly over the wall, trying not to wake the elephants, giraffes, caribou, or vultures, I drag my feet through piles of sawdust and palm fronds, and whatever else is on the ground, getting the animals' scent on my shoes; dropping one of the socks in the pen, and the other as I jump back out. Tiptoeing to the other side of the pen, I kneel down in a dark corner just outside the fence and wait. It only took moments for the clicking to return and quickly get loud.

Five Speculari happen upon the wet sock; the Big Spec carries the scarf clamped tightly in his teeth. The four smaller Specs jump wildly; excited at the find and quickly jump the wall into the pen; the larger one spits out the scarf and clicks and clacks away what seems to be a warning that's far too late. The small Specs have found the matching sock, but their exuberant chatter has awakened the caged beasts that will not stand for the noise or the intrusion.

As the Specs dance around, the larger of three gray African elephants trumpets and charges them, stomping mercilessly until one Spec is nothing but muddy road kill. A nearby vulture with clipped wings bounces in to claim the remains as the elephant takes off after the other Specs who scurry off into the personal space of the delicate giraffe that rears up on its hind legs and stomps on the forelegs of the loudest, chattering Spec turning it instantly into a quadruped. The maimed Spec limps away and trips, falling into a puddle of rainwater, dissolving into goo instantly. The two remaining Speculari, far more brave than their co-conspirators, run full-force at the elephants and land on their backs. They trumpet loudly, signaling the baby elephant to scamper to the corner for safety.

The Speculari attempt to sting the adult elephants with their scorpion-like tail, but they cannot penetrate their tough hide. As with any other pests, parasites, or bothersome nuisances, the elephants fill their trunks with water from their trough and spray the Specs repeatedly until the bubbling ooze washes away to the ground beneath their feet. The Spec *General* looks over the gruesome scene and shudders, snapping and popping his jaws in discontent and disgust as he slinks back into the dark.

Realizing this is my moment to move, I stand much too abruptly and the bottle of rainwater tumbles out of my pocket. The General quickly comes back into the light and faces me, meeting my eyes with an icy stare.

"Oops," I say, just before I take off, sprinting for the exit at my top speed.

Climbing over the entry gate, I exit the zoo quickly through the parking lot and run across the street. Rounding the corner, I listen for the galloping clatter of the sharp nails of the General close behind. Making my way to the middle of the overpass, I listen and watch for my opportunity to escape on the freeway below.

With my attention drawn away to the giant southbound Bekins moving truck, the Spec sneaks up behind me and pops his heavy jowls at me in disgust. Then I laugh: loud, long, hard, without control.

The Spec is confused, popping and snapping his teeth in a constant stream of what I believe to be obscenities. He's furious with me for setting the trap for his Sagittarians?…No, no…three clicks, a pop, then two snaps…his *Sergeants*. He has stopped trying to blend in with his surroundings. His spindly legs, scarred from battles of the past, one leg missing its claw; his eyes weary, yet firmly focused on mine; he shakes from the anger he feels for me. Every move I make in retreat makes him tremble more with fury.

"I know what you want," I say to him in my best Specularese; uncertain if I emphasized the clicks and snaps correctly, "but I'm afraid I can't oblige."

Feeling the curb of the sidewalk against my heel, I step up and then take advantage of the shift in weight of my feet; bending my knees I vault to the freeway below. Allowing my body to fall backwards over the edge of the overpass towards the southbound traffic, toss my hiking boots to the top of the Bekins truck; I simultaneously reach out and grab the edge of the green highway sign. The double thud they make as they bounce draws the attention of the Spec. He flies over the edge towards the sound, landing hard on the top of the truck and skidding to a stop as he drags his claws in the metal.

Hoisting my body to the top of the green sign, I brace myself against the concrete and manage to scale the short distance back over the wall and onto the sidewalk. Knowing I don't have much time to dawdle, especially knowing the tracking abilities of the Specs; I jog back over to Golf Links Road and make a sharp left to Mountain Boulevard, wanting to stay parallel to the freeway just in case the Specs find me again. Feeling the key stir under my shirt, I pat it calmingly as if it's a frightened child; it settles and falls; I feel the silkiness of the ribbon against my skin and once again remember the young girl who gave it to me. I left her in the capable hands of a Royal Courier, a truck driver, carrying a load of books and clothing to The Dominion for the start of the school year. A lovely girl, traveling alone, crying in her car while parked in a quiet, unpopulated alley near the back door of the roadside diner I was working at as an assistant to the cook. A Sous Chef at any other four-star establishment; but to my boss, Otto, an assistant. Sue was the name of his ex-wife so he wasn't about to call me that, too. I served myself a coke with a lot of crushed ice, then went to the alley to take my break, sat for only a few minutes when the Specs made their presence known.

He jumped on me without warning. I batted him away with my hand, dousing it with the icy soda; but not before he scratched me with his claws, creating three deep gashes across the inside of my arm.

"Oh, my God!" she cried, having been witness to the attack.

"Get out of here!" I yelled, as she ran to my side. I took a handkerchief from my pocket and held it against my arm.

"Let me help you," she said, trying to pull me to her baby-blue Carmenghia.

"No," I told her, gently pushing her away; but just as quickly I pull her to me as a Spec jumps on her and becomes entangled in her hair. Wrenching it free, as she whimpers from the tugging and pulling, I toss it into the puddles of melting ice. The Spec rolls away through the ice, suffering only a few burns and one broken claw.

That was my first meeting with the General, a mere Private then.

The young girl, shaken and scared, held on to me to keep from falling. Walking her through the kitchen to the diner, I sat her down in a booth closest to the door hoping that I wouldn't need to exit quickly.

"Wait," she said stopping me before I turned to go. She took the burgundy ribbon from her jostled hair and tied my handkerchief in place over the wound the Spec made. "My name is Yvonne. Thank you…"

"No, no, it's me that should be thanking you," I said. "Do you have somewhere to go? Somewhere safe?"

"I...?" A blush came over the young, innocent face of Yvonne; her designer shoes, hand bag, and perfectly-manicured nails belying her jeans and flannel-shirt disguise.

"We need to get you somewhere safe," I said, as my boss, Otto, yelled for me to get back to work. I noticed Darius, one of the Royal Couriers, taking a seat at the end of the counter.

"Quit flirting with the pretty girl and get back to work; I need my coffee hot and my burger mooing," Darius laughed; good guy, old friend, met through Stolas; I knew I could trust him.

"Darius, I need your help. The girl I was talking to? I need you to get her somewhere safe. Please? She and I were just attacked in the alley by Specs."

"*That*...girl?" Darius stuttered with his big, green eyes open wide and clearly taken with her; then he suddenly realizes what I'd said, "Specs? Here? Why? Your arm? Crap! Did it sting you?"

"No, No...just clawed," I said, remembering the warning Stolas gave me about their venom and their sting. "Please, Darius, she needs to get out of here. Her car is in the alley. Once I leave and draw them away, you can bring her back and get her car. Just give me till tonight. Okay?"

"Yeah, I'll call Edna. She can make up an excuse to tell the King why I'll be late," Darius said, knocking his Oakland A's cap back as he wiped his brow with his hand. "Just do me a favor?" he asks, glancing up at the cap, then removes it hastily and stuffs it in his back pocket.

"What?"

"Introduce me? A face like that, and I'm bound to forget my own name," Darius said, running his fingers through his dark-brown, wavy hair and straightening out his clothes.

Laughing, I nodded for him to follow me; introduced Darius to Yvonne, watched as they walked out of the diner, and I hoped for the best. Showing Otto the cut on my arm, I told him it was a giant rat; loud enough so that patrons heard me; he sent me home without a second thought. Once there, I grabbed my backpack, some water, snacks, and hit the road, again.

From Sparks, Nevada to Aurora, Colorado; up north to Anchorage, Alaska; back down to Milwaukee, Oregon and all over California; traveling wherever the weather takes me. If it's wet, rainy, or snowing, I move there. It seems my skin is always in some state of water-wrinkled or chapped; need to be if I want to stay ahead of the Specs. When I tire of the wet, I come back to

California but make sure I stay near the coast; close to the ocean's shore; and in each place, I take a different name.

Sometimes I forget who I am.

Sometimes I wish I could get lost for good

Seeing the Moraga Avenue turnoff coming up on the Warren Freeway, I look both ways and cut across the street. Hearing a sound like ball bearings hitting a snare drum, I look behind me and gasp at what's broken my peaceful, silent memory. The General has returned, and he has a new platoon.

Row after row, the Speculari march toward me; climbing trees along the street and jumping from branch to branch; coming at me with aggressive speed; readying for attack. Stepping up my pace, I run full stride. The clickity-clack sound getting louder; claws hooking the heels of my shoes because of sheer exhaustion, cold, and the fact that I'm not the young wide-receiver I once was. Noticing the tall, concrete wall that surrounds Mountain View Cemetery approaching, I try for just one last burst of speed. Turning on the afterburners, I get a cramp in my right leg but try to run through it. Looking down at my failing leg, I see it isn't a cramp but a small Spec, grinning at me as he digs his sharp claws into the flesh of my calf and readies to sting me. Grabbing the bottle of rain water, I try and twist off the cap; but the Spec's claws are cutting in deep, and I lose focus from the pain.

"Please, God, a little help?" I ask, limping down the street of the quiet, residential area.

Lightning streaks the sky with a bold, white announcement, illuminating a cyclone fence in the backyard of an old, brick, colonial home; a large, manipulated hole at the bottom waves to me with rusty, metal fingers just before the sky opens up to a rumbling roar and falls to my rescue.

Leaping in the air and cheering jubilantly in my mind, I carefully shake off the remains of the gooey, melted Spec, wincing from the burn of the cuts. The inside of my shoe is wet and squishy from the blood running down my leg, pooling in the heel and soaking my sock. Limping to the hole in the gate, I carefully crawl through and then drag my backpack behind me. Once through, I throw the pack over the stone wall.

Struggling with three good limbs, I hoist myself up the wall and grab onto a nearby Bay tree; inching my way up the longest branch, I then roll over the top of the wall, falling to the ground, mere inches away from the resting spot of someone's dearly departed. Realizing where I've entered the graveyard, I grab my backpack, nod respectfully to the orphans in the unnamed graves for disturbing them, and then limp my way to a nearby fountain. Taking shelter at a large Oak tree, I take my first-aid kit from my pack and gingerly attempt to roll up my pant leg. The wet khaki is not cooperative; so again, begging the pardon of the dearly departed near me (*always be respectful of the dead; one day, you'll be one of them and in consideration of what I've seen in my life, you never know when they might come back*) before I remove my shoes, my bloody socks, and my ripped pants.

My Demon transfusion is already clotting and closing the wound; bruising from the cuts will take longer; damned human blood. I laugh at this; Stolas would scold me for such a thought. What I always found to be weakness in humans, Stolas found strength.

The Demons of The Dominion are amazing: they care for the sick and wounded without a thought, feed the hungry, shelter the homeless. No one goes without. No fees. No taxes. No questions. A far cry better than some humans I've encountered in my life; I can think of two examples now. The two that attacked me. Called me names. Shot me. And why? Because I'm *different*.

After covering my still-healing wounds with gauze and tape, I pack up the first-aid kit and put it back in my pack, take the clean pair of jeans and socks out, and then dress quickly; thanking the surrounding deceased hosts, once again, as I ready to make my way through the rain. Stopping briefly, I admire the beauty of the peaceful, final resting spot.

"Place still looks great, Mr. Olmstead," I think aloud, finding the splendor in the designer's work, even in the pouring rain. The six perfectly manicured hills intertwined by wide, curved lanes lined by Lebanese Cedar, Italian Cypress, regal Pines, and the indigenous California Oak. The man had a vision for building this cemetery, and he was right; nature isn't in *us*, we *are* nature.

As I round a bend in the walkway, I happen upon a path of large and artistically-designed crypts. Seeing the name on the largest one and the lovely, pensive angel seated in front tells me I have happened upon Millionaires Row.

From bank moguls and chocolatiers, to world-renowned architects, the who's who of the birth of the San Francisco-Bay Area rests here in this palatial, peaceful spot, where the sunrises and sunsets are always breathtaking against the backdrop of the Oakland Foothills and the Pacific Ocean's shore. The stories of the lives of those who lay in eternal slumber here vary and carry forward in the population of the area; that's what makes it so rich and alive with layer upon layer of flavors of the history we all hold and bequeath to the next generations.

The rain is steady but not hard. Wanting to stop and rest, but uneasy about rudely taking shelter in a family crypt, I continue walking over the next couple of hills and around a bend. Seeing a gothic chapel in the distance, I head for a broad path leading there that's covered by a winter-barren arbor canopy; tentative at first, considering my last experience. The peal of bells fills the air; and in the distance, fireworks light the sky over the Bay Bridge. A new year has begun, and with it comes a cloudburst overhead to reassure me that my original path is clear and safe. Taking my time and enjoying the smell of the rain-washed trees, I stroll leisurely down the arbor path and make my way to the waiting chapel. The pointy steeples of the Chapel direct my attention to the large, dark cloud mass above. Quickly making my way to the covered doorway, I set my backpack down and then settle my old, weary body on the ground beside it.

Sitting in the protected, arched cove of the chapel, I lean back against the double doors and sigh as I watch the rain pour from the sky above. Trying not to dwell on the negative aspect of my current situation: cold, wet, hungry, scared; I try to view the positive: I have a clean and semi-dry set of clothes, a Mylar blanket to fight the cold, beef jerky, peanut butter and dried fruit to eat, a sky the color of charcoal that will keep me safe from Specs for a good, long while, and when I stop to consider my current company...I am above ground and breathing.

After changing out of my rain-soaked jacket and shirt to a flannel button-down and an insulated running jacket, I open the Mylar blanket and tuck myself in, but not before grabbing a midnight snack of banana chips and peanut butter. Using my backpack as a pillow, I rest my head and find my eyelids growing heavy. Listening carefully for any sounds to be wary of, but only hearing the rush of the rain from a nearby drain pipe, I drift off to a much-needed sleep.

I awaken startled to a glare from the sidewalk in front of the chapel. The sun, brightly shining down from the East, beats down upon the rain-soaked cement; precipitation continues, not as hard as last night or early this morning, lightly tumbling drops which makes the foliage glitter in the sun. In the distance, a double rainbow begins somewhere South and ends, by only an estimation on my part, near Berkeley. My mere thought of the city stirs my traveling companion.

"Soon, my friend, soon," I tell him, and gaze again at the rainbows. Dad always told me that rainbows are sent to us by those who have passed on; they miss us so much that they want to reach out and say hello. The first time I saw a double rainbow, I didn't know what to think.

"You're twice as loved, Son," he would say.

"Thanks, Dad," I think aloud, harkening back to days long since passed and wonder who the second rainbow is from. One the many who knew me? Helped me? Lost their lives because of me? Otto, at the diner?

Neal, at the library? My poor young friend, Ignatius? Or perhaps Stolas. Placing my hand over my heart, I bow my head humbly to the rainbows and thank whoever cared enough to send them. Taking a now-thawed blueberry Pop-Tart from the zip-loc freezer bag in my backpack, I enjoy a nice, leisurely breakfast while I watch the rainfall in the first sunrise of the new year. After breakfast, I clean myself up a bit, using a small bottle of anti-bacterial gel, then once again take out my journal and the maps for a quick review.

Having strayed from my original path when Declan sent me through the golf course, I find myself a little further North than I'd planned. I take the key from its safe place and let it tell me where we are to go. It bids me on; still urging me to Berkeley.

Pulling on my old, beat-up Cal Berkeley baseball cap and my trusty backpack, I head on through the sun-drenched rainfall. Exiting the gates, now open for families and friends to visit, I head up Piedmont Avenue on my way to Broadway when the rain comes to a sudden and abrupt stop. Feeling distinctly uneasy and naked, I trust my gut and walk briskly. Approaching the corner of Pleasant Valley Avenue, I feel the key stir excitedly, as my ears prick at a familiar and fearful sound; growing and filling the quiet morning with its furious and intense chatter.

Speculari, hundreds of them, waiting at the corners and hanging off the buildings; disguised to blend in with the city's surroundings: crawling along the sidewalk, hidden behind a mask of concrete, scaling the walls with a brick and glass façade, and high above atop a corner bar another boldly attempts to appear as a hump on the back of a gargoyle.

The General.

The key, giddy and excited, expects me to turn right and move on, but a hoard of Specs spring to action from the corner and force me in the opposite direction. Backing up, I remember Stolas and all his warnings. Looking up I see there is not a cloud in the sky. The new year is starting beautifully, and I fear this will be the only day I see.

Glancing to my left, I see only two, maybe three, of the knobby-jointed beasts at the gas station. Removing my backpack, knowing I can run better without it, I reach inside quickly and take the last two bottles of water out. Dropping my pack, I twist off the caps of both bottles and take off running.

Kicking the first Spec out of my way and into the locked, propane-tank cage as I run past, it stumbles and rolls into the second one who clicks and clacks furiously at being knocked down. Running hard and fast, I don't make time to stop and listen to the rest of the conversation because the key distracts me as it slips around my neck and pulls so hard in the opposite direction: trying to remind me of our original destination. Regaining my focus, although choking from a lack of air, I continue to run until I arrive at my old childhood stomping ground.

Feeling a little more sure of myself; probably more than I should; I brazenly jay-walk across Oakland Avenue; turn to go towards the neighborhood that welcomed me so warmly fifty-plus years ago, and neglect to see or hear a Spec jump from a yellow fire hydrant. Yelling from the pain as it stings the top of my hand, I yank the Spec off and slam it into a flooded gutter. Feeling the venom rush through my veins as I continue down the street, numbness overcomes my hand, my arm, and works its way up to my shoulder.

Paying far too much attention to the lack of feeling spreading in my right side, I watch as my grip loosens on the water bottle and it falls. Another Spec, hiding in the awning of the camera store two doors down from my dad's old shop, springs to the back of my neck. Fearing it's trying to steal the key, I reach up with my left hand and pour the open bottle of water on it, but not before it stings me twice in my neck.

Anger consumes me and brings my already racing adrenaline to an uncontrollable speed. Feverish and growing continually numb, I struggle past the next two storefronts to Dad's old shop that has since become a trendy candle store. Falling to the ground at the door, I'm unable to feel much of my body except my left arm. The half-empty bottle of water rolls away as I hoist myself up on the one working arm and then slowly pull myself to the safety of the puddle-ridden alley beside the shop.

After dragging myself half-way down the alley, I hear the familiar pop-pop-pop of the General giving orders to his troops: commending their work and expressing remorse for their lost comrade. Still having some sensation in my body, but not having any ability to move, I feel the General walk slowly up my back to my face, digging his foreclaws in my skin with every step; but he stops suddenly and backs away, chattering something about being a traitor.

Very confused by it all, I turn my focus to moving my body forward. Feebly reaching out with my only working hand, I touch a giant, scaly foot the color and texture of shale rock, with long talons. Using that same arm like the kickstand of a bicycle, I raise my upper body and see a beast burst forth from a double-breasted, navy-blue trench coat; growling with great ferocity and baring his scissor-like teeth at the Specs. They are not the least bit afraid as the horde fills the alley, carefully avoiding the puddles.

The Specs laugh. The beast, which I can now see is a gargoyle in his live form instead of stone, fully extends one of his leathery wings and with one sweep he whips the numerous pools of rain water into an exacting and controlled Tsunami, wiping away every last Speculari there, except the General whose cowardice propels him up and over the rooftop.

"Nasty buggers! They breed like rats," the gargoyle sneers, as he takes a deep breath and retracts his wing. He picks up the remains of his coat and sighs, "Damn, I really liked this one."

The gargoyle kneels down beside me and I flinch; at least, in my mind, I did; no longer able to speak, all I have are my thoughts.

"Oh, no, please, I mean you no harm. I got here as quick as I could, but you run pretty fast for an old guy," the gargoyle laughs, but stops suddenly. "Oh, no, no, no…you were stung!"

The gargoyle sweeps me up in his arms and carries me around to the back of the shop, nods at the door, and it opens on its own.

Once inside, he places me on a couch and leaves me to go into another room behind a red door. I hear a series of beeps; then the gargoyle speaks in a flat tone, leaving a message for someone named Peg; he asks her to call him immediately. He emerges from the room, carrying with him bits of what looks like moleskin and a beaker of liquid that looks and smells like an opalescent balsamic vinaigrette.

Pouring some of the sparkly liquid in a novelty coffee mug from Alcatraz Island, he drops the pieces of fabric in the cup and then swirls them around. Picking out the soaked cloth, he places them on the three spots where I was stung.

Almost instantly, my body starts to awaken; tingling from head to toe with a prickly, stabbing feeling like after your foot awakens from falling asleep; but it's excruciating. The gargoyle can sense this, I think; either that, or he could see the tears welling up in my eyes.

Gently, he lifts my head and brings the beaker to my lips and says, "Drink. You *must* drink. It's the only way to fight the venom. That pricking you're feeling? It's the venom fighting to stay active, and it's getting ready to attack your major organs. Drink. Please?"

I do my best and let the shiny potion slide down my gullet without choking. Then everything goes black.

I awaken alone: no longer on the leather couch of the old shop in Piedmont, but on a bed, covered by a blanket, in a stark, yet well-lit bedroom. Moments later the gargoyle enters, dressed in a long, black-velvet, Victorian-style, day coat with the Royal Crest embroidered on the pocket. He smiles broadly and comes to my bedside.

"Much better! You had me worried," the gargoyle says, walking in with my backpack. He places it on a chair beside the bed. "The elixir I used drew the venom to the surface, and I feared you were too fragile to expel it yourself, being human...but, somehow your body fought it off." The gargoyle looks at me, puzzled, and trying to see through me.

"Where am I?" I ask, as I try to feel my feet and legs.

"*Circles,*" he says, "It's a restaurant...bar...a good place. You'll be safe here. I need to...um...go somewhere. Will you...?"

"The Dominion?" I say, filling in the obvious blanks he was avoiding as I instinctively lift myself up in the bed and sigh when I realize how, not long ago, I couldn't do anything but think about it.

"Yes...you know?"

"Yes...I know the crest," I say, pointing to the adornment on his breast pocket. "I've been there many times with Stolas...long ago."

The gargoyle's eyes grow huge when I say my friend's name, and his broad shoulders extend back as he breathes a silent gasp. Shaking his head in disbelief he smiles, "It's true. It's *you*. You're...*him!*"

"*Him?*"

"You're...*the Teacher!*"

I laugh, "That's what people and Demons keep calling me. All my life it's all I ever wanted to be, so...I think so."

The gargoyle's face is a mixture of amazement, joy, and concern; I'm tickled by how often he just stops and smiles. My curiosity gets the best of me.

"You act as if you expected me."

"Well, yes...and no. There was a prophecy told to me...by Stolas, but I gave up on it ever coming true. The Erudite sometimes..."

"Talk in circles?"

"Yes. They do. And the Sentry..."

The gargoyle instantly stops talking because at the mere mention of '*The Sentry,*' the key springs to life and points to the mirror on the far-right wall. He backs away briefly; seeing it's not a weapon, he comes close again.

"It belongs to the Sentry. I made a promise to Stolas that when the time came, I would deliver it to him. Almost didn't make it; but thanks to you...," I say, extending my hand to my new friend.

"Galen. My name is Galen."

Taking a deep breath, I recall the past and how the name Galen always came about: both times trying to help Dad. I sigh and smile, relieved to be in friendly company. He looks at me with a familiar, ornery glint in his eye, common to all *non-rogue* Demons, not to mention my dad, and then asks, "You are?"

For so long I feared to say it aloud, using fake names and initials to stay hidden and unknown. Wiping away the tired and useless need, I look Galen squarely in the eyes and speak proudly to my new, *old friend*.

"My name is Tempus. Tempus Raleigh."

...Today

Eli

I had the strangest dream last night.

Nothing new for me, my dreams always are a little strange; even before I got my powers. I was walking through a cemetery; I could hear whispers. It was daylight and I was walking along a twisted, hilly, path. A breeze would blow through the trees and whisper that blasted phrase the Erudite told Uncle Sage so long ago.

"Time will tell you all you need to know."

Over and over the whispers went on and on the further I went along the path. I passed a fountain and saw something scurry behind a headstone. I took another step and again something ran away. Then, I heard clicking sounds like castanets but they weren't just sounds…they were words.

"Stop the Sentry! Stop the Sentry! Stop the Sentry!"

I kept on walking but could feel someone behind me, so I turned quickly…but no one was there. I caught a slight movement from the corner of my eye; then another; and another; until my eyes adjusted to see all the movements of the spindly creatures camouflaging themselves in the cemetery, like giant rocks with legs; and they all crawled out in front of me.

Then someone called to me. I turned back to the pathway and saw a man: forty-ish, tall, handsome, Black, with a warm, friendly smile,and an ornery twinkle in his eye like Grandpa. He was reaching out to me. He had something in his hand. He was running but kept turning around behind him. I started to run: suddenly scared for him, or of what,or who was behind him. We both slowed down as we got closer; and just as we are within arm's reach, the man's eyes become huge and a look of terror takes the place of the smile of relief; in seconds he's shriveled up and dry like tissue paper. I reach out to touch him, and he dissolves into sand in my hands. I stand there just staring at the sand pile; not knowing what to do; then a man, dressed in a blue-grey, hooded overcoat and bedroom slippers, shuffles in front of me, moaning. He is older and disheveled: his hands in shackles and ankles in leg irons. His long, dirty, white hair covers his face; but I can hear him sob between moans. He stops walking and turns to me suddenly. Holding out his bound hands to me he says, "Help her? Please, help her?" He looks to me; and a breeze brushes his hair away, his eyes white and cloudy, like watery milk. He whimpers then speaks again, "Help us?"

That's when I woke up.

Was it prophetic? Something I ate? I've no clue. I don't usually dream about strangers; except for the time when my family erased my memory, and I dreamt about them; not knowing it was them at the time...because...well, I didn't know them, then.

Sometimes I think back to those days and get angry, but it's really a waste of time and energy. My family erased my memory to save me from being found out by Corson; and then, even when he did find me, he was looking for a boy...not a girl...so, I guess it was all for the best...besides, there's nothing I can do about it. And if I can't change it, why worry about it? Right?

Yeah. Right.

"Mornin', Sweetie! Ready for the big day?" Mom asks, her eyes twinkling with pride as she holds her arms open to me. I scurry over to her and hug her, feel her arms wrap around me tightly.

"Ready as I'll ever be, I guess. It's all kind of strange, really. There's so much I don't know about the job yet, and I'm already being sworn in. Shouldn't there be some training involved? Or at least a secret handshake I need to learn?"

Mom laughs at this and tries, why, I don't know, to tame the random hairs on my head that are trying to reach the ceiling; but I stop her just short of doing the *Mom-thing* by licking her fingers to style my unruly locks.

"Mom?"

"Baby, just let me try. Maybe we can pin-curl it."

"Mom! No!"

"Don't you want curlies, like me?"

"Oh, Mom...," I laugh and kiss her beautiful face.

"Are you hungry, Sweetie? I made your favorite Sticky Buns."

"Mom, you've been here since six this morning, and all you've made are Sticky Buns?"

"Don't be silly. I was getting the family dinner started. I promised *The King*, I'd make Cioppino."

"And…wait, let me guess. Rocky Road candy with a glass of Port wine for dessert."

"Hey! You remember!"

"Oh, yeah…I remember. More and more, little details come back about the family. Some sad; some funny. Once in awhile I'll be out walking or talking to someone on the phone; and then I'll remember a moment and just start laughing, hysterically sometimes. The other day, right before New Year's Eve, we had a beer delivery; and the delivery man wore the same after-shave as Uncle César, and I burst into tears because I remembered him and the Chili Verde." Mom's face went white. "It's okay, Mom. It's a good memory. I only cried because…"

Mom takes me in her arms again; sobs gently. She, too, remembers the day; the day before my thirteenth birthday: Last day of school before winter break, early day at school, then lunch at Mom's bistro because Uncle César made me his famous Chili Verde. *'Perfection in a pot'* Dad used to call it. I told Uncle César I could eat it all day; so he made enough for lunch, dinner, and breakfast the next day. We brought it home; Mom warmed it up and fixed a salad and rice on the side.

Then we left for Aunt Peg's.

Then…

Never got to have it for breakfast. And Uncle César…

A door slams, and we hear Connie swearing up a storm in Spanish.

"What the…?"

Turning to face the door as Connie storms in, Mom turns away and wipes her face.

"Did you know about this?" Connie yells at me, as she grabs her purse and keys; barefoot and still in her fuchsia-pink sweats.

"Know about what? Where are you going? We have to be in The Dominion in a couple of hours," I say, trying to keep up with her erratic behavior; racing from room to room picking up a weird combination of things: a pair of 3-D glasses from the last movie we saw, her empty Betty-Boop Pez dispenser, and her bubble-gum-pink, water socks.

"Answer me, Eli! Did you know about this?" Connie demands, hopping on one foot at a time while stretching her water socks on.

I shake my head, "Connie, I…"

"Your family's *brilliant* plan to save *your life*; keep *you* safe and away from harm. Remember?"

Nodding to Connie as Aunt Peg walks in, she goes to Mom's side. Mom looks at her and asks how she is with her body language. Aunt Peg is clearly *not* all right.

"What about…?"

"They killed my parents."

"Con, what…"

"Oh, no, no…pardon me, let me rephrase that…Corson pushed your dad's car into them and then the car exploded. Officer Reinhardt pulled you to safety; then your parents were carted off. No one gave my parents any assistance at all…just left them there to burn."

"Connie, Uncle Dave…"

"No one helped them!"

Breathing too hard to speak and not knowing what to say anyway, I turn to the obvious guilty party and wait, but she says nothing.

"Well?"

"Eli, your Uncle Sage's vision showed Connie's parents didn't survive the impact."

"But no one checked," Connie barked. "You know his visions are flawed. You don't…you didn't…"

Connie is starting to grind her teeth; I step between her and Aunt Peg, "You've known about this all this time? Why didn't you…?"

"No, I didn't know until I met Connie's grandmother at Graduation," Aunt Peg replied, fingering a gold serpentine chain Uncle Dave gave her for Christmas.

"Con's grandmother died a year after we graduated from high school, so you're obviously not talking about college graduation," I deduct with a heavy sigh. "You've known for seven years?"

"Yes."

"And, you decided to tell her *now*?"

"We couldn't tell her before, it would have broken the protection spell and…"

Connie, swearing in Spanish again, runs out the door before Aunt Peg finishes her sentence.

"Eli, please, you have to understand."

"That's the problem, Aunt Peg, *I do* understand; but I also understand the pain in that little girl's heart all too well. I lived it, remember?"

A long and heavy pregnant pause hangs in the room as the three of us stand and stare into the emotional void that's been perpetuated by a need to survive; then a familiar voice gives the silence a much needed break.

"Knock, knock…hope I'm not interrupting anything; but, I just wanted to ask where we're supposed to meet up today? Hey, Eli, is Connie all right? She blew past me so fast and didn't even say 'Hi' or 'Go to hell'…or anything. That's not like her."

"Um…yeah, Robert,….Connie is…Connie is not feeling well; and I'm going to go get her. You should go on ahead to The Dominion. Use the mirror here. You remember how, right?" I ask, grabbing my purse, keys, and cell phone. Pressing Connie's number on my speed dial I hear Bobby McFerrin telling me not to worry and be happy, loud and clear from her bedroom.

"Shit," I sigh, knowing the clock is ticking, my friend is hurting, and I have no way to locate her than to feel where she is. Not so easy with Connie. When she doesn't want to be found, chances are, you won't. She knows how to pack her bags and run, both literally and emotionally.

"Come on, Eli, you *know* where she'll be," Robert says, his shit-eating grin emphasizing his sadistic glee at my circumstances.

"Yeah, yeah, yeah…I know, I know," I answer, as a chill goes up and down my spine.

"Want me to come along? Better yet, why don't *you* go to The Dominion; and let *me* go bring her in. I am *the Hunter*, am I not?"

"No, no, it's okay. You go on to The Dominion. Someone needs to tell Grandpa and my Dad that I might…*we* might, be a little late," I ask, as Robert nods and turns to go. "You two," I say, turning to Mom and Aunt Peg, "You're coming with me to find Connie."

"Where are we going, Eli?" Mom asks, as she grabs her jacket and purse.

"To the Holy Land," I sigh.

"To the *what?*" Aunt Peg asks, stopping me with her hand to make me face her and help her understand.

Taking Aunt Peg's hand from my shoulder, I hurriedly drag her along behind me and say, "The Mall, Aunt Peg. We're going to the Mall."

Asmodeus

"Here, Son, put this on your neck. It'll make you feel better."

"Thanks, Pop," Sage says holding the ice pack I made in place, still looking green from the last vision. I remember his mom getting bad ones like this, and I fear what these may mean. For her, it was a blessing in disguise; the foretelling of our son Ash, but also the end of my brother's life.

"Can you tell me what you saw? Or is it just fractals and fragments?" Sage looks at me with his mother's eyes and cocks his head; a crooked smile starts to appear ever so slowly from the side of his mouth. "What? Don't look at me like that…Your mom used to get them, remember? I know what they're like. I also know what you go through getting them. Here. Put your feet up," I say, pushing an ottoman up under Sage's feet, and I notice the shoes he is wearing.

"Son?"

"Don't worry, Pop, I plan on changing them," Sage assures, seeing my disapproval of his neon-green high-tops with his new gray suit.

"Kings can wear sneakers, Sage. Just not on Coronation Day."

Sage smiles and pats my shoulder, but his smile is short lived.

"What is it?" I ask hesitantly.

"It isn't over, Pop. Corson and Lilith's influence; I think it spans further than any of us imagine. He was one busy son of a bitch."

"Influence? What do you mean influence? On whom?"

"He was doing more than just trying to ruin our reputation and kill us. I think he had several back up plans, just in case…."

Waiting for Sage to finish his thought; even though he really doesn't have to; I can see in his eyes how bad the danger is. What I can't tell is a time frame.

"Are we in immediate danger? Should we get Bill in on this? Maybe we should postpone the Coronation?" I say, already motioning to the phone and calling it to me.

"No, no, don't postpone; we need to go on as planned. We'll get Bill later. First, tell me what you know about *The Brotherhood*?"

"Well, they're like the associations that humans have: Lions, Elks, Rotary; been around as long as I have, maybe longer. They have officers and sponsor charities. They're also a Royal-approved faction."

"Royal-approved?" Sage questions.

"Yes, your Uncle Stolas was a member and even president for a while. The family agreed that they would be given a few more privileges and access to Royal properties and provisions, and why do I suddenly feel like I'm being set up for the punch line of a bad joke?"

Sage smiles; not a happy smile, but more apologetic and remorseful, as he reaches out and touches the side of my head and shows me what is coming; the new horrors awaiting our family and a possible outcome if we don't act fast.

"We can turn this around. We have the means to do it," I say, feeling slightly more than uncertain but also not entirely lost.

"Yes, we have the Kindred now. And the Sentry," Sage thinks aloud; he looks like the wheels of his mind are never going to stop.

"What? Are we missing something?"

"From here on out, we need to be extra cautious; more careful than we've ever been. As King, I can activate *The Eternals*, right?"

"They've never really been out of commission, just sort of freelance…But I think you're planning to bring them back to the Royal House staff level?"

Sage nods, "We'll need their eyes and knowledge. The Kindred can do the job, I have no doubt. My niece will make sure of it," Sage said, with a wink.

I nod; he's right.

Standing up, I start to head to the door, "I'll be in the waiting room outside the proscenium steps. Come join me when you feel ready to."

Putting my hand on the doorknob, I start to turn it but instead make a u-turn and go back to my son; he stands up with a single tug, and I hug him tightly and kiss his cheek.

"You may be the next King, but you're still my little boy!"

Sage blushes as I walk away and out the big, double-doors of my *old* office; now the office of the new King. Heading down the marble corridor, I hear a familiar voice.

"He's going to make a grand King!"

"Yes, my Love, he is indeed."

"He's fighting the visions again."

"So did *you* I seem to recall. Can you blame him after what he's seen? Talk to him, Liz, you know about these things. I can only help him like I helped you."

"I will. He has a lot of work ahead of him."

"You were listening?"

I hear my wife's light and carefree laugh, and my heart flutters.

"You know me, Modie,...I always listen."

The Hunter

I was in the middle of doing my homework, struggling to find 'X' and not really caring why, when Dad, on the verge of yet another Jim Beam induced confessional, first told me about the Demons.

"Robbie!" Dad whispered, "Robbie, she's here! She's here, again! In *here*," he said, slapping at his forehead like he was swatting at bugs, staggering towards me, twisting and turning abruptly trying to avoid the imaginary enemy chasing him.

"No one's here, Dad. It's just you and me," I said, getting up and gently guiding him into the chair next to mine at the kitchenette table.

This was just one of many times he had fallen into this state since Mom died. After the fourth or fifth time, I was used to it. Numb really. It was the same thing every time: I'd sit him down, listen to him ramble on about how much he missed Mom, put him to bed to sleep it off, then have a nice quiet dinner for one with Captain Crunch.

This particular instance was different. He was more lucid, and I could feel an inner terror for what, or rather *who,* he felt was in his head. The look on his face told me there was something tangible that was scaring the shit out of him; and in turn, it was scaring me.

"Robbie, you don't understand; it's *her*. I can hear her! Smell her! She's inside of me!" Dad said, wringing his hands, wiping at his face, arms and body to remove the disgusting invisible filth that was blanketing him.

"Dad? Who's 'her'? Who are you talking about? Is it Mom?" I asked, trying to understand as Dad suddenly looked me in the eye, glared, and then slapped me hard across the face.

"Your Mom was a good and beautiful woman!" Dad yelled. "This shit is nothing like her! Don't you *ever* mention your Mom to me while this bitch is inside of me!"

"Who Dad? Who is…?" I asked, trying to rub the sting away while fighting back the tears that were struggling to break free from my eyes.

"Her! The Gypsy Moth!" Dad said in an emphatic whisper; looking to either side of him in case the paneled walls of our trailer grew ears and were listening, too.

"Dad, I have no idea who you're…?"

"It was a lifetime ago, Robbie. Way before I met your mom and before you were even a prayer in my heart," Dad said, no longer looking or sounding like the drunken, old sod he'd made himself into, bottle by bottle. He reached out to my face, and I flinched not knowing what to expect. I saw the tears of remorse well up in his eyes and his entire body tremble with regret. I sat down, took his hand and asked him to explain.

"I'd been with the County for a little over a year when the bodies started turning up. Unexplainably gruesome murders; the bodies were dried up like mummies but without the bandages. The coroner had to be careful handling the victims because they were so fragile, like tissue paper. I was working side by side with more seasoned officers. As far back as I could remember, I wanted to be a sheriff. I always wanted to be a cowboy; that was the closest I could come to it growing up in the city, I guess. None of them had seen anything like this. None of them knew what to make of it?"

"We went out one day on a tip called in to our dispatcher, Edna Blue. She had accidentally intercepted an anonymous call from a witness who claimed a blonde-haired woman that was reportedly last seen with one of the victims, was now at a local watering hole. Stan Davies, you know, Pete's daddy…? He and I went out to look into it. We weren't at all ready for what we found when we got there," Dad said, eyes vacant as he drifted back to that day and was reliving it moment by moment.

"The parking lot was full, but it was as quiet as a graveyard. Stan and I walked up to the door cautiously. He looked at me funny, but I knew instinctively what he was thinking. We drew our weapons and stood by the door. Stan signaled that he was going in first, and I was to cover him. I waited at the ready as he walked in, announcing himself as he moved. He stepped just inside the door and stood motionless. I stepped in behind him and stopped just as he had."

Dad was standing now, acting out what happened. His hands started to tremble with the imaginary gun. I stood up and went to his side and put my arm around him. He looked at me and smiled.

"They were dead; every one of them. Men in suits, the delivery guy with the kegs of beer, the bartender…all the patrons. Some seated at the bar, one at the jukebox…two of them in mid-stroke at the pool tables. All of them dried up and lifeless, like a leaf in autumn. A door slammed in the back, and we rushed to see what or who it was."

"The back door was cracked open. I took the lead this time. I could see in Stan's face the same hesitation I felt, but something inside me said to push on. I opened the door carefully and stepped outside…That's when I saw her for the first time."

"At first, it looked like she was just kissing some guy; but his arms fell limp and then shriveled up. She looked at me, and I met her stare. Her eyes penetrated mine like shards of crystal. I felt like she could see right through me and all my deepest, darkest secrets on the way out. She smiled at me and dropped the body; it fell into a pile of dust and powder. I held my gun on her but couldn't fire. A shot rang in my ears from Stan's gun, and I heard her cry out as she fell to the ground. Stan moved around me to get to her. He had only taken a few steps, and she was up and gone in a blink."

"That was the first time…first of many times I would meet up with her. She would always smile at me before she would make her escape. Time after time, tip after tip…she eluded us over and over again. Until one night, after a long shift of bodies and paperwork, I arrived home to a visitor in my apartment."

Dad suddenly stopped. A confused expression came over his bloated face as he tried to piece together the events. He put a hand on his forehead and held it there for a long time before he spoke again.

"She was beautiful. Like nothing I'd ever seen before. Her skin was like porcelain, but her eyes terrified me: black and cold like a shark. Her voice was smooth and sultry. She told me she wanted me. I should have been scared. I should have called for help. Something in her voice…I was compelled to go to her. She held her hand out to me and I went to her willingly; to this day I don't know why? In the back of my mind, I was certain that she would kill me like the others… I wanted her. Needed her."

"The next morning I woke up, surprised and even angry that I was still alive. I jumped up and ran to the bathroom to heave. I turned on the shower and tried to scrub her stench from my skin. I couldn't get clean. As hard as I scrubbed and as hot as I could stand the water, I couldn't get the feel of her body off of me. It was like her scent and touch were tattooed on me."

Dad came and sat back down at the table with me. He was somber and visibly exhausted. Reliving the emotions from that day had taken everything he had left in him.

"I vowed that day to catch her…And I did, eventually. The next time I saw her she looked different. She looked human. At first I didn't recognize her. It was the child. He looked just like her...Like when I first saw her! She kissed him...The same way she kissed me that night. No mother kisses a son like that! It made my stomach turn. We trapped her, Stan and I...I served as bait. She's in Napa now. God only knows what happened to the boy; CPS probably threw him in a group home somewhere. Sometimes, I hear her. Calling me. Telling me she still wants me...Needs me! Touching my body...!" Dad was wiping away at the invisible dirt again. "I'm tired Robbie. I'm gonna go lie down."

I walked Dad to his room and pulled back the covers on his bed. He laid down and closed his eyes. Covering him up, I started to leave; and then he grabbed my hand.

"You're a good boy, Robbie. Your momma and I love you very much."

Leaning over, I kissed Dad on the forehead and turned to go; turning the light off before closing the door behind me. I went back to my homework and tried to concentrate. It was two weeks till the two biggest events in my young life: turning eighteen and high school graduation. What the hell did I care about 'X'? Let it find its own damn self. My dad just dumped a shit load on me that I wouldn't soon forget.

The next morning, Dad didn't wake up. The coroner said he didn't feel any pain; his liver had failed and threw a clot; the bottle won the battle, and he died in his sleep. At his funeral, Edna Blue came up to me and put her arm around me.

"Jon Benoit was a good man, and he raised a good son. Your parents were proud of you, don't ever forget that," she said, looking up at me. Edna had always been like a grandmother to me growing up. Making me cookies and knowing to say a kind word when I needed it.

"I feel so alone now, Edna. I don't..."

"Hush now. You're not alone, Robert. Listen to your heart; your family will always be there.

As I sit here in the lobby of the Royal Home in The Dominion, waiting for the rest of The Kindred to arrive for the coronation, I replay this whole event in my mind. It isn't the first time; I've replayed it many times. With the events that have led up to now, I've replayed it more than I can count. Especially the night Corson came to Circles.

Looking in his eyes, facing him down, all the while wanting to protect my friends and seeing the eyes of my father staring back at me. Confirming the story that my Dad had told me long ago.

Not to mention those damn cats and what they did to Sean! I felt lost and all alone again like the day of the funeral. I froze. All I could hear in my head was Dad saying, *'She's here Robbie, she's here again'!*

Then the night we almost lost Eli…Edna's words came back to me that night. I listened to my heart like she said. I tried to get Eli away from Corson and the mirror, but I couldn't…I don't know what I would have done if…? Thank God Zach was there to…

"Hey! Are we the first one's here?"

Speak of the devil himself, Zach walks in with his signature goofball grin.

"No, the family is here somewhere. I was instructed to wait here," I say, as Zach pulls up a chair and sits down. "I've been meaning to say something to you; but, well, thanks for saving me after, you know…?" I say. Sort of. I'm not good at saying thank you, or please. I don't usually ask for help and have trouble accepting it when it's offered. Fiercely independent, but then I had to be; I was forced into it by a succubus. Zach grins at me.

"Your welcome. How much did *that* hurt?" he asks.

I laugh, "Just a little, smart-ass! Are we always going to be like this?"

"Like what?"

"Sniping at each other?"

"We're family now, Robert. Isn't that what family does?"

"I don't know? I never had siblings."

"Me neither. Just the band, but they're like family. We pick on each other constantly, but we're also there for each other, too; so, yeah, I think we're always going to be that way."

I think about this for a bit and then answer, "I think I can handle that."

"Me too," Zach says, with a nod and that damn goofy grin again.

I wonder what Dad would think? Would he approve of my association with Demons, Witches, and goofy Nephalim? Would he think I went to the other side? I close my eyes and again take Edna's advice. All I can hear is Dad's voice telling me that he and Mom love me very much.

That's a good enough answer for me.

Sage

Walking from room to room and then hall to hall, retracing every single step I've made, and I still can't find my damn shoes.

"Excuse me, *Your Highness,* did you lose these?"

"My shoes! My shoes! Where did you find them?"

Handing the loafers to me with a broad smile, Helen immediately takes to fixing my tie.

"In the bathroom cabinet. They were next to an open container of hair gel, sitting in front of a toothbrush with the toothpaste still on the bristles that lay atop a coupon for fifty cents off shaving cream, right beside a half-eaten bagel. Nervous, Sage?"

"Oh, no, not at all," I say, rolling my eyes in disgust at myself; remembering the blinding pain of the vision and why I left my shoes there.

"Don't worry about it, kid. You're going to be great! Bill and I both think you are made for this job."

"Really?" I ask curiously. After all that we've endured? Through the more than obvious doubt she had in me? The sacrifice I asked her to bear by leaving her child behind for her safety? Her confidence in me is not only fantastic but startling.

"I know we've had our differences, but I also know that you wouldn't have asked them of me on some kind of whim or flight of fancy. You're a family man like your brothers and father. You sacrificed, too. You lived without and in fear, just as I did. I know where your heart was and still is. It's here, with us," Helen says, patting her hand on my chest as she fixes the handkerchief in the pocket of my jacket. "I tend to be a little hard on men that appear too ambitious, not that it's a bad thing. It's just a hard habit to break."

"Because of your dad?" I ask.

"Yes, that and the losers that Peg married; but we both have good men now," Helen says happily, as she hands me a parchment-wrapped package. Lifting the warm, paper-wrapped bundle to my nose, I breathe deeply and take in the comforting aroma of my favorite treat she makes...Sticky Buns.

"You spoil me," I tell her, as I remove one and re-wrap the rest to save for later. Taking a bite, I enjoy the buttery-sweetness and, for a moment, lose myself in the indulgence. Still contending with the residual throb in my forehead from my mega-vision this morning, I hold the warm package of rolls to my aching head.

"Uh-oh."

"No, no...it's all right. The vision was early this morning. This is just the leftovers," I reply, as Helen comes to sit beside me on the couch.

"It's nearly noon, Sage, and you're still feeling it?" she asks, reaching for my forehead like any good mom would. "It's *bad*, isn't it?"

"It could be."

"Can I help?"

"Maybe...What do you know about Necromancers?"

"Umm...well, umm...why...why do you ask?"

"Because...my vision...it was..."

"STOP IT!"

"What?"

"YOU'RE READING MY MIND!"

"You stammered..."

"I know!"

"Why?"

"Why, what!"

"Why did you stammer?"

"Because..."

"Helen?"

"Because...I know...well...I knew...a Necro," Helen admits quietly, avoiding my eyes with everything she has.

"And?"

"He was a Traveler. Romany. A *Gypsy*. We knew him through our mom. He was very powerful. We went to visit once or twice; but after her husband died, we never saw him again. I've no idea if he's even still alive. They move often."

Helen's eyes meet mine, finally; she smiles tentatively, but warmly.

"I'm sorry," I say, and she nods thankfully. "You liked him, this Necro you knew."

Helen nods cautiously, "So, Peg and I know a *bit* about Necros; we'll help you all we can."

"Thanks, Helen," I reply. Puzzled by a feeling that she is hiding something, I fight the desire to pop into her head again for a look-see. Instead, I clear my throat and quickly change the subject. "Now, tell me what happened with Connie."

Helen sighs angrily, purses her lips, and punches me in the arm. Shrugging my shoulders, I accept the blame, "I just took a peek and landed on something else when you yelled at me to stop."

Helen's minor annoyance with me reading her mind boils away quickly as her body slumps, surrendering to her regret of the event. Shaking her head, she speaks with faded hope.

"We planned everything right to the letter: what we would say, how we would say it, and even where. What is the thing you and Peg always say? *We act with the best intentions...*Eli is still out looking for her."

Wishing I could reassure Helen of the outcome, I half-smile and pat her shoulder; all the while hoping that this morning's vision was just as flawed as the others because I can't recall seeing Connie in it. Helen takes my hand from her shoulders and holds it tightly. She looks in my eyes deeply and smiles.

"Don't worry. Eli will find her."

Turnabout always being fair play, I smile at my sister-in-law's use of her talents to read *my mind.* "Touché, mon ami," I say, as she laughs lightly.

"Our ordeal with Corson and Lilith isn't over apparently. There's a group called The Brotherhood, loyal to their beliefs. They're going to be our biggest adversary in our goal of the Reformation. My vision proved that today. We have another fight on our hands; but we're better equipped now, and we'll be more prepared...."

"Cut to the chase, Sage. What is it?"

"I'm not certain yet, but I think we're dealing with The Dominion's *Most Wanted.*"

The Healer

I love looking at old family photos.

Walking up and down the halls of the Royal Home waiting for the rest of the team to arrive, I'm admiring the old pictures that are displayed.

There are pictures of Grandpa as a young man, later with his wife, and even later with his boys out fishing. Bill and Helen on their wedding day, and another of my Elizabeth as a little, bitty girl sitting on a tackle box with a half-eaten, fried chicken leg in her hand. So many great memories committed to paper for everyone to share and remember.

I used to have some great pictures of my family, but they were destroyed in a fire…All but one that I have in my room. It's probably why I love looking at the pictures of other families so much.

I grew up on a farm in Jackson, California. We had chickens and goats, grew our own vegetables, and had a small grove of fruit trees: apples, cherries, peaches, pears, and one white nectarine tree that was my favorite.

Sharon, my mom, was a registered nurse, studying at night to become a nurse practitioner; and she knew my dad, Nathanial, inside and out before they got married…literally. My dad was a klutz. You would think being an angel, he'd be agile and graceful; and being a healer, he'd fix himself. But just like me, he couldn't fix his own wounds…and when I asked how he came to earth, he simply said, "I fell." I believed him. I can't remember a day when Dad didn't have a band-aid somewhere or an ice pack on something. Dad could walk across a flat, hardwood floor of an empty room and trip.

Dad and Raffa were paramedics; and without fail they'd go on a call, take the injured or sick person to the hospital, and Dad would end up on the gurney in the next, curtained exam-bay. After Mom had administered one hundred and forty-eight stitches, sixty-two butterflies, thirty-three ice packs, fourteen ace bandages, six slings, two crutches, and a tetanus shot, Dad finally got the nerve to ask her out, tell her he was an angel, ask her to marry him, and ask her to move to Jackson.

Secretly, they both yearned to get away from the fast-paced city life. When Dad mentioned he'd flown over an old, run-down farm with a small orchard for sale, Mom jumped at the chance sight unseen. Of course, knowing Michael, Gabe, and Uri had its advantages to it all: the guys could practice all they wanted in the barn, day or night, if they rebuilt the house, the animal pens, and the produce stand.

Dad couldn't heal himself, but he sure could heal plants. I remember Gabe telling me how dead and brown the leftover fruit trees were, and how hard and clay-like the dirt was; but we had one of the biggest and most bountiful farms and frequented stands in the valley. Restaurants from counties away would order Dad's vegetables, fruits, and nuts. Then, when Mom got the bright idea of starting an herb garden, things started clicking in a different way.

Using Mom's knowledge of medicine and Dad's ability to heal, they started creating organic, herbal tonics, and elixirs. Word got around of Mom's medical experience; and people would come to call, asking for help with all sorts of ailments and illnesses. Keeping it all very quiet and low-key, they enjoyed their life together and their successful business, helping their friends and neighbors on many different levels.

One day, an unusual and ominous force entered their lives. Me...I told you dad was accident prone. Being born half angel in a human world can be...shall we say...interesting.

My earliest memory of my healing powers was at the age of three. Dad was holding me in his arms talking to a big, burly, dark-skinned man; and I caught a glimpse of a baby looking at me from over the shoulder of a woman. The baby reached out to me and smiled. It was then I noticed his face. He had what looked like a split-lip that went almost up to his nose. Later in life, I would come to know this as a *Cleft Lip*.

Reaching out to the little dude, I held his hand; and I remember thinking to myself *fix the boo-boo*...the little boy giggled loudly and covered his face.

"Are you playing peek-a-boo with the baby, Son?" Dad asked, then suddenly his tone changed. "Wave bye-bye...time to get more produce from the back storage."

I turned to wave to my little friend and saw his perfectly healed face. The split gone; only a great, big smile with scattered baby teeth.

As Dad and I rounded the corner, we heard a woman scream, "Madre de Dios!"

Dad set me down and told me to go inside and help Mom. Doing as I was told, I walked inside but turned to see Dad hurriedly go back to our market.

I was sitting at the kitchen table eating a snack of crackers with home-made peanut butter and plum jam when Dad came in the door, calling to Mom. He followed the sound of her voice to the kitchen and stood at the door looking at me; half with pride half with worry. "Sharon, I think we need to talk." From then on, we had rules.

House rules.

Outside-the-house rules.

Town rules.

Market rules.

Company-comes-over rules.

Then, there was the one rule that scared the crap out of me.

Mom always said, "If anything happens to me and Dad, find Michael." I thought to myself, 'Yeah right...What could happen?'

Life was so simple...And perfect! Man, I was so wrong!

One morning, just after I turned thirteen, for some reason I woke up earlier than usual; got dressed and ran up the hill to my favorite tree to get some fruit to take to school in my lunch. I climbed up to the branch facing the East and sat down to watch the colors of the Amador Valley come up with the morning rays. As the sun came up over the hill and illuminated my home and my town, four cars; fancy and expensive; like I'd only seen on TV; came roaring up the road to our house. They pulled up in front of the door and raised a cloud of dust when they parked abruptly. Seven men and six women got out, slamming the doors of the cars before going up to the porch. Dad came out of our house; I could see he was putting his hands up in defense, like he was trying to calm the man down who was talking to him.

The man's voice grew louder. I couldn't make out what he was saying; but he was shouting at Dad, and the other men moved in behind him. Mom came out then, and one of the women came right up to her and slapped her. Dad turned and pushed the woman back, knocking her to the ground. One of the men in the group was carrying some kind of club; he broke through the middle of them and hit Dad square on the side of his head, knocking him down.

Jumping from the tree, I tumbled to the ground but got up as fast as I could and started running to them; all the while the man was still beating Dad with the club. Mom went to stop the man; but instead he turned and hit her, knocking her to the ground in one swing. I screamed over and over for him to stop; then took a running leap at his back as he raised his arm high to hit Mom again. I took the club from him, threw it away, and grabbed onto his head with everything I had in me.

The man struggled to breathe; he staggered and stumbled around aimlessly, then started to twitch. He fell to the ground; but I never let go, keeping my arms wrapped tightly around him. Suddenly, he stopped twitching and lay perfectly still. I heard one of the women scream, and then everything went black.

When I came to, the sun was going down and the cars were gone. I had a headache and a goose egg growing out the back of my head that was throbbing. There was no sign of Mom or Dad...except for the blood. The porch was covered, and the walls and door were sprayed. I ran inside calling their names as I entered every room. The only reply I heard was the echo of my sobbing as I cried out to no one. My legs betrayed me, and I fell to the floor crying uncontrollably.

I must have fallen asleep or maybe passed out.

The smell of smoke and the feel of intense heat from the flames lapping at the walls all around woke me; I ran upstairs to my room and grabbed my backpack, a stack of clean laundry Mom had just left in my room last night, an old cigar box I kept my allowance in that I'd saved up, and my bass guitar that Michael gave me for my birthday last week. Running down the stairs, I covered my face with the collar of my sweatshirt.

The front door was completely consumed by flames. Car lights shown through the windows where curtains used to hang; I counted eight lights; my guess is it was the same four cars from this morning. There was no getting out safely there, so I headed through the kitchen to the back door.

Someone was banging on the back door when I got there; kicking it, obviously trying to get in...And possibly get me? I could see a silhouette only as the moon cast a backlight on *him:* male, tall, but slimly built. I grabbed the new bag of Oreos that was on the counter and Dad's thermos that I was certain was filled with milk, (It was Dad's, what else would it be filled with?) still sitting on the counter from this morning. Taking the latest family picture from the fridge before heading to the garage, I leave through the side access door.

The flames hadn't reached the garage yet, but there was enough smoke to foretell its close approach. I entered cautiously, looking for more of *them* looking for me; but as it turned out, they had already been here.

By the light the full moon cast through the skylight Dad and I installed last summer, I could see in the front seat of my parents' car were the bodies of Mom and Dad, bloodied and broken, posed side by side.

Crying out, I quickly covered my mouth in fear that *they* might hear me. I walked carefully to the access door on the opposite side of the garage, but I trip on something blocking my way. Something...or *someone* was on the floor.

I held my breath. Heard no sound; felt no movement. Stepping back, I looked for the flashlight Dad always kept on his work bench. I turned it on and pointed it to the floor in front of me. It was the man with the club.

I started trembling. His eyes and mouth were open, and there was no sign of him breathing. He was motionless, silent...dead.

Did *I* do this? Did I *kill him*? As far back as I could remember, I was able to heal and repair humans, animals, and other Nephs...but can my powers to give life also *take life, too?* My healing is usually controlled by what I think... All I could remember was thinking the word, *Stop!"*

I felt sick and dizzy: partly from the smoke that was billowing now from under the door to the house, and partly from the discovery of what I'd done.

Stuffing the flashlight into my backpack, I headed out the door. Taking one last look to the bodies that used to be my parents, I said a silent prayer for them; asked them to forgive me for what I'd done, and then carefully crept into the darkness of the corn stalks in the vegetable garden.

I stayed there for awhile, waiting for the cars to leave as I heard the siren of the Amador Valley County fire truck coming up the road. When the last one pulled out, I made my way to the fruit trees up the hill. I climbed up my nectarine tree and stayed there into the morning, watching the firemen's feeble attempt to control the blaze. Remembering Michael used to play at a bar in Paloma, about seven miles south, I started walking there hoping to make it by night fall.

The owner, Daniel, an old friend of Michael's and Dad's, said that Michael had moved on with the band to a gig at another bar in Stockton. I asked where the bus station was, but Daniel said he was driving his wife there that afternoon to visit her mother; if I could wait, he'd give me a lift. I accepted and waited for the ride. When I got to Stockton, the bar wasn't opened yet; so I walked to a luncheonette and sat at the counter.

While waiting for my order, the man sitting next to me opened his newspaper to the front page. There were pictures of Mom and Dad and the man who killed them. The headlines read that it was a murder suicide over an adulterous wife. The man sitting next to me asked me if I was all right. I nodded and wiped the tears from my eyes. The waitress brought my order, and I immediately asked her to make it to go. Taking a few bills from the cigar box, I paid for the food and then left. I walked down to the park across from the bar and climbed the tree that was furthest from the street. I've no idea how long I was there, but I woke up to a voice of someone saying hello.

"Hi," I replied, looking to the bar across the street to make sure it hadn't disappeared while I dozed in the tree.

"Are you here all alone?"

"Yes."

"Where are your parents?"

"Gone."

"Are you all right, Son? Can I help you…?"

Looking to see the face belonging to the sweet voice, I found an older, grandmotherly-looking woman; wavy gray hair, short and a little round, wearing a blue, flowered-print dress with running shoes.

"No…no one can help me," I said, feeling tears come to my eyes again.

"Why don't you come down here? I'm sure we can figure something out together. My name is Edna, what's yours?"

"Zach."

"It's a pleasure to meet you, Zach. It looks like you're traveling? Where are you headed?"

"The bar across the street."

"I see…Aren't you a little young to be drinking?"

I laughed a little, "I'm looking for my Uncle Michael. He's a musician. His band is supposed to be playing there."

"Are you a musician, too? I see you have a guitar with you."

"It's a bass. I'm still learning, but maybe someday."

"Perhaps you can play in your Uncle's band? Hmm? I bet that would be fun for you."

I nodded. The little lady sat down at the table closest to the tree I was in, opened a bag and took out a sandwich.

"Would you like half? I can share with you?"

"No, I have a sandwich, thanks."

"I really hate to eat alone. Do you mind if I eat here with you?"

I shook my head and decided to take out my sandwich and eat, too.

"May I ask how old you are, Zach?"

"Just turned thirteen last week."

"Oh! Well, a late happy birthday to you."

I nodded. Not much to be happy about really, not anymore anyway.

"You said your Uncle is *supposed* to be playing there at that bar? What if he isn't? What will you do?"

I shrugged my shoulders; I hadn't thought about what I would do if I didn't find him. I had money; and I'd already planned to take the bus wherever I needed to, but…

"Zach, I don't know you; and you don't know me…but I get the feeling that you are a very sweet, young man who's very troubled; and if there's anything I can do to help you…."

"My parents are dead; they were murdered. Mom and Dad told me to find Uncle Michael if anything should happen to them, and that's what I'm doing…but, truthfully, I have no clue *what* I'm doing, or *where* I'm going. I feel so alone," I said angrily to a woman that I'd never seen before in my life, but somehow felt as close to now as if I'd known her all my life.

"Hush now. You're not alone, Zach. Listen to your heart, your family will always be there."

And with that statement, Edna packed up her bag, wished me luck on my journey, and then left. I stayed in the tree until dark.

As soon as I saw patrons going in and out of the bar, I climbed down and walked over. Stopping a couple coming out of the bar, I asked if a band was playing there. The lady said, "No, they haven't had a band here in weeks." Thanking her, I headed back across the street to my tree where I climbed back up and contemplated my next move. Fighting back tears of frustration, I took Edna's advice; closed my eyes and listened to my heart to see what it would tell me.

"Are you going to sit up there all night, or are you going to come down here and give us a hug?" said a familiar, deep, raspy voice with an English accent.

Opening my eyes, I leaped from the tree and hugged Michael tightly. Standing behind him were his band mates and long-time family friends: Uri, Raffa, and Gabe. I pulled away from Michael and looked at all of them.

"Mom and Dad are…"

"We know, we heard," Raffa said, stepping forward.

"What they say in the papers isn't true."

"We know, Zach. Your folks were good people," Michael said, looking to the guys.

I started to cry again. "The man who killed them...? Oh, God, Michael, I think I...!"

"We'll talk about that later...Let's get you home and safe. You're what? Thirteen, now? Got your wings yet?" Uri asked, stepping in closer.

"No, not yet."

"Slow bloomer like your Dad, huh?" Gabe said, ruffling my hair. "That's okay...the slow ones are always the strongest," he said, winking a bright, blue eye at me.

"That's right! We are!" Raffa said, patting me on the back.

"Well, better hang on tight," Michael said, grabbing my backpack and bass and tossing them to Uri and Gabe. He threw me over his shoulder and onto his back. Wrapping my arms around his neck, we shot up into the air like a bullet; never saw when he extended his wings, they were just suddenly there. Each wing just as long as he was tall: white, fluffy, and glistening in the moonlight.

We flew over the San Joaquin Valley; passed the lights of the refinery in Martinez; to a house with a barn in Castro Valley, surrounded by fruit trees, rows and rows of vegetables, and off in the distance a well-grown vineyard. The guys welcomed me into their home, gave me my own room upstairs, and there I've stayed.

The guys each gave me pictures that they had of Mom and Dad from before I was born. My favorite is of Dad, same age as I am now, perched up in a tree. The resemblance between him and me is startling; to look at it, you'd say the picture *was* me.

I've gained a greater appreciation of photographs, now...they are precious and important and deserve as much respect as the people in them.

"Oh...my...God, is that 'E'? Look at those cheeks? Cute little thing, wasn't she?"

"She still is," I say to Marco as he looks at my favorite picture of Elizabeth.

"Hey! That's my *baby sister* you're talking about!" Marco says, punching me in the arm.

I put my hands up in surrender, "Sorry, man, I can only speak what's in my heart."

Marco smiles, pats me on the back, and then asks, "Are you alone?"

I had to think about that question for a moment before I answered. Looking to the pictures on the walls, I recall the pictures I have at home and remember all the pictures I used to have in Jackson. I guess Edna was right after all.

"Never," I say.

"What?"

"Nothing, Bro...come on, let's go find Robert," I say with a laugh, walking to the lobby with him; taking one last glance down the hall at the precious memories being shared there.

Helen

"Damn, Girl! Give an old broad some warning before you walk in here carrying that kind of an emotional load. I have enough hot flashes as it is on my own," Peg says, poking her head out of the closet as I exit the portal into Eli's apartment. "You brought a bigger load of crap with you than I have packed up to throw out! You nearly knocked me down!"

"Sorry, Peg, I...What *are* you *doing?*"

"Isn't it amazing how much *stuff* you collect in a lifetime? When Dave and I packed up to move into the new house, I couldn't believe how much...well, *crap* I had collected...and I thought I had everything. Then Eli calls me and says I left an entire closet of linens and knick-knacks. Well, she actually said 'linens and shit'; but I thought she was just being a smart ass, but she was right! I have all the linens packed and ready to go, and a garbage bag filled with various papers and miscellaneous odds and ends that I collected for really no reason other than it might come in handy one day. Honestly, Babe, I am *never* moving again...*ever*! The only thing with any real worth is this," she says, handing me a zip-lock bag full of old pictures of her, Mom, and me.

Amid all the old Polaroids and negatives was Mom's locket: a gold heart with two enameled, etched flowers and a heart-shaped ruby in the center, inside was a picture of her girls on one side and of her husband on the other. I prefer to acknowledge him as her husband than *Dad* because, well, he simply wasn't there as a dad to us. He was always on the road; and when he was there with us, he was always so timid around Peg and me, like he was afraid of us. Then when he learned that we got our powers early, all he left was a pile of smelly laundry and a vapor trail.

Never felt sad when Mom told us he died. I felt, nothing, actually. Mom was devastated because I think deep down she never gave up hope that he would eventually come to his senses and come back. I felt bad for her; not him. That was the beginning of the end. If anyone can die of a broken heart, I think Mom did.

Peg dragged the over-stuffed garbage bag from the closet to the door, and then came running back fanning herself with her hand as she plopped herself down on the couch.

"Okay, so, what gives? Your mind is all closed up; I can't see what's bothering you. Either let your guard down or…Oh! Crap!"

Taking a deep breath, I let down the brick wall I'd built in my mind and let it all come tumbling out.

"Whoa! A necromancer? How much did you tell Sage?"

"Only that I knew one…not that…"

"Maybe we should tell him…after all, we don't even know if he's still alive."

"After Mom's husband died they all moved…but, I don't know where."

"You *still* call him *Mom's husband*? What are you? Thirteen?"

"What should I call him? *Daddy*?...I can't call him what he wasn't, but I won't call him what you call him."

"*Shithead* is a far better description."

Thumbing through the pictures in the bag, I come across a picture of our happy little family, the day before the infamous breakfast.

"I'll call him *Julian*. That was his name, right?"

Peg nods as she slides to my side and leans in to peek at the photo. Taking the plastic bag from my hand, she reaches in and takes out Mom's old locket and examines it closely.

"What are you looking for?"

"Look at that picture closely."

Examining every dot on the frame, I go over the photo carefully, until my eyes fall upon what Peg caught.

"Oh! But…*he's* wearing it…and it's…"

"Glowing," Peg said, still looking at the locket. She was turning it around and around and opening the latch when something caught my eye.

"Peg, what's that there?"

"Where?"

"There."

"Where!"

"Here," I say, taking the locket and pressing on the red enameled hinge pin, opening a third section of the locket holding an interesting collection of stones.

The heart-shaped locket has a secret opening lined with small, diamond chips; a mixture of ruby and fire opal chips fills the center, up to the edge of an eye-shaped sapphire.

"Peg, do you know what this is? This is a third-eye amulet…why was he…*Julian*…why was he wearing it? And it was glowing. It never glowed when Mom wore it. She always told me…Peg, why are you staring at me like that?"

"Look. Can't you see it? Look!" Peg says, turning me around to face the mirror; and I finally see what she is talking about.

"Oh, my…"

"He knew."

"What?"

"Shithead knew…when he saw us use magic…he knew…that's why he ran. He wasn't afraid of what we were. He was afraid of what we might become…"

"That *we*, one of us, would carry on *his family's ways*… that means *he was…*"

"Yes. *He was.* Have you told Bill about *all* of our heritage…ancestry…roots?"

Feeling a little stunned by everything I've just discovered, I don't answer and can't answer her.

"Helen?" Peg brushes my hair back from my face.

"No, not all of it. Just bits and pieces. I need to tell him the whole cohesive story," I say, feeling guilty for always shying away from telling him. He knows how it upsets me and never pushes me for an answer; not that he didn't try…he always seems so concerned that it's something more serious. Well…it is now.

"Sage!"

"What about him?" Peg asks, startled by my outburst.

"His vision…this could be the piece he needs to change the…"

"We need to tell him…everything."

Nodding, I take the locket and put it in my pocket, "You tell him. I need to find Bill. Where do I start?"

"Like everything else," Peg says, pricking her finger to activate the portal. Patrick discovered that only a drop is needed; Bill and Eli are thrilled.

"At the beginning?" I say, finishing Peg's thought.

"Yes, at the beginning," she says, stepping through the mirror. "We'll start...with our grandfather...Valko Ivanova."

The Soldier

The last time I felt this many butterflies in my stomach was the day I enlisted in the United States Army.

Today, just like that day, I don't know what to expect. The only difference is I don't have an ounce of hesitation about being part of The Kindred. Back then, I had more than just doubt about enlisting.

I was seventeen and mowing the lawn in the backyard so I wouldn't be in the house when Pop came home and saw the letter on the table with my SAT scores.

"Alessandro! ALESSANDRO!" he yelled.

Oh, shit! He used my *real* name!

"Yeah, Pop?" I answered, as I pushed the mower into the rusty aluminum garden shed.

"What does this mean? Huh? Explain this to me!" he said, waving the letter at me.

"It means I'm not going to Stanford, or Cal, or any of those other schools you wanted me to," I said, picking up the rake to start in on the clippings.

"After all that studying you did? Or were you really studying? You weren't out with that little…?"

"POP! DON'T START! HER NAME IS CONNIE, AND SHE'S JUST A FRIEND! AND YES, I WAS REALLY STUDYING!"

"Don't you raise your voice at me! *I'm your father*, and you still live under *my* roof!" Dad said, walking towards me with his chest puffed out. "You know what they say about her family don't you? Witches! Into black magic and shit! Carving chickens up under a full moon...Naked! That's how her parents were killed, ya know! Rival covens! *Her* mother didn't like *his* father! How else do you explain an empty car just careening into them and killing them? Huh? Goddamn witches! I'm just glad your mother isn't alive to see you going around with that little…!"

"*Pop! Please?* That's enough!" I said, holding my hand up as he blessed himself and kissed his crucifix. "Connie's my friend, nothing more. Besides, she has a boyfriend," I said, packing the grass clippings into a garbage bag.

"Why can't you date Eli? Now there's a cute little thing I could see you with! Huh? *HUH?* What about her? You ever think about that…?" Pop said, nudging me in the ribs.

"Pop, Eli's my best friend…she's like my little sister," I said, getting really grossed out by what he was insinuating. Finishing the clean-up of the clippings, I put the rake away and started to take the bag to the garbage when I noticed that Pop was just staring at me.

"What?"

"What are you going to do?"

"Throw this in the garbage."

"Damnit, Alessandro! I mean with your life?"

"I don't know…be a mailman like you," I said, really not wanting to get into this with him right now.

"The hell you will! You're going to college whether you like it or not!"

"Pop, I'm not cut out for college! I don't have the grades. Besides, I don't think I really want to go."

"What if you had gotten that football scholarship to Notre Dame? What then? Would you have gone?"

"Pop, that's not even relevant now…?"

"Answer me!"

"I guess."

"You guess? It's been your dream your whole life to play professional football!"

"No, Pop, it's been *your* dream to play pro football; but you didn't have the size or ability," I said, slamming the lid of the garbage can down. "I do; but it isn't what I want."

"Then what *do* you want? Give me something to go on here, Son? I'm worried about you! Where are you leading yourself? What is it you want in life?" Pop asked, turning around and walking away. He was rubbing his face, attempting to keep his emotions under control. At heart, a mushy old fart, but he hides it under his grumpy-butt exterior. He stopped at the back door and turned to me, "Did you purposely lose it?"

"What?"

"The scholarship? You're head wasn't in the game that night. Then you nearly left it on the field."

This was the conversation I never wanted to have. I knew we would have to talk about this one day, but he'd never brought it up until now. I took a deep breath and went for it.

"You're right, my head wasn't in the game that night; but, no, I didn't lose it purposely. I knew how important it was to you that I impress the scout; and the harder I tried to focus, the more I screwed up. I had other things on my mind that night," I said, walking up to Pop and looking him in the eye. I stood nearly a foot taller than him now...when the hell did that happen? "I met with an Army Recruiter that day...what he told me...Pop, it all sort of just clicked."

Dad turned white and his eyes were huge. He started breathing hard and tried to make his way to the patio table to sit down.

"Pop, you okay? You want some water?" I asked, helping him into a chair.

"No, no I'm fine...." He was rubbing his face again. I could see in his face he was searching for the right words.

"The Army, Marco? What...? Why?"

All my life, Pop had been pushing me, encouraging me, to set goals and reach higher. 'Strive for greatness' he'd tell me! I think he always felt that he had to be two parents in one, even though he really didn't have to. He was great all by himself.

"Pop, did you ever feel like there was something waiting for you? Something you were supposed to be a part of? Something you were born to do? Something big? But you just didn't know what it was?" I asked, watching him listen intently.

"And the Army is where you feel you'll find it?" he asked, still an air of uncertainty in his voice and demeanor.

"I think so..."

"You *think* so? You better *know* so, young man! You can't just drop in and drop out of the military, like going to the mall!"

"Pop,...let me finish. I think it's the beginning of something. I think I'll get the training, discipline, and education I need to get to whatever it is I'm destined for."

"But this *big thing*? You have no idea what it is? *Your destiny?*" Pop asked, mocking me.

"You don't want me to do it, I know…"

"Did she put you up to this?"

"What? Who?"

"The witch?"

"Oh, Pop,…not this again?"

"Just answer me! Are you doing this for that…? For *her*?"

"We're just friends, that's all. I told you already, she has a boyfriend. She's dating our backup quarterback."

"The backup quarterback?"

Oh, shit! I can already see where this is going. *Our Father, who art in heaven…*

"You *SEE*! *A witch*! She was trying to get her boyfriend into the game. Probably said some mumbo jumbo to you when you didn't know it, killed some little critter and that's what's got you all confused about this army thing! I'll just bet *he* got a big football scholarship! Am I right?"

…hallowed be Thy name…Thy kingdom come, Thy will be…

"Made you lose your focus in the game, too! You could've been seriously hurt! Goddamn witches! Are you missing any hair?" Dad asked, instantly jumping up and scrounging around my head.

…done.

"Pop? What's gotten into you? No, I'm not missing any hair! Seriously, what's wrong? What's got you so freaked?"

"I DON'T WANT YOU COMING HOME IN A BOX WITH A FOLDED FLAG AND A LETTER BEING THE ONLY THINGS I HAVE LEFT OF YOU!"

Pop stormed off and went inside the house, slamming the screen door behind him punctuating his statement. I finished saying my prayer in my head, because I don't think it's respectful leaving them half done, and then got up to go find him.

I walked in the kitchen, through the dining room to the living room and his bedroom; but he was nowhere to be found. Hearing rustling coming from the hallway, I turned the corner and found the door to the basement open. Going downstairs I found Pop sitting on the floor in front of an open, old, oak chest, holding a glass-encased American flag, folded in the traditional triangle. I sat down on the floor next to him.

"Your Grandpa was in the Army. Staff Sergeant Alessandro Marco Conti; your Mom and I named you after him. One night, we're tossing a football around, the next thing I know, this is all I had left of him. He went out on maneuvers; just practice for the real thing. He came home in a box. I remember the priest coming to the door and your Grandma collapsing...she couldn't stop crying," Pop said, holding back tears. "I promised your Mom I'd take care of you. How do you expect me to keep my promise if you do this?"

I wrapped my arms around him and held him. I never knew that much about my Grandfather. Pop never talked about him; now I know why.

"I've already lost your mom; please don't make me go through life without both of you? Please, Marco?"

Pop spent the rest of the evening telling me about my Grandfather and what life was like moving from base to base. From his time spent in Germany, to how big the bugs were at Fort Hood, and how it was hotter than Hell at Fort Irwin; I finally got to know the man I was named for, and why Pop became the man he was.

"Eli will miss you if you leave," Pop said quietly.

"She has another year of high school. She'll be busy being a Senior. Besides, the Army has phones. And she can write. So can you."

"And Connie?"

"She'll be fine. Eli will watch out for her."

"Who'll watch out for you, Marco?" Pop asked, getting teary eyed again.

"I guess that'll be up to me and God," I said, wiping a stray tear from his face.

"Better to make sure," Pop said, taking off his crucifix and handing it to me.

"Pop,...I can't take...!"

"You have to. Don't make me break my promise to your mom. Besides, can't very well stand in the way of destiny," Pop said, no longer sounding angry, hurt, or scared.

I put his crucifix on, and I've never taken it off.

Months later, the day after Graduation, while on his route in Alameda, Pop suffered a heart attack; he died on the way to the hospital. A week later, I turned eighteen and found myself outside the Army Recruiting Office, unable to bring myself to go in. Something was holding me back. I sat down at the bus stop and tried to regroup.

"Gee, it sure is warm today!"

"Oh!...Um, yes. It is, isn't it?" I replied, answering the elderly lady seated next to me.

"Has the bus come by already? Did I miss it?" she asked.

"I'm sorry. I don't know. I just stopped here for a minute. Trying to get my courage up," I said, pointing to the recruiting office.

"Ah! I see! May I ask what's holding you back?"

"I'm not sure, really. Couple of months ago I was all ready to join...Now? I just don't know."

"What's changed? What happened between then and now?" she asked.

"I...?"

"Oh, my stars! Where are my manners? Here I am prying into your life, and you don't even know me from the mailman! My name is Edna," the little lady said, offering her hand.

"Marco...Marco Conti," I replied, taking her hand. She was grandmotherly-looking, wearing a bright-yellow, flowery dress and running shoes.

"Well, Marco,...I don't know you; but you look like a smart, young man. I'm sure you'll make the right decision."

"You think so?"

"Certainly! Why wouldn't you?"

"I don't know? I had more confidence when my folks were here. They're both gone now. I've never felt so alone."

"Hush now...you're not alone, Marco. Listen to your heart, your family will always be there."

A bus arrived. Edna stood up, not much taller than when she was seated and patted my shoulder before walking to the doors. She boarded the bus and waved to me from the window.

Holding onto Pop's crucifix, I kept hearing Edna's words going round my head. I closed my eyes and listened ...and, instead of Edna's words, I heard my Pop's voice.

After boot camp at Fort Sill in Oklahoma, I based at Fort Irwin; Pop was right, it *was* hotter than Hell; but it was also exactly what I needed to be ready for my future... with The Kindred!

Standing in the living room of the Royal Home, I admire all of Bill and Grandpa's medals they earned in The Dominion Army; and I feel a pair of arms slowly wrap around my waist from behind. Seeing the bright pink finger nails, I know exactly who it is.

"Well, it's about time you get here. I thought *you* of all people would be here early...Connie? What's wrong, Baby?"

Turning to face my woman, I see something I thought I'd never see: Connie's makeup was everywhere except where it was supposed to be. Her mascara was running down to her chin; lip gloss smudged to her ears; her nose and eyes as red as an autumn sunset.

"Nothing...really...just having an emotional day...I'm okay, Marco,...really."

"I know better than that. I have never seen you this upset. What happened? Tell me. What...?"

"Marco, I told you...I'm fine."

I've learned over the years...when a woman says "I'm fine," she really isn't...but she doesn't want to talk about it...whatever 'it' may be. When she's ready, she'll tell me.

"Baby, I'm sorry. I think I left a face print on the back of your shirt," Connie whimpers, as she turns me around.

"That's all right; not to worry. I've been preparing for this day all my life. I brought another shirt."

"But, Marco, this is going to stain..."

"Connie, Honey, it's okay! There is no way I will allow a little smudge of grease pain to stand in the way of my *destiny*."

Peggilyn

Watching a captive tiger furiously pace in his cage as he calculates his escape is exhaustive work, especially when that tiger is my brother-in-law. I've been standing at the doorway of the kitchen for the last ten minutes as he paces with a twenty-ounce coffee cup in hand and his thoughts racing loudly at an incredible pace.

"How did this happen? How the hell, did this happen? That lousy excuse for a Demon! It wasn't enough that he nearly killed my daughter and brother, plotted to kill the rest of the family, and planned world domination by opening The Gates. No! He has to set back up plans! BACK UP PLANS! After he made us lose all that time together because his MOMMY wanted her revenge, too! Stinkin', no good, son-of-a-fucking...!"

"Bitch? I think the word you're looking for here is *bitch*," I say, winking at Bill as I startle him out of his mental tirade. He laughs.

"Yeah, okay. Maybe I do think loud."

"Well, who wouldn't, considering what's going on?" I say getting a cup and joining him in his caffeinated brain storm. Taking a seat at the kitchen table, Bill joins me. His tie hangs undone around his collar.

"Peg, about your...about Valko. We...?"

"Wait. Bill, please, let me try and ease your mind here. I know out of courtesy you never brought the subject up with Helen but you need to know how we feel. You and your team need to do whatever it is you need to do. NO MATTER WHAT!"

"But, Peg, we may...!" Bill says, but I stop him.

"Our connection to Valko ceased to be a very long time ago. We don't even know where he is, if he's still living...or what state of mind he's in? Necros aren't always able to keep all their marbles in the bag, ya know what I mean? Crossing the plain of life and death can be...hazardous to one's brain cells."

Bill takes his handkerchief from his jacket pocket and hands it to me. I hadn't realized it, but I have tears flowing from my eyes.

"I don't cry. What the hell's the matter with me?" I say, wiping the waterworks away. Bill reaches out and holds my hand.

"You love him; so does Helen. The powers of the Necromancer may have passed onto her, but she won't…we won't let her lose her mind to her powers. Besides, she's one tough cookie. She wouldn't allow it, either."

Folding Bill's handkerchief, I stuff it neatly back in his pocket. Wiggling my finger at his tie, I fix the Windsor for him.

"Thanks, Peg," Bill says, with a shy smile.

Bill takes our cups and goes to the sink to wash them. Grabbing a towel from a nearby hook, I dry the first of the two clean cups.

"She's scared, Peg. She wouldn't say it; but I know my wife…she's terrified of this power."

"She should be. She'll need your strength more than ever now."

"She has it. Always. But then, she's a 'Young' woman. You all come with your own quiet, inner strength."

"Yes, we do…and we're also *Ivanova's*."

The Empath

Did you ever look in the mirror and suddenly not recognize the person looking back at you? With the way mirrors are around here, it gives one pause when you look into them. But this morning, after learning the truth that was kept from me, I'm not so sure I know that person I see looking back at me.

I was born Consuelo Dorotea Valentia Gutierrez to wonderful people named Humberto and Ernestina.

Bert and Ernie; my parents, not the Muppets; met and fell in love against all odds. It wasn't quite a Romeo and Juliet, star-crossed lovers, or West Side Story of rival gangs breaking into song and dance at the drop of a switchblade kind of thing; but it was definitely one family against another. We moved all around Southern California a total of twelve times; we lived in Glendale, Ontario, Pasadena, Torrance, Pomona, Brea, Santa Monica, Anaheim, Placentia, Fullerton, Escondido, and Orange.

We kept moving because…well, something weird kept happening.

My folks first met in grade school; Mrs. Burton's third-grade classroom in Tucson, Arizona. Mom was the new kid in town, and she sat in front of Dad in class. From the moment they met, they were inseparable.

Mom, orphaned as a baby, was being raised by her foster parents, Juan and Patricia Seguidor. She was watched carefully and never really allowed to do anything except go to school. When she was sixteen, she was allowed to get a part-time job at the local book store. Little did the Seguidor's know, my Dad was already working there.

Dad would write Mom these beautiful love letters. Sometimes there would be a poem, a drawing, or pressed flowers. He'd hide them in a section of the bookstore, then leave a book from that section somewhere out on the sales floor. Mom would then have to re-shelve the book and low and behold, find the letter.

This went on for two years while they worked there; Dad would profess his love to her, page after page, picture after picture, flower by flower…day after day. When Mom turned eighteen, instead of finding a letter, she found my Dad waiting for her with a ring. She said, "Yes," but knowing how Mom's foster family would react, they eloped and left for California that afternoon. This would have all been really romantic and sweet if it all ended happily ever after right there…but this was *my* family. Nothing was ever sweet, simple, or, God forbid, *easy* for long.

When Mom and Dad made it to California, now husband and wife thanks to a judge who wanted to hurry up and make his afternoon tee time; they rented a bungalow in Glendale. Mom found work at a tailoring shop, and Dad went to work at a local coffee house.

One morning a few months later, Mom didn't feel well and went to the doctor. He told her it was just the flu, and she should go home, rest, and drink plenty of fluids. Six months later, the *flu bug*, now named Consuelo, came kicking and screaming her way into the world. A few days after Mom and Dad brought me home, there was a knock at the door.

It was the Seguidors. They'd come to collect Mom. Dad said he would have nothing to do with them and slammed the door on their faces. The Seguidors wouldn't leave. They camped on the front stoop taunting Mom and Dad and the neighbors, calling them names and being a nuisance. Dad wanted to call the police, but Mom made him promise not to….

During the night, Mom, Dad, and little me, snuck out the back and over the fence to the neighbors. They helped us out by taking us to the bus station where we left for Anaheim. Dad would make the trip back later to get our car when it was safe.

Dad had friends in Anaheim that we stayed with until we got a place of our own. Another year went by; and then here come the Seguidors again, bringing their brand of mayhem to our door. This pattern went on once a year, every year, on or near my birthday. I started to anticipate it coming on by the time I was three; the energy in the air would get thick; and when April Fool's Day rolled around, I started packing. By my birthday on April fifteenth, we had already moved on, trying to stay three steps ahead of them. A month before my eleventh birthday, we were in Pasadena; a few weeks away from having to plan our next move. Dad got several consecutive calls on his cell phone; I lost count after the ninth one.

Mom and Dad were not fighters; I can't remember a time prior to that day that I'd ever heard them say a cross word to each other; but those phone calls set off an argument and a chain of events that would eventually turn my world upside down.

The tension that built up in the house as the phone kept ringing was incredible. There was something in the taut atmosphere that made me want to eavesdrop; and then again, it scared the hell out of me and made me want to hide. I could tell in my stomach that I really didn't want to hear it. I kept trying to make myself busy so I wouldn't pay attention, but I couldn't help listening as the voices rose higher and higher.

Dad had been calling on old friends that we made along the way in the previous cities we'd lived to see if there were any places to move back to; or if we could possibly stay with them, until we found a place of our own. The answer was a resounding, "No". But it wasn't the no's that started the initial fight...it was the 'reason' behind the no.

I heard Dad ask Mom why she didn't tell him? Tell him what, I don't know; but Mom wasn't at all defensive about it. She was genuinely surprised and hurt by his tone. I could feel her through the wall. She wanted to cry, but she remained strong and told him that *it*; whatever *it* was; was not at all important.

I believed her, but I also believed the fear I could feel coming from Dad. Sneaking quietly out of my room, I took a look at their faces. Dad's was stressed; Mom's was held high and without fear.

"Do you know what Francisco in Ontario told me? The Seguidors broke into their house looking for us and for information of *your* whereabouts. And when Paulo in Pomona wouldn't tell them, they cut off a finger! Jorge in Torrance said the same thing! Marta Santos, Efrem's wife...? She said...!" Dad took a breath and swallowed something from his memory that looked like it would come back up any minute. "She said...the Seguidor's cut out Efrem's tongue because he wouldn't tell where we went to! Ernie, tell me, please? What is Nahualli? Why do they all keep calling you that? Why won't the Seguidor's leave us alone?"

Mom let her proud front down and started to cry. She walked to my Dad, hugged him, and whispered something in his ear. His eyes grew wide and fearful. He pulled away and looked at her, nodded, and hugged her again.

I couldn't hear what she told him; but I could tell by the way he was standing, he wasn't afraid anymore. Still concerned, but the fear had dissipated in the air.

One year later, the old familiar knock at our door came as scheduled.

Dad ignored it.

The knock came again, but louder.

Dad still ignored it.

The knock came again, but this time it felt and sounded like a battering ram was being used; the entire house shuddered. Mom stood up and went to the door. She opened it slowly and carefully. Dad came and stood with me, putting his arm around my shoulders.

"We have come for you, Ernestina. It's time to come back where you belong," Juan said.

"No. I'm not leaving. This is my home," Mom said proudly.

"Ernestina, *you know* you cannot stay here!" Juan said sternly, stepping forward.

Mom held her hand up and stopped him. "Please, don't make me…!"

"Ernestina, *your kind cannot*…!" Patricia started to say, but Mom cut her off.

"*Silence*. That will be enough out of *you*," Mom politely scolded.

Patricia was silenced. Not out of fear or because of the scolding but because she literally could not speak. She tried to open her mouth and couldn't. She turned to Juan in a panic as tears rolled down her face.

"What have you done?" Juan cried out, turning to the neighbors that by now had come out to their yards. "Nahualli! She is Nahualli! She is…!" He shouted pointing to my Mom.

"I wish both of you would just disappear and never return!" Mom said sternly.

I blinked and the Seguidors were gone.

Dad held me tighter, trembling slightly. I couldn't figure out where the Seguidors had gone to. One moment they were there and the next…Poof! I could sense from Dad that it wasn't a good thing, especially since the neighbors saw.

"Ernie, close the door. Close the door!"

Mom closed the door and turned to look at both of us; her eyes were wild and intense. Dad, still shaking a little, took a deep breath and headed off to do what needed to be done. So did I.

"Guess I'll go get packed."

We moved to the city of Orange after that, but Mom and Dad were never the same. They were distant and quiet; there was always an edge of anger in the air. I was happy in Orange: good school, nice neighbors, and I actually had friends.

One day, when I was walking home from school, I felt like I was being followed. I kept stopping to look behind me, but I never saw anyone there. The feeling never left me. I got home and went to the kitchen to get a snack before doing my homework.

"How was school, Honey?" Mom asked.

"Good! I really like it here, Mom. Do you think we can stay here...you know...for awhile?"

"Well...?" she started to say, but was interrupted by Dad running in the house. He was panting and sweating; an air of terror followed him. His left hand was wrapped in a bloody paper towel; his face, pale and drawn.

"Ernie, Connie,...pack up; we're going to visit my mother's new home in Berkeley!"

"Bert, what's wrong? What happened to your hand?" Mom asked, as she unwrapped the towel. She gasped at what she saw and hid it from my view. I could feel her pain and fear compounded by a nauseous roll in her tummy, and I could only imagine what she saw.

"They came back, Ernie! But there's more of them now!"

Once again, we packed up and hit the road. The departure of the Seguidors was obviously only temporary.

Berkeley was...in comparison to the L.A. area, quiet and different. Dad's Mom was...well, not the grandmotherly type.

She was perfectly coiffed and dressed in a spotless, crisply-pressed, off-white, linen suit. Her gray hair had a slight blue tint to it, nails were perfectly manicured, her shoes showed no wear and tear at all. She looked down her nose at Mom and me like we were something left in the cat box, and she insisted I address her as Grandmother. Not Grandma, Granny, Grand, or even Abuelita, like my friends referred to their grandmas.

Coming from L.A., I dressed like the girls there: trendy and bright, with a little flair. So, in Berkeley, I really stuck out. I wasn't like everyone else, more like a square peg in a round hole; but I was all right with that.

Grandmother wasn't! She gave me a list of rules and regulations and expected me to follow them to the letter; including a dress code.

I hadn't been enrolled in school yet because this *visit* was supposed to be temporary. Then Mom and Dad sat me down and told me they needed to go back to L.A. to take care of some *family business*. I could feel their intensity and knew it was the Seguidors again.

"They're coming *here* aren't they?" I asked.

Mom looked at Dad and then back at me. The fear in his eyes as he looked at his hand where his index finger use to be, was all the proof I needed. The temporary visit was going to be a little longer. I wasn't happy at all. Not only were my parents leaving to deal with those horrible people, but they were leaving me here alone with 'Grandmother'. They said they were only going to be gone a few days; so, I made the best of it by finding ways to get around Grandmother's edges by anticipating the things she had trouble doing and then did them. Reading was difficult with her failing eyesight, so I read to her. Cooking became troublesome with her arthritis, so I cooked for her a few dishes Mom taught me. Whatever I could *feel*, I did, to keep her *happy*; and, in turn, I was happy, too.

A week went by; Mom and Dad finally called to say they were on their way home. They didn't say exactly what happened or what they said to the Seguidors to make them go away, but they assured me that they were gone for good and never coming back. They both sounded very happy and like their old selves. They were laughing together on the phone; that was something I hadn't heard in a long time.

"We love you! See you soon," were the last words I heard them say. Ever.

After the accident, I sort of freaked out and ran away; but I didn't get very far; I only had enough money to ride BART to Oakland. I was sitting on a tiled bench in the station watching a man talk to something or someone inside the lapel of his trench coat.

"I love your pink sweater!"

"Excuse me? Are you speaking to me?" I asked the elderly woman in a brightly-flowered, purple dress seated next to me.

"Although, I must say, it doesn't go at all well with that blue funk on your face, or the gray cloud hovering over your head."

Looking away I tried to subtly scoot over a little, away from the lady. I didn't feel like talking; especially to strangers; I didn't want to offend her either just in case....

"Forgive me! I don't normally just start talking to strangers, I didn't mean to frighten you," she said, turning away from *me* this time.

I didn't mean to be rude; but with my past experience with my family, I just don't speak to strangers even if they don't come to my door.

"Thank you," I said, "about my sweater. Thanks."

The little lady in running shoes nodded and turned back to the train.

"I'm not very happy right now. That's why I don't look...happy," I said to her.

She nodded and smiled. I turned my back to her again and tried hard not to cry. I didn't succeed. A hand was in front of my face holding a pink handkerchief with the name Edna embroidered on it.

"Life sucks right now!" I said, accepting the offer.

"Sometimes it does, Dear...I have to admit I have seen my share of poopy days, too; but everything gets better with time, if we want it to. Changes happen and life isn't always what we'd like it to be; but it *is life none the less;* and we have to take the good with the bad. What is your name, my dear?" Edna said, sitting next to me; not too close, but not so far I couldn't hear her.

"Connie. Connie Gutierrez."

"Well, Connie, I believe we get in life exactly what we are capable of handling...no more, no less. I can't say that it's always what we deserve, but...."

"But it's just so hard now. My parents are gone, Grandmother hates me, I don't know anyone here, and...I've never in my life been so alone!"

"Hush now. You're not alone, Connie. Listen to your heart, your family will always be there," Edna said.

A train pulled in, and Edna stood up. I handed her handkerchief back to her, but she pushed my hand back towards me like she wanted me to keep it. She patted my shoulder and smiled, then turned to run to her train.

After that day, Grandmother and I formed a *special* relationship; as long as I kept anticipating her needs and helping her around the house, she would look the other way where her *regulations* were concerned. I kept to her dress code and the other rules most of the time, but she allowed a slip here and there so my true self could shine. She still made it clearly known that she didn't approve of me, but we were in each other's lives whether we liked it or not.

After Grandmother died, it took me awhile to figure out who I was. I still liked my bright colors and fun, flashy outfits and immediately jumped back into them; but I learned the art of subtlety from a perfectly-polished woman. I never walk out of the house in shabby clothes, my hair is always combed, my nails are clean and nicely kept. I took the best of both worlds and made it my own. It isn't prideful to care about the impression you make as a person. You are not only representing yourself to the public, but also honoring the ancestors who came before you.

Grandmother would have smacked me with a ruler if she had seen how I arrived here. What a mess. After cleaning myself up and changing into the new outfit I picked up at the mall, I find my way through the Royal Home and then enter the Library. Looking through the shelves, I come across a book on the Aztec culture and their religious beliefs.

"Is that a good book?"

Waking from my daydream, I realize I'm staring in a mirror holding a book open to a page with a familiar name.

"Um…actually, yes. I was looking for some information on this," I say, showing Sean the page describing a Nahualli.

"Oh! An Aztec witch? They're very powerful; they can transform themselves into animals and even remove curses from other witches…they are associated with the shamanistic practices of the Aztecs. Their personality dictated their craft; some were good, and some were very evil. I have more books on them back home; I can loan them to you if you like?" Sean says, looking closely at the picture, then at me, noticing the resemblance that I saw when I first opened the book.

"Sure, I think I'd like that."

"Ya know, Connie,…this picture …sort of looks like you," Sean says, taking the book and holding it up to my face; looking at the picture, then back at the reflection in the mirror.

"I don't know, Sean. When I look in the mirror…I only see my parents."

And that just happens to be the very best of me.

Bill

Heading down the hall, my brain still going ninety miles an hour, I pass by the Royal Hall and see Ash, air jamming to a tune on his iPod. It must be some hard, fast, rocker from the way he's thumbing the imaginary strings. He jumps in the air, spins around and finds me standing there, applauding him. Turning twelve shades of red as he pulls the earbuds out, the rock star speaks, "Hey, Bill, how long have you been there?"

"Oh, just long enough that I was ready to yell out for a rendition of *Free Bird* and then get my lighter out," I reply, smiling at my baby brother. He laughs, shyly.

"It's a recording of Zach and the band; damn but this kid can play. He asked me to sit in for him one night next week. He has some big evening planned for Eli; an official 'date night', I think."

"Are you going to incorporate that last move into your performance? I get the impression that Michael is pretty meat and potatoes when it comes to a gig."

"No, I won't be adding that in. That's just me, being...me," Ash laughs. "It's a good day, Bill! Don't you think so? We're all together, and there's *change* in the air.

"Yeah, it is. You're right," I reply, but I'm not very convincing.

"Aw, hell, man, what's wrong? I know that look. Dad used to get it when either I was in big trouble, or something really bad was happening," Ash says, coming up and putting his arm around my shoulders. He's taller; don't know when that happened, but he stands six inches taller than me now; guess I just never noticed it before. He walks me over to the couch, and we sit down.

As I download all the new information that Sage told me, I watch Ash's happy face disappear in an instant. The second I say *Corson*, all the joy just evaporates from him. The man's name just seems to suck the life out of anyone who hears it.

"How are Helen and Peg holding up?" Ash asks.

"Peg is…all right. Helen…scared and not about to admit it. All we have is a vision; a picture of a possible outcome. Still so much we don't know.

"But it's the not knowing that makes it worse. It's that 'what if' that always looms larger than the cold hard truth. *If* is a mighty big word for being only two, itty-bitty letters."

Ash is right. We really know nothing; nothing cohesive, anyway, just bits and pieces.

"Ash, what would you say to being a special agent? Work with me, Dave, and The Kindred?"

"Special agent? You mean like covert missions with cool clothes, fast cars, and I get to sleep with all the hot babes?"

"Well, sort of. Definitely covert missions; but the babes, the cars, and the clothes I can't promise. I'm thinking more along the lines of a 'Corson' expert."

Ash grimaces at the name, but he's really thinking.

"Will I still get to jam with the band and fulfill my destiny to be a rock God?"

I laugh. Damn, how I missed talking to this little dude!

"Yes, Ash, you can still rock out to your heart's content."

"And we'd be together? Working side by side, you and me?"

I nod and grin; Ash returns the response.

"Count me in, Bro! Whatever you need, I'll be there. Now, Pop mentioned a project for me; some structural changes and repairs he wants drawn up, but I got the impression that's a long ways off. So, barring that, I'm all yours. I'd love to work with you guys."

Grabbing him by the scruff of his neck, I pull him into a one-armed hug. A month ago, had things been different, we might not be sitting here. *Thank you, Helen.*

Hearing voices in the courtyard below, Ash and I move to the picture window to see what's going on. The Royal Courtyard outside our home is called Sapphire Square; aptly named because of the octagon-shaped tiles that are accented with real sapphires. Volunteers are setting up a podium, chairs, microphones, and decorations in preparation for the coronation. In the distance, citizens of The Dominion are already milling around the entrance, waiting patiently to be let in. A flash from a digital camera startles Ash; he's pale, sweating, and shakes his head to clear the episode. Ash turns away from the window; I hand him my handkerchief which has come in pretty handy today. He blots his face and breathes deeply.

"I...I, um...still get some, I don't know...flashes, glimmers, mini videos of things to do with Corson...weird shit...like just now."

Ash's face is so serious and stern that he's actually scaring me. "Somehow...I get the feeling I don't want to know...but, I *need* to know, don't I?"

"He...*Corson* had a friend who...liked to take pictures. He dragged me along several times. We should go to his house and look for them. Can't leave those around if Sage's vision of The Brotherhood is even minutely accurate...there's...there are pictures of Circles and Eli's apartment...and..."

"...and what, Ash?"

"Pictures of her sleeping..."

Trying to keep my eighty ounces of coffee from coming up at the thought of that rat bastard or his friends being that close to my baby when she is in her home and so vulnerable, I go to the house phone and call down to the Royal Guard Dispatch and request a crew to go to Corson's home, tear the place apart, and gather any and all photos they find and then tape it off; it's officially a crime scene.

Hanging up the phone, I turn to see Ash, who is on the couch again, his head flung back, hands covering his face.

"You all right, Ash?"

"Are *you*?" he asks, mumbling through his hands.

"Yeah, I'm all right. All I have to do is remember Eli chopping off that asshole's arm, and The Void gleefully screaming as it sucked him down."

Ash nods and sits upright as I sit down on the couch beside him.

"Remember that thing the Erudite said to Sage? That 'time' thing?"

"Time will tell you all you need to know?...yeah, what about it?"

"What if 'Time' isn't *time*, as in watch...or even thyme as in an herb."

"What other time could it be? You have to admit, Ash, both a watch and an herb helped us."

"Yeah, yeah, yeah…it's just that, there's *still* so much we don't know…what if…what if *'time'* is a person?"

"You think we need to find a *person* named 'Time'?"

"I don't know…I don't know. It's those flashes I was telling you about…, one in particular. I get it everytime I pass the vault. Corson and *his friend* were taking pictures of it and talking about opening it…it's probably nothing. The douche was a lunatic, right? It's nothing…nothing," Ash brushes at the air with his hand to erase the idea he's been dealing with; he says it's nothing; but considering whose mind he was in for so long, it *may not be nothing*.

Feeling something poking me in the ass, I reach beneath me and yank out Ash's iPod.

"So, what's the song?" I ask, handing the player back to Ash.

"Well, it's a little more alternative than you're probably familiar with; but it opens with a killer bass solo. Here, listen!" Ash says, putting one of the earbuds in my ear and the other in his, and then pressing play.

Ash is right. As we sit and share the song, I find it is a little more modern and alternative-rock than I'd listen to normally, but it does have a killer bass line. And I like it. 'Cuz it rocks.

Just like, Ash.

The Scholar

Biology, by definition, is the science that studies living organisms: examining the structure, function, growth, origin, evolution, distribution, and classification of all living things. In my new position with The Kindred, I'll need to learn a whole new group of beings and their categorizations. Before joining, I just sort of made up my own. In my mind's eye, Demons fell into one of the following four categories: Super Yucky, OMGs, Holy Crap and SMPs.

SMPs (also known as "Shit my pants") are the most current and nasty list of one: Vorax. Had I met up with them before the others, I don't think I'd be here now, in The Dominion, joining this team. I had to build up to it.

The Holy Crap list was the first one I made up because they were the first I encountered way back when I was at that awkward age: not quite a rookie, but not nearly a grizzled, old veteran. This list consisted of every movie monster I ever knew existed: Vamps, Lycanthropes and Zombies.

It was Halloween. Me and my first wife, Andrea, were invited to a costume party. We went as a convict and a warden which wasn't a far stretch from the truth, in hindsight.

These two characters, dressed up as a Vampire and a Werewolf, started arguing; cursing left and right and getting really belligerent. Next thing you know, costumes were ripping apart; and they were morphing like the Vorax did, and they *became* their costumes.

The Vamp looked more like a giant bat than what you see in movies: grey, supple wings, pointy ears, blood-red eyes, and, of course the pronounced canines. The Lycan was a dead ringer for the standard matinee creature of the newer cinema: extended nose and jowls of the canine class, reverse knee joint, and a dew claw just like his smaller, domestic counter parts. I'd always felt it was the shiny, black, wet nose that made me feel sorry for the Lycans; made them more vulnerable and familiar like the family dog. But this? This was *no* mutt from the pound!

One of the guests, dressed as a bumblebee with running shoes cried out, "Oh, my stars! Somebody, do something!"

Remembering my Saturday-morning-boyhood education at the capable hands of the masters: Lugosi, Chaney, and Karloff; I grabbed a wooden tiki torch from the patio and shoved it in the chest of the Vamp. As he lay twitching and spewing, I took a sterling-silver serving fork from the buffet table and shoved it in the chest of the Lycan.

The beast howled; my wife screamed and ran out of the house with everybody else, leaving me behind in my convict's costume to call for backup and explain the bloody pile of smelly shit with the tiki torch stuck in it right beside the dead, naked man with a sterling-silver serving fork embedded in his chest. Luckily, I make friends easily and had buddies in forensics.

They found unknown materials in the blood of the naked man and attributed his aggressive behavior to "steroids"; the bloody, smelly-shit, remained bloody, smelly-shit, or 'BS' as it was labled in the file. I'd been visiting my buddies in the morgue when they gave me the good news…that was when the Zombie attacked.

Dude stumbled right off the slab in the back of the freezer. Before we could slam the door on him, he was out and baby-walking his way to me and my buds. Pulling my gun, I fired one-round right between his eyes and decided to thank George A. Romero in my prayers for the rest of my life.

When I got home that night to my wife, who was already uneasy after witnessing the party high- jinks, I proceeded to share with her about my adventures at the morgue and the living dead. I apparently tipped the scale too far for her, and she packed a bag to go visit her mother in Kalamazoo. The next time I heard from her was in the form of divorce papers.

Next were the OMGs, which were usually not really bad as much as they were annoying. This list included: Banshees, Harpies, Goblins, Jinn, Sirens, and, on occasion, ex-wives, namely my second wife, Barbara. She started off a Siren, quickly turned into a Harpy, believed she was a Jinn, and ended up a Banshee when we went to divorce court, citing me as a Goblin. Well, that's not what she called me, really; but she may as well have. Barb and I were both getting our Masters when we were married. We were learning and growing and unfortunately that included learning to grow apart.

The Super Yucky list is short and sweet: Ghouls. Brazen and bold, these sick, disgusting fucks make me lose my appetite just thinking about them.

I had just come off a bank standoff; on SWAT then, with long hair and an attitude to match. Directly involved in a fatal shootout, I was given a few days off to deal with the stress and regroup. I spent that day off like any other I had; I went to Hayward to visit my folks.

Walking into Lone Tree Cemetery, I took the footpath to my folks' plot, just to the left of the Vietnam Memorial. In the distance, right between their headstones, you can see the giant, praying hands. Cleaning the bird crap off the stones, I removed the old flowers from the cups on the side and put fresh ones in for both. It's so peaceful and serene there…Usually.

I noticed a dark figure scurrying from stone to stone, tree to tree, sniffing the air, and licking its lips. Sticking mostly to the shadows, *It* made *its* way to an open grave where a coffin had just been lowered in from a funeral service earlier that day. *It* stood close by snorting at the air, jumping up and down excitedly like a child. Then *It* disappeared. Shaking it off at first, I figured it was just stress like the gal in Internal Affairs said…I waited around for awhile to make sure *It* was gone.

The cemetery caretakers were completing the task of putting the deceased to bed for the last time. They placed the headstone, smoothed the soil, laid the sod patches down, and took a thoughtful moment of silence in respect. One of the workers looked up and made eye contact with me. We nodded to each other as he walked to the tool shed at the top of the hill.

Saying my goodbyes to Mom and Dad, I headed to Val's to grab a banana milk shake and a burger while I was there. I was single again, having just been served with divorce papers from Catherine, wife number three *(Yes, I realize I married my wives in alphabetical order; I'm just organized that way!)*. That's why Catherine divorced me. She labeled me *anal retentive* like it was a bad thing! Once a biologist, always a biologist, I guess? At least I know what letter my next wife's name will start with.

I was sitting at the counter, finishing off the last of my shake when someone spoke.

"Could you pass the mustard, please?"

"Sure thing," I said, giving the little lady the bottle. She was grandmotherly-looking, dressed in a bright-red, flowered pantsuit and running shoes. She poured the mustard on her plate and proceeded to dip a French fry in it.

"My only vice!" she said with a smile, before she devoured the crispy potato. "You look familiar to me. You've come here before, no?"

"Yes, I grew up around here. I was visiting my folks and stopped for a bite. Dad and I always used to come here for a banana shake," I said, not certain why I was so comfortably telling my life story to this woman. There was something about her…something soothing in her voice.

"Such a nice boy. You're folks must appreciate that," she said, eating more of the fries.

"I hope so," I said, eating one of *my* fries. "You must come here a lot if you remember me?"

"Only when I visit my husband. He's at Lone Tree. I come by and spend some time with him. Make sure that nothing's happened…you know…?" she said, with a nod and a strange look in her eye.

"What could happen to him?" I asked hesitantly.

"Well, sometimes…strange things happen there. Stones are moved; and once, a body was…moved. Then…well, that was a long time ago. I'm sure its fine now, but I still like to go and keep an eye open."

"WHAT?!"

"Oh, my stars, I've startled you. Please, forgive me!"

Something was very familiar about the lady; something in the way she spoke and what she said…like déjà vu all over again.

"No, no…I'm fine. It's just kind of strange to hear things like that. That stuff only happens in movies."

"Mm-hmm," was all she said, stuffing the last of her mustard-covered fries in her mouth. "Well, I should be going," she said, as she hopped off the stool. We nodded to each other, and then she walked out the door.

Her words made me uneasy, to say the least, so I paid the check and hurried back to Lone Tree. The peace and serenity of the daylight were gone now, replaced by the ominous full moon and the shadows of the night and what owned it.

For as many times as I'd come to visit my folks since they died, which had only been two years, this place of radiance and warmth suddenly seemed murky and cold. Parking my Harley at the top of the hill, I walked down the street to where the fence is lined with trees; there, I could climb over and not be seen by the neighbors. Hopping the fence, I used the tree branches to help me over.

Moonlight lit the familiar path I had just walked hours before, casting strange shadows from the memorial statues and family monuments; mere phantoms for my peripheral vision. The silence played tricks with my senses, making my ears just as acute and over-active as my eyes. Every pop, crackle, and snap…creatures of the night, taking part in the evening symphony of sounds. The biologist in me kicked in, and I thought about which nocturnal organisms were taking part in the musical masterpiece. Then I heard the laughter, and the cop took center stage.

Trying to reason with myself and stay calm, I decided it was probably just kids hanging out here on a dare, or a pledging frat house. It was one voice laughing; one and only one.

Creeping quietly away from the laughter I made my way to the other side of the memorial wall, a few yards away from the Davies' family crypt with the eternal burning flame. The hot waxy smell of the paraffin oil with its Citronella scent wafted from the old, rusted torch; stifling, even from this distance. Waiting quietly, I stood motionless; then I heard the voice again. Closer than before, just on the other side of the wall; an odor blew over to me in the evening breeze, sickeningly sweet and familiar from seeing my share of murder scenes. I heard shuffling feet along the pathway as *It* conversed with *itself.*

"Decisions, decisions….. New one to the left …new one to the right. One is aged to perfection…the other is young and sweet!"

My mind racing, I took a breath through my mouth to keep from losing my banana shake right there and then. Instincts, honed well from both sides of my worlds, instantly told me what *It* was referring to. *It* was scavenging.

But I only saw one open grave today; where is the other one *It's* talking about?

Turning my back to the memorial wall I was leaning against, I looked straight ahead at a small area surrounded by flowers with pink ribbons and banners that was glowing and iridescent under moonlight. The flowers by the headstone, nestled in place with stuffed animals of all shapes and sizes, were accented by a Mylar balloon with 'We miss you' stamped across the front that floated aimlessly and lost in the breeze. The largest wreath in the shape of a heart said 'Littlest Angel'.

My heart stopped, and my face burned as anger raged inside me. I clenched my fists but had to stop because my knuckles cracked. If I was going to act and stop *It,* I needed to keep my presence hidden. But if *It* is scavenging and can smell the bodies, why hasn't *It* found…?

Something wet hit the top of my head and dripped down the side of my face; I stopped thinking. Wiping it away with the back of my hand, the thick, slimy liquid wreaked of death.

It was drooling on me from atop the wall.

It was then I realized that *I* was one of the ones *It* was scavenging.

Reaching behind my back out of habit, I remembered my off-duty weapon was at home. I had nothing to defend myself with against *It*.

Think, Donohue! Think!

I made a run for it.

Aiming for the Davies' family crypt and the old, rusted torch, I ran as fast and hard as I could; the torch came closer and closer. Reaching out, I grabbed the rusty pole as *It* tackled me from behind.

The old torch snapped from the pressure as we both fell to the ground, exposing the conduit feed from underneath. The paraffin oil; apparently in some type of pressurized reservoir; was spraying erratically all over *It* as it rolled and screamed. (Citronella has many more uses as a repellant than for just bugs apparently.) Grabbing the torch; still burning from the oil absorbed in the wick; I stood ready to defend myself should *It* get up.

It stood and faced me. His eyes were milky and almost translucent, skin a mottled mass of decay; but he was still recognizable. He was wearing the jumpsuit he and his team robbed the bank in yesterday. The hole in the left, breast-side pocket where my bullet went in and killed him was still apparent with powder residue. I'd heard rumors from SWAT that the body disappeared en route to the lab, but I blew it off because the morgue dudes insisted it wasn't true. A new Assistant Coroner also disappeared; they left that part out.

It moved too fast to be a Zombie. *It* spoke, so *It* definitely wasn't a Zombie. *It* had teeth that were gnarled and misplaced, with a careless appearance and colorless, vacant eyes…can't be a Vamp. No self-respecting Vamp would be caught dead (no pun intended) looking like *that*! My best guess…*It* was a Ghoul.

Since my live and in-person experiences with my Saturday matinee idols, I'd been doing a little more research into the classifications of the things that went bump in the night. Every book says the same thing about Ghouls. They take on the form of who they ate last; and the best way to get rid of them, is fire.

The Ghoul started to laugh hysterically; I laughed with him for a bit because of the situation I'd found myself in once again. Then I remembered the little girl; the *littlest angel* he could have eaten instead of me, and I stopped laughing. He lunged at me; I didn't move. Instead, I turned the flame on him; and for the second time in two days, I burned his ass.

This time for good.

Ten feet away are Martha and Jim (Mom and Dad, to me). Walking over, I sat down with them and watched the Ghoul burn to nothing from the safety of the quiet glen, feeling better about what I had to do yesterday and today to protect the innocents.

Dawn came and I awoke, still seated between Mom and Dad's headstones. A familiar face was looking down at me.

"Good Morning, Handsome! Do you make it a habit of sleeping in cemeteries?" the mustard-and-fries lady asked me.

"No, ma'am, I don't usually," I said, standing up and brushing off my clothes.

"Are these your parents?" she asked.

"Yes. I came back last night after...what you said...I...."

"Oh my!" the lady said, putting a hand to her face, "I *did* scare you, didn't I? I'm so sorry, Handsome! I didn't mean to!"

"No, please! Don't feel bad. It was a good thing that I came here...and by the way, it's Sean. Sean Donohue," I said, offering my hand.

"I sort of liked calling you Handsome! But I like Sean, too! My name is Edna...Edna Blue."

Edna wrinkled her brow and sniffed the air; the smell of the Ghoul's ashes caught her attention.

"Oh, my stars! What happened here?"

We walked together to the burned spot on the lawn and the broken torch.

"Um...you know those awful things that you said happened here? Well, they won't happen again. I took care of it. But I had to use the torch to do it." The look on Edna's face was telling. "Is this your husband's crypt? Oh, I...I'm so sorry...I didn't know...Mrs. Davies, I'm so...I'll pay for a new one."

"Don't be silly! Pete would have hated that lamp. I was looking into a smaller one; something more reserved and dignified like him. His mother bought that garish, old thing. You did us a big favor," Edna said, patting my arm. "Tell me, Sean, did it have white eyes?" she asked, nodding to the burned spot.

"Yes, how did you know?"

She smiled slightly, "I'll talk to the caretaker and let him know that it was just kids here, and you stopped them; but the lawn couldn't be saved...it'll be fine."

"Edna? How did you know? You've seen it before, haven't you?"

"When I came to visit last. It was circling the baby's grave on the side. Poor little thing; her parents have had their share of grief; they don't need anymore."

"I knew he was going there to the little girl; he said he was until he found me. I didn't know what to do…but then I remembered what my folks told me when I became a cop. They said 'protect those that can't protect themselves'. I didn't want him to get the little girl; but the…I was so scared, Edna…I felt so alone…I…."

"Hush now. You're not alone, Sean. Listen to your heart; your family will always be there," Edna said, squeezing my arm just before she made her way to the office of the caretaker.

Walking back to Mom and Dad, I couldn't help but smile. I closed my eyes and listened…Edna's right; I could hear Mom telling me 'Good job, Son' and Dad telling me to get a haircut. I hiked back out to my bike, rode home to clean up and stopped at the barber on the way.

Three days later; after my imposed leave was over; I accepted a promotion to detective. I'd doubted the move originally; but after the things I'd seen, it was the most opportune position I could be in to continue protecting the innocent on all fronts and continue to study the new species I'd encountered.

Put my Harley in storage; even though I told everyone I sold it; and bought a white, Shelby mustang. Reworking the trunk, I installed racks and storage cases to house wooden stakes, crossbows, iron chains, several guns, and a long-range rifle all equipped with silver bullets, and an occasional salt round. In my glove box is my notebook of every *thing* I've met.

Looking out the window of Grandpa's office, Sapphire Square is assembled for the Coronation; and samples of all the new classifications I'm currently studying are there (the real ones, not mine). Not to mention my own personal study since I'm technically one of them now; thanks to my *blood sister* saving my life.

"Amazing isn't it? Who knew they all existed?"

"I know, Cap. I've been chasing the rogues for years…I'd no idea there were good ones doing the same thing just hoping for a break," I say.

"There's a lot of work to be done, yet. You ready for it?"

I thought for a minute about everything that's happened, everything I've learned, everyone I've met along the way, and the innocents we've already saved.

"My heart's in the right place, Cap. I'm ready for anything!"

Ash

Surrounded by walls that are familiar, I feel I've been here before.

Getting up, I walk out of the room and down a long hall to a stairwell. Climbing down carefully, I see him. I'm not afraid of him, in fact I'm happy to see him, a hooded figure with a face hidden in shadow wearing a heavy, wool, navy-blue, peacoat.

"Eli is a girl," I say, "We've been deceived."

"Boy or girl, doesn't matter; it's still The Sentry," comes the reply.

"Are you scared?"

"Never," comes the answer from the peacoat.

"If you don't hear from me by the New Year, you know what to do," I say, as I extend my hand to the peacoat.

"Yes," comes the answer, as a man's hand, completely covered with tattoos and perfectly manicured fingernails, shakes mine. In a whispery voice he asks, "What about your mother?"

He has a grip on my arm. I try to pull away, but he grips tighter. The tattoos are moving on his skin; cockroaches and rats pad their way from his hand to mine. A snake slithers off his arm and onto my wrist, creeping up my arm slowly; its tongue darting in and out, testing the air for my fear. Again, the voice asks, "What about your mother?"

The snake leaps from my arm, but its head is no longer a serpent. It's Lilith. She wraps herself around my neck, cutting off my air, coiling her scaled body around and around whispering to me, "It's all about me! It's all FOR me!"

Lilith's gaze meets mine. I see my reflection in her cold, black eyes.

I'm Corson. I'm scared. I'm shaking, or I'm being shaken. A voice says, "Come back. Come back."

Struggling, I strain to turn my head, trying to find the voice. Lilith is squeezing herself around me tighter and tighter. I can't breathe. Can't bre...

"ASHTEROTH! WAKE UP! SON! COME BACK TO ME!"

I come to with a gasp that makes me choke. My earbuds are wrapped tightly around my neck; Dad is trying to undo them for me, kneeling beside me on the couch I'm sprawled over in the Royal Hall.

"What? What happened? Was I dreaming, or was it another one of those...?" I start to ask, holding my arms out in front of me like Frankenstein, moaning and staring blindly into space.

"I'm afraid it was another *episode*. You haven't had one in awhile; I thought they'd finally stopped. Especially after Corson was sent to The Void, I'd hoped they'd stopped for good."

My head was pounding, with a pressure building up behind my eyes, like I still had the snake slithering in my head trying to pry its way out via my sockets. Dad's right; I haven't had an episode like this in awhile, but these players invaded my sleep last night, too; although at the time, I thought it was the alcohol from too much New Year's cheer. I wanted to talk to Sage and Bill about it first, so as not to worry Dad. Too late now.

"Dad, did I say any names?" I ask, hoping maybe he heard something more, as I reach for a sheet of paper and a pen on the end table.

"Lilith and Corson were the only names. You described another character, but I don't know anyone like that. Do you remember any mention of The Brotherhood?"

"No, none; but Bill mentioned that to me earlier." I sit up straight, feeling more focused. "Dad, didn't The Brotherhood disband? I thought I remembered you telling me that they were dissolved?"

"They were, just after Stolas was killed; but after a while, they came back; and they are still going strong."

Burning the few remaining brain cells I have, trying to come up with something more, I could see the shadowy shape of the stranger; but my gut told me nothing.

"Dad, I'm sorry. I've written down everything I saw; there's nothing else," I say, rubbing my forehead. Just as I expected, Dad was shocked when he read my notes.

"What about your mother?" Dad repeated. "And, you're sure you were Corson?" Dad looked at me with worry. "A vision?"

Shaking my head 'No' doesn't relieve his worry.

"Lilith used to send Corson these images; mini nightmares whenever she was feeling…I guess, ignored. I'd seen that one before. Makes me wonder though? Was that just a summer rerun, or does she not know that Corson is…?"

"Or *is* Corson really…? There's a reason Sage saw a Necromancer. I think its time we get your brothers in on this," Dad says, looking more than concerned.

Bouncing up, I pull Dad with me, "Let's go, Dad. The family's in the Green Room waiting for the ceremony to start. I don't think this can wait a second longer."

The Peacemaker

There are certain events in history, place markers in time, that people always ask about in retrospect; and everyone, I don't care who you are, always remembers.

"Where were you when…?"

From assassinations to world wars, everyone knows where they were, what they were doing, and who they were with at that moment in time.

When I learned my brother died, I was fighting Jesse Santos in front of the auditorium of my high school, with his girlfriend, Vera, watching from the wings. I was going to kill him.

School came easy for Andrew (Drew as I called him), but not for me. I had to work hard to achieve even half of what he had. Drew was the golden boy: good grades, good athlete, good looking, and an all-around good guy. Plus, he was *my* big brother. All I ever wanted as a kid was to grow up and be just like him. And I tried! Believe me, I tried.

Drew was older than me by five years. He was already out of college and training to be a cop when the Oakland Unified School District realigned and closed a few schools. The enrollment at my high school doubled after that, and we had a very wide and diverse cultural explosion. In most aspects, it was cool. For one key aspect, it was my undoing.

Jesse Santos had a big mouth, a chip on his shoulder, and an attitude about anything that wasn't Jesse Santos. When I found out he would be coming to my high school after the realignment, I was none too pleased. Jesse and I already had a history…his dad was my brother's partner. The summer they'd been teamed up, I met Jesse for the first time at an OPD picnic.

My folks and I joined Drew at Knowland Park by the Oakland Zoo for the festivities; it was his first company function out of the academy, and he wanted us to meet the officers he was working with. This was the first time I met Rudy Santos, Jesse's dad.

Rudy was a big man with an even bigger heart. He took my brother under his wing and guided him. He had a wild, raucous laugh and a brilliant smile; and I knew that with him watching out for my brother, Drew would be all right. He wasn't a social climber like some of the other officers we'd met. He wasn't looking to make a name for himself or to move up the ladder using others as the rungs; he just wanted to be the best cop he could and make the city a better place for families to live in safely. How he wound up with a kid like Jesse, I'll never know?

Jesse was flashy, loud, obnoxious, and desperately needed to be the center of attention. He was the absolute antithesis of his dad. He had a girlfriend named Vera O'Neil. Pretty girl with auburn hair and green eyes; she was very quiet and stayed in the background. Jesse dragged her around like a security blanket and made a habit of telling people she 'belonged to him'.

"So, *your brother's* my dad's new partner?" were the first words out of Jesse's mouth to me when I offered my hand to him after Drew introduced us.

"Yes, he is. I'm Dave…"

"Your brother better not fuck up. If anything happens to my dad, I'm coming after you," Jesse said, poking a greasy, half-chewed-on chicken wing in my chest, leaving a stain. He laughed out loud and pointed out his signature on my shirt to his buddies and girlfriend. When Vera didn't laugh, he grabbed her by her hair.

"Laugh, damnit! It's funny! I was funny!"

Vera forced a half smile and let go a gasp more than a laugh. Rudy stood up from the table behind him.

"JESSE! KNOCK IT OFF, OR GO HOME!"

Jesse looked at his dad, let go of Vera, and then looked back at me with a smirk.

"You watch your ass, Pendajo!"

And so began my next few years of Hell at the mercy of Jesse Santos.

Without fail, I had at least one class with Jesse each semester; and no matter what class it was, several times during the year my homework would turn up either missing, or miraculously, his name would appear at the top of it instead of mine. I had to work hard as it was to get the grades I had, I didn't need his help lowering them any more! The one and only 'F' on my school record was because of Jesse.

In my Senior year I took photography as an elective and was actually pretty good at it; of course, Jesse was there. For our final at the end of the semester, we had to turn in a notebook with all of the weekly assignments: pin-hole cameras, contact strips, contact sheets, using filters, pushing and pulling of film, shooting at different speeds, using the Zone system. I completed my notebook early, turned it in, and then suddenly it disappeared. Jesse, who never did a single assignment, turned in a notebook early also. His notebook had pictures and negatives of my house, my dog, my parents, and our family reunion. A coincidence? I doubt it.

By the way…Jesse got an 'A'.

One day during the class, a couple of weeks before graduation, I was in the dark room printing some extra copies of the pictures taken at my family reunion, when a voice came booming out of the darkness.

"My dad came home limping last night, Pendajo! Do you know why?"

I knew who it was.

My folks and I had talked about Jesse harassing me; and we decided, collectively, that I would ignore it as best I could but was given the green light should he ever physically touch me. So, I ignored him. Big mistake.

"I know you hear me, *Whine*-hardt! Do you know what your hot-dog brother did to get my dad hurt yesterday? He broke up a fight at a gas station; and when one of the dudes tried to get away, he opened his car door right in my dad's shin. Remember what I told you, Pendajo? If anything, *anything,* happened to my dad, I was coming after you!"

While Jesse was talking, I took the paper I'd exposed with a negative of me and Drew and put it in the developer bath. Suddenly a blinding pain in my shin sent me face first into the table. Putting my hands up to block my fall, I knocked the developer tub on Jesse.

He screamed like a girl, stumbled to the door, swung it open wide and went running, wiping his eyes, spitting developer out of his mouth, and cursing me along the way. The teacher came running in, demanding information. A quiet voice came from another enlarger booth.

"Jesse kicked David and made him fall; he did it on purpose. The developer bath spilled on Jesse. It was an accident."

It was Vera. She flipped on the safety light and started cleaning up the tray and mopping the floor. She took my picture from the floor and tossed it in the stop bath.

"Here," she said, handing me a wad of paper towels. "You're bleeding. Jesse's wearing his steel-toed boots today."

Looking down, I saw there was blood pooling up in my shoe, soaking my sock. My teacher said to go to the nurse. Hobbling my way there, I walked inside and took a chair.

The nurse came out, took one look at me and my bloody shoe. "Let me guess? Jesse Santos?" she said, with a furrowed brow. I nodded. She ushered me into her station with a wave of her hand. "Go to the back table, David; you know the routine."

The fact that Mrs. Barnes and I *had* a routine was bad enough; but for her to know by the injury *who* did it...somehow made it worse.

The next day, Jesse was nowhere to be found. I thought sure he'd be there looking for payback, but he wasn't. I actually had a nice, quiet day at school. The next day, the same thing; as well as the day after that. By the following Monday when he wasn't at school again, I started to get concerned. Not concerned like a friend; but selfishly, I was coming up with all manner of horrible events because I was anticipating the consequences of my actions: concerned that he was blind, maybe he swallowed some of the developer and was sick in the hospital. Finding Vera at her locker at the end of that day, I asked her about Jesse.

"You didn't hear?" she said, her big, green eyes wide with surprise.

"Hear what?"

"His dad...Rudy? He was killed. He went out on a call, and he was shot. They had him on life support since last week. The family let him go, and he died yesterday. Didn't your brother tell you?"

"No...I haven't talked to Drew in a couple of weeks...," I said, trying to remember the last time I talked to my brother.

"Oh! Before I forget...I finished this for you...," she said, handing me the picture of Drew and me. "Remember when Jesse...? Well, of course you do...I put it in the stop bath and then washed and dried it with mine. I thought you might want it. It's a good picture. Your framing's a little tight, but it gives it character. Like it's squeezing the two of you together. I've been meaning to give it to you; but with everything going on, and then graduation and...well...here."

"Thanks."

"Sure. I gotta go. See ya, David," Vera closed her locker and walked away.

After school when I got home, I grabbed the phone and rang Drew's line four times; but there was no answer. Heading to the kitchen to talk to

Mom about what I'd heard, she was coming down the stairs when I passed by.

"Mom…!"

"Shh…your brother's sleeping. He's…."

"I know. Jesse's girlfriend told me. How's Drew?"

Mom just gave me that half-smile that told me he was as good as could be, considering the circumstances.

"Was he with Rudy when…?"

"No, Davey…he wasn't. That's why he's so upset. He's beating himself up over it all. Let him rest. You can see him later. Okay?"

I nodded and followed Mom to the kitchen and headed out the backdoor to shoot some hoops on the half-court Dad built us on the back side of the garage. Drew and I spent a lot of time there growing up. I came here now just to clear my head. I'd been shooting from all spots of the key and couldn't make a basket to save my soul. My concentration was nil. Rudy was a good man; and even though Jesse was a shithead to me, I wouldn't wish for this on him or his family in a million years. In the back of my mind was another thought…what if it had been Drew?

"Kid, get your head in the game. By my count you have *H, O, R* and *S.* One more blown shot, and you're out of your own game and *THAT really sucks!*"

Drew took the ball from me and started shooting from the same spots I missed previously and made every one cleanly, and he then handed the ball back to me.

"You're up."

Grinning at him, I took the ball to the opposite side of the court; his presence alone always upped my game. Dribbling the ball, I shot; made a clean basket, never even hit the rim. Grabbed the rebound and passed it to Drew.

"I suppose you heard, right?" Drew asked, making another clean shot from my selected spot.

"Yeah," I said, taking a pass from Drew.

"Do you want to ask me anything?"

"Nope," I said, making another clean shot and passing the ball to Drew. He took his shot and missed.

"H," I said. Drew shot me a look that told me the game was on and passed the ball.

Moving to another spot, I took aim, made another clean basket; Drew shot, missed, and continued to miss until we were tied at four letters each. Moving further outside of the key, I took aim. As I was about to release the ball, Drew spoke.

"I love you, Davey. Don't ever forget that."

Never looking at him I smiled, shot the ball, and missed. Retrieving the ball, I passed it to Drew; he shot and missed, too.

Everybody I know has their own rules when it comes to ending a game of Horse that's a draw; Drew and I did, too…but we never had to use them. Drew always won.

"First one to miss?" he suggested. I nodded, aimed, shot, and made a clean basket. Drew retrieved the ball and made the same shot effortlessly. Taking the ball, I moved to a new area and made another shot; Drew followed in step. This went on for the next twenty, maybe thirty plus shots I made. I'd toss up a clean one; and Drew would follow in rapid-fire succession, one after another, without stopping. The faster he'd rebound the shot, the faster I moved; challenging each other with every jump. Tired and winded, I threw the ball up carelessly and missed. Drew grabbed the ball and made ready to win the game dribbling into position.

"I love you, too, Drew. Don't *you* ever forget that!"

Drew never looked at me. He just smiled and shot the ball.

…And missed.

We both collapsed on the ground, giggling like a couple of little kids.

The next day was Graduation…and still no Jesse. The word going around campus was he wouldn't be making the walk with us; he would pick up his diploma later. I was relieved, but felt bad for him and his loss at the same time. Needing to be at the school early to get in our alphabetical lines, I left before Mom and Dad; Drew said his shift would be over in plenty of time, so he would meet us there.

Sitting in the chairs on the football field, I was looking to the bleachers for my family; but they weren't there yet; they were only calling the C's and D's, so they had time. Glancing down the row, I noticed Vera. She had her bangs snugly held down by her cap, almost completely covering the right side of her face. She looked really uncomfortable; but then which one of us didn't, sitting up there in ninety-five degree weather wearing bright, yellow nylon?

They reached the M's and still my family wasn't there, and I started to get a weird feeling in my gut. Even as my freshman homeroom teacher,

Mrs. Whitaker, signaled our row to stand, I looked and they weren't there. We walked single file to the podium; no Mom, no Dad...no Drew.

Stepping up as Principal King read off my name, a smattering of cheers from my underclassmen friends could be heard; but no cheers from my family. No loud, two-fingered whistle from my best friend...my brother.

My heart was racing. The ceremony could not get over fast enough for me. The principal presented the graduating class to a round of applause from the crowd; some kids threw their caps, others hugged and cried; I bolted from the stands and ran to the quad area to see if I could find my family.

Was Mom sick? Was the heat too much? Did Dad twist his ankle walking through the field to the bleachers? Did Drew...? I suddenly had a sick knot in my stomach that crept up to my throat.

"What's the matter *Whine*-hardt? Lose something?"

Jesse looked like he was twenty pounds lighter, and he hadn't slept in weeks. His eyes were narrow and full of pain. Ignoring him, I headed to the pay phone to call home.

"They won't be there," Jesse said.

Turning to look at him briefly, I tossed a coin in the phone and dialed our number.

"Your mommy and daddy aren't home *Whine*-hardt, but I do know where they are."

After six or seven rings, I slammed the receiver down and headed to the parking lot. I walked up and down the aisles looking for Dad's car. Drew's car. No sign of either.

"I told you they weren't there. They have more important things to do. So sorry, Pendajo!"

"Jesse, leave him alone!" Vera said, coming up from behind him.

"You shut your mouth, Bitch, or I'll make your eyes match!" Jesse yelled, as I saw Vera quickly bring her bangs back down over her face to cover the shiner Jesse just admitted to giving her previously.

"Okay, Asshole. You're dying to tell me, I know. Where's my family?"

"They're on the way to the morgue to get your hot-dog brother," Jesse said, smiling. "I couldn't have wished for a better resolution to the mess he made. He got my dad killed. Your brother deserved what he got!"

"You're full of shit, Jesse. It wasn't his fault. My brother wasn't even *with* your dad when he was shot. You don't know anything," I said, walking back to the phone as my stomach tried to come up. My head was telling me he was lying, but my heart said he wasn't.

"My cousin works dispatch. She called my mom and told her the great news. The hot-dog met his match. He's dead, just like my dad. Did you hear me *Whine*-hardt? COLD AND *DEAD!*" Jesse said, taunting me with every phrase, punctuating that last filthy word with a finger in my temple from the imaginary gun he made of his hand. Pushing his hand away, he came back with a backhand to my face.

"Is that the best you got, Jesse? It's no wonder your dad liked my brother better than you. At least he hit like a man and not a little girl," I said, throwing a left to his gut and a right to his jaw that sent him tumbling back, hitting his head against the brick wall of the cafeteria, and bouncing him forward from the impact. Clasping my hands together, I brought them both down on the back of his head as hard as I could, and knocked him to the ground. He scrambled at my feet and got up enough leverage to knock my legs out from under me.

Jesse rolled over and grabbed at my gown collar, yanking me back till it choked me. Reaching behind, I grabbed his ears. Feeling the stud in one, I pulled as hard as I could and felt the flesh give way. Jesse howled and released my collar. I turned around to see him holding his bloody ear with his hand; anger flooding his eyes.

He charged me like a bull with everything he had. Standing perfectly still, I waited for impact. He hit me with all his weight and shoved me into the locked, glass doors at the entrance of the campus, shattering them on impact. I grabbed his face and head butted his nose, breaking it with a sharp snap. He let me go, moaning and holding his nose; I sucker punched him and knocked his wind out.

My rage; having built up for years; had taken on a life of its own. I had him pinned against the auditorium doors, pounding at his body with everything I had.

"Didn't your dad ever teach you to fight, Jesse? He taught my brother. Took him to a ring and showed him how. Then Drew taught me! You should have asked him? Should have taken a greater interest in what he did. Maybe you would've been closer to him, and my brother wouldn't have been his favorite."

Jesse was on the ground now, battered and bloody. I was just about to kick him and crack another rib when a hand on my arm stopped me. It was Vera; tears streaming down her face, making her bruised and beaten face even more heartbreaking. Touching her cheek, I wiped away a tear; anger raged in me again as I turned to Jesse and kicked him repeatedly, this time for Vera. I heard feet running hard and loud behind me.

"Go, Dave! Run!" Vera said, pushing me to the parking lot. "Run now! I'll take care of this! Go!"

Running to my car in the parking lot, I found my dad pulling up as I got there. His eyes were red and glassy. From the pained look on his face, I already knew why.

"Is it true?"

"Davey, get in the car…"

"IS IT TRUE? JUST TELL ME. *YES OR NO? IS IT TRUE?*"

My dad's bottom lip started quivering as he shook his head in disbelief. He said nothing, and spoke volumes.

Leaning against my car, I was unable to control my emotions any longer; and there was no Jesse in front of me to pound on. Dad must have parked the car because the next thing I knew, he was standing beside me with one arm around me and the other stroking my hair.

"Where's the blood from, Davey? What happened? Are you hurt?" Dad asked me. Before I could answer, we heard a deep, formidable, but familiar, voice.

"David Reinhardt? We need to speak with you?"

Dad and I turned around and saw Principal King standing there with an officer from the Oakland Police. "This is Officer Wood. He has some questions for you?"

"Jesse Santos was beaten; he's being taken to the hospital. We need to ask you a few questions. Vera O'Neil and his mother, Elaina Santos, filled us in on what happened; but we need to confirm the story with you," Officer Wood said, looking at his notepad.

Wiping my face, I stepped forward and stood ready to take whatever I had coming to me. I explained what had happened to me that evening, step by step, punch by punch; Officer Wood nodded as I spoke and made notes now and then.

"That's fine, David. Your story confirms what both Miss O'Neil and Mrs. Santos told us. We may need to contact you later for more details regarding Miss O'Neil's case and the charges she's pressing, but I don't think any charges will be filed against you. Mrs. Santos has corroborated her son's actions. From what I've learned, this has been an ongoing scenario that culminated tonight," Officer Wood said, putting his notebook away. "Mr. Reinhardt, David…please accept my condolences. Drew was a great, young man. I'm proud to have known him and been able to call him a friend. We all suffered a great loss today; his family, the department, and this city included."

Officer Wood shook our hands and walked away with Principal King, leaving Dad and I there in the parking lot at a loss for words.

"Davey…? I'm sorry you had to find out like that. Your mom and I…we handled this all wrong."

"Dad, I don't think there's a right or wrong way to handle tragedy. Everybody has their own way. You handled it your way…I handled it mine."

We each got in our cars and drove home.

Four days later, after we buried Drew, I sat in the cemetery on a bench looking at all the people milling around; all the people that Drew touched along the way who came to pay their respects. Hundreds of people attended the service, including Vera and Mrs. Elaina Santos.

Vera offered her condolences to me and my family. At that time there was no sign that four years down the road she would become my wife…but then again, maybe there was? I always was a little slow when it came to girls.

Jesse didn't attend; he was on his way to prison. No charges were placed on me. Vera nailed Jesse with repeated rape and assault with intent to kill.

Sitting on a stone bench, watching the crowd, a little, round lady came and sat down, grandmotherly-type in a Sheriff's Department dress uniform, one of the many representations of the brotherhood of law enforcement that was in attendance.

"Sure is warm today," she said, taking a tissue from her pocket and blotting at her face.

"Sure is," I said, loosening my tie.

"I understand you're his brother?" the lady asked.

"Yes, I'm David."

"Edna Blue," the lady said, shaking my hand. "Drew was a wonderful young man from what I've heard. I'm very sorry for your loss."

"Thank you; yes, he was quite a guy."

For some odd reason, I sat there with Sheriff Blue and told her all about my brother; all the way back to when we were kids, what happened with Jesse, Vera, and also the tremendous decision ahead of me.

For a long time, I'd thought about going to law school; but in the back of my mind, criminal justice called to me. I knew after losing Drew, Mom and Dad wouldn't want me to do it; the loss was still too new; but day after day, moment after moment, that's where my head and heart had been leading me. I'd already been accepted to Cal-State Hayward; my future was wide open. I just didn't have my best friend to talk it over with.

"Sounds like you have a mighty big decision to make," Edna said.

"Yes, I do. I wish...I wish Drew were here to talk it over with me. I wish I didn't feel so lost. So alone...."

"Hush now. You're not alone, David. Listen to your heart, your family will always be there," Edna said, as she patted my hand and said goodbye.

Summer flew by, and time came for me to decide what direction I was going in. Closing my eyes, I listened to my heart like Sheriff Blue said. Hearing Drew loud and clear, I told my advisor of my decision; and I never looked back, clear through to my graduation from the Academy.

"Excuse me, Dave," Patrick is looking at me with wide eyes full of excitement, "is it true?"

"Yes, Son," I say, looking at the little kid who always seems to look at me like I'm some sort of Super Hero. "It's true," I say, watching him smile broadly.

"So, you're not only The Peacemaker; but you're also the Deputy Marshall? Second in command to Bill? I mean, what an honor! So much responsibility! And such a huge wealth of knowledge you're bringing to them! I'm so excited for you! For all of us! I mean I'm excited by what's been offered to *me* alone! Well, nervous more than excited...no, no...excited, too! Well, half and half nervous and excited! No, more seventy-thirty...maybe sixty-forty...?"

Trying to keep up with his rapid-fire speech, I give up; I can hear Drew in my head, laughing at how the tables have turned.

"Kid! Get your head in the game!" I bark at Patrick, as I see him finally breathe and calm down. "You keep that up, and you won't make it through the ceremony," I say, winking at him.

"Sorry, Dave. It's just that...it's such a huge decision to make. I'm just so impressed and respect you so much, because I know I could never make a choice that big. I just don't think I have it in me."

He's referring to my decision to step down from the Berkeley Police Department; still protecting the world I know and love from the evil that I've come to know, helping Bill create a new kind of police force.

"No, Patrick, you're wrong. You *do* have it in you. I know, because you and I are similar in a lot of ways," I said, patting my chest over my heart.

"And *I* have everything I need, *right here.*"

Asmodeus

Sitting in the White Room on the stiff, plastic, non-conducive stool, I clear my frequencies.

"Liz? You there? Lizzy?"

"Of course I'm here, Modie. What is it?"

"I need to talk to you."

"I'm all ears…figuratively speaking…well, you know what I mean?"

"It's the kids, Honey…I'm worried."

"Anything in particular?"

"*Everything* in particular! I'm not certain we'll make it to the coronation; and if we do, we may not make it *through it.*"

"Modie, you're letting your fears get the best of you. Stop it, you know how your stomach gets," Liz says, her words punctuated with a gurgle and moan from my intestines.

"I think I have good reasons to fear, don't you?" I ask. Liz sighs, then takes a breath as if preparing to say something.

"Liz! Don't answer that," yipped a nasaly, irritative voice.

"I wasn't going to, *Ezekial*. I know the rules," Liz reputed, irritably.

"Zeke? Zeke the freak is an Erudite?" I laugh. The thought of my lovely wife's whiney cousin as an Erudite puts me in a state of hysterics.

"Are you quite finished, Asmodeus? And it's Ezekial, if you don't mind…a little decorum would be nice…*Emporer.*"

"Lighten up, Freak…it's just me. We have way too much history to let such triviality come between us."

"Liz, would you kindly tell *your husband* to refrain from such use of familiarity. There needs to be a greater sense of humility and respect when addressing the Erudite."

"I wasn't addressing the Erudite, *Freak*...I was addressing my wife. You interrupted a private conversation...*Freak*."

"There is no such thing as a *private* conversation where the Erudite are concerned."

"You're wrong, Ezekial...there is so," Liz says, using her don't-mess-with-me voice.

"I beg your pardon, *Liz,* but I am very much right!"

"No, *Zeke*, you are very much mistaken. Get your handbook and look it up. Section forty-two, addendum 'C', paragraph eleven, sub section six."

Hearing pages flutter, I imagine Zeke hurriedly shuffling through his handbook, mumbling to himself the directive Liz just gave him.

"Ah, here...private conversations," Zeke clears his throat. "Private conversations between the Royals and the Erudite may occur only when there is absolutely no chance of war, famine, disease, destruction, death of family member, ritual sacrifice, reckless endangerment, severe magical or paranormal weather."

"So, Zeke, any sign of severe magical or paranormal weather, ritual sacrifice, or death of family member?"

"No"

"Any sign of reckless endangerment, famine, or disease?"

"No, nothing."

"And...what about war and destruction?"

"Well, not war per se; but, there is a small battle that could lead to destruction, but it's really nothing and...*Oh!...You!* You *tricked* me!"

"EZEKIAL!" yelled the deep booming voice of the Erudite Collective.

"Oh, crap!" Zeke mumbles, as he shuffles away to answer the call of the group.

"Well, I'm sorry, Liz. I guess we can't have that *private conversation* we wanted.*"

"No, I guess not," Liz responds quietly.

"Another time perhaps, *my darling?*"

"Yes…another time…"

"Pretty slick move you pulled there, Liz…Thank you."

"Take care of them, Modie. Try not to worry. *Time will tell you all you need to know.*"

I sigh; hearing that confounded phrase again brings back so many scary moments for me and for our family.

"Did you *really* need to say that?"

"Yes, I did, Modie. Because it's true. Now…more than ever."

There was something different in Liz's voice. A true honesty that I only remembered hearing in our most private moments; warmth only I knew and miss terribly with every breath I take.

"I miss you, too, Modie."

Smiling to myself as my wife weaves her way through my mind, reminding me of those private moments we shared and the not-so-private ones with the boys.

"I love you, Liz…I always will."

"And I love you, Modie. Take care of them."

Exiting the White Room, I run into my daughter-in-law.

"Dad, are you all right?" she asks, taking a tissue from her purse and dabbing at my eyes.

"Yes, Helen, I'm fine…Why…?"

"You're all teary…what's wrong? Are you hurt…?"

"No," I say, taking the tissue from her. "I was chatting with Liz, your mother-in-law."

"Oh, yes…Bill told me you speak with her," Helen replies, looking as if she has more to say.

"The Royals and the Erudite have a kind of open-door policy…similar to what you may experience soon with the Necromancy. It's nothing to be afraid of."

"Dad, I've heard stories; people are known to lose their minds from this. They die early sometimes; meet up with angry spirits who kill them…I…"

"No, …my darling girl…you are surrounded by family that loves you. We simply won't let that happen. Besides, I have an 'in' with some pretty knowledgeable people."

Helen smiles, "You have 'people'?"

"Yes, Helen…and my 'people' aren't going to let anything happen to any member of our little family."

The Inventor

I love being under pressure!

That sudden, rush of energy you get after six cups of espresso have worn off; but you still have to meet that deadline; so you push, bear down, pull out all the stops at the last minute, and reveal that diamond you always knew was there! Because if it's worthwhile, you have to go for it; and give it all you've got!

Some people get off on drugs, some alcohol…but for me, it's the adrenaline coursing through my veins from the intense urgency and excitement of the challenge.

The last few days have not only proved to be challenging but informative. Reworking The Void with a release door that's activated with a remote trigger was first, then working on new and improved weaponry for all the different rogues, and the best one…figuring out that the portal only needs a drop of blood.

Finally I feel like my education and experience are being put to good use; no longer feel like I wasted Mom and Dad's money going to such an expensive school. I can't help but wonder what my folks would say? I was adamant when I told Dad I didn't want to work for the Lab in Livermore making weapons. Yet, what am I doing? I'm protecting humans from monsters…by making weapons. Isn't that the same thing? Does that make me a hypocrite? I'm not doing this for the money…which was my problem in the first place. What they wanted me to do felt like blood money. They were intended as tools of protection like I'm making now; but they were going to inevitably end up as weapons of destruction, and I wanted nothing to do with that because I wasn't raised that way. Mom worked really hard to give me a normal, happy childhood and teach me the value of a dollar, which wasn't easy for her since she was one of the richest women in the United States by the time she was eighteen. Life kind of threw her a curve when she met my dad.

My real dad. The biological one.

Quinn is my adoptive dad's name; I've no idea what my real dad's last name is, and neither did Mom. He was a truck driver she met when she tried to run away from her financial legacy.

Yvonne Marie Bertrand, having lost her parents in a freak plane accident, found herself the sole heir to the Bertrand-Rousseau fortune, made from a long line of attorneys at a major firm by the same name; a merger and a marriage of her great-grandparents' doing.

Men, young and old, were calling and visiting or sending flowers. Being the heir to a fifty-billion dollar fortune can make any woman attractive, but Mom was a looker to begin with. She always dressed down and tried to look plain and frumpy; but she looked like a runway model, no matter what she did. One day, after the twentieth bouquet arrived, she packed a backpack and hit the road.

On her way to anywhere-but-here in her baby-blue Carmengia, she took a wrong turn and ended up in an alley in Sparks, Nevada. She told me there was some trouble there, and she was caught in the middle of a fight. She helped a man, and he in turn helped her. He introduced her to a truck driver with a lime-green semi, a sweet, inviting smile, and a lyrical voice who offered to help. One thing led to another: a cup of coffee became drinks, drinks became dinner, dinner became breakfast, nine months later she came home with a souvenir…Me! Forever trying to downplay her financial status, she sold the mansion in Danville and moved into a two-bedroom apartment in downtown Berkeley.

Mom still drew the attention of admirers and gold-diggers alike, who were familiar with the name; but now with me on her hip, she had her own personal screener. If I didn't like the dude, I started wailing like a siren; and the suitor was gone in a blink. Once I learned to talk, I just flat out told the guy I didn't like him; and then he was gone. She was *my mom* and I wasn't about to let just anyone into our lives.

One day, Mom and I went for a walk to our favorite place; the library. We stopped at the park on the way back to sit and read what we had borrowed that day. Mom was deep into her novel; and I was reading a book about trains when I was distracted by a young guy at a picnic table whose stacks of papers were flying everywhere in the light, bay breeze.

Just as he picked up the last stray sheet, the breeze would swoop in and pick up the next batch. I laughed at first, but then thought he was struggling way too much and could use some help. Walking up to one of the groomed trees, I picked up two potato-sized stones and placed one on each stack of papers as he ran back from retrieving the last two escapees.

"Thank you, little man! That's smart thinking! My name's Kevin Quinn; what's yours?"

He was tall, thin, with light-brown hair and freckles; and he offered me his hand to shake like a grown-up. Being only five, this was quite impressive to me; he didn't do the customary, cautious, puppy-dog-pat on my head like some of the other guys Mom brought home for me to meet. Taking his hand, I shook it with all the strength I had.

"Patrick...Patrick Bertrand."

"Well, that's some handshake there, Patrick Bertrand. Thank you very much for the help. Hey! Wait a minute! Are you here alone?" Kevin asked, looking around and suddenly appearing very concerned.

"I'm here with my Mom. We came from the library. Come on, I want you to see the books I got," I said, taking his hand and dragging him away from his work. He protested all the way to the bench we were sitting on until he saw Mom. Then he forgot all about his work,...and Mom didn't mind at all that I'd been talking to strangers.

Kevin Quinn was a grad student at Cal Berkeley when I made his paperweights. He was working towards his PhD in Nuclear Engineering and carrying a 4.0 average; but more importantly, he was nice and very polite to my mom.

From that day on, our little threesome was an every-day thing. Even after I started Kindergarten, Mom would take me to the library after school; and we would stop at the park on the way home and meet Kevin. I'd show him my books, and he would always show a genuine interest in them and me. Mom was very pleased with this, but she was still cautious and guarded around him; that money thing rearing its ugly mug again. One day on the way to school, I decided it was time to tell her what I really felt.

"Mom, I think you need to marry Kevin."

"WHAT?!" Mom said, nearly swerving to the curb.

"I like him. I think he'd make a good dad, don't you? And I know he likes you! You should marry him."

"Patrick, I..."

"Mom, you've been alone long enough; and I think its time you did something for yourself and were happy. You like Kevin, right?"

"Yes, but, Pat...."

"No buts, Mom. Like you always tell me; if it's worthwhile, you have to go for it and give it all ya got!"

"How do you always remember the hair-brained things I say; yet you can't remember to clean your room?" she said, grabbing me and kissing my face. I smiled, and gave her an Eskimo kiss before I hopped out of the car and ran to my classroom.

That afternoon, Mom came and picked me up with Kevin because he was taking us to his house for dinner. From the way Mom and Kevin were looking at each other, I knew that this was the beginning of something big for all of us.

Then I saw Kevin's car (the green Jaguar I drive) and his house (the same house I live in now). Mom was worried about coming from money? As it turned out, so was Kevin. He, too, had inherited a small fortune and tried to live quietly and cautiously. They married later that year; and, Kevin, *Dad,* officially adopted me as soon as he legally could. Lots of hoops to jump through since Mom didn't know much about my real dad, but Kevin wasn't worried. Neither was I. Kevin was my dad in every sense of the word, from the moment he let me drag him away from his work.

Right about that time, I blossomed at school. Maybe it was the stability. Maybe it was Dad's encouragement, inspiration, and love of learning.

Mom and Dad were always proud of me but were beside themselves when I tested in the genius bracket in a district-wide exam. Pushed ahead in my curriculum, I was always far beyond my grade level. By middle school I was taking college-prep classes; and with Dad's guidance and influence, easily graduated high school more than ready to enter MIT. I graduated at the top of my class because of Dad. I don't think I ever thanked him for that.

The Sheriff's Department called me to identify some of my parents' belongings yesterday: Mom and Dad's wedding rings, Dad's wallet, my brass ring from MIT that Eli said Mom wore around her neck on a chain.

"I'll be damned, Eli was right," I thought aloud.

"She usually is," the little, round lady behind the counter says. She wore a standard-issue Sheriff's uniform, but instead of work shoes, she wore white, running shoes. Her name tag said 'BLUE'.

"How did you know Eli was a 'she'?" I asked, still a little wary of people who know things that I think shouldn't.

"Pardon me?"

"When I mentioned Eli, most people assume Eli's a male; you referred to Eli as 'she'.

"There's an Eli that comes in here, a bounty hunter. Maybe I thought about her; maybe just a lucky guess," Sheriff Blue said, with a shrug of her shoulders. She looked at me with a puzzled stare, "Are you all right, Son? You look like you've seen a ghost."

While Sheriff Blue was talking, I was looking in Dad's wallet. I found an envelope with my name and the names of our attorneys on the outside of it, folded in half amongst the dollar bills. Stepping away from the counter, I sat down in an empty chair against the wall to read it.

Patrick,

If you are reading this, it means that I'm gone; and the attorneys are enacting the will. They will inform you of the contents once the documents are ready.

I want you to know that you brought me more joy than I ever knew possible in my life. You and your mother are the most precious gifts I've ever been given, and I'm so thankful for the breeze that blew you both into my heart that day in the park. You and I may not share a blood bond, but you are my son in so many more ways than blood can ever connect two people. For so long, I was missing something in my world; you came along and made it whole. You gave me purpose, strength, and light. I love you, and I am so very proud to call you my son.

Dad

Sitting there in the Sheriff's Station, I tried hard to hold back the tears but didn't succeed. Dad really wanted me to work with him at the Lab, and I never gave that to him; always unsure of how he felt, if he still loved me or not, and if I hurt his feelings by saying 'No.' And Mom, I never knew if I hurt her by saying 'No' to the man I called 'Dad'. I was stubborn. I was wrong.

"Patrick? Are you all right? Can I get you anything? Is there something I can do?"

It was Sheriff Blue holding a tissue in front of me. Taking it from her, I wiped my face.

"It's from my dad...I never got to say good-bye, and I had so many unanswered questions. This helps," I said, folding the letter back into the envelope and putting it in my pocket.

"Maybe this will, too," Sheriff Blue said, looking inside my brass ring. Mom and Dad had it engraved with the date I graduated and three words: '*SO VERY PROUD.*'

I sat there stunned and frozen. "I've been surrounded and consoled by so many friends the last few days, but I've never in my life felt so alone...."

Sheriff Blue closed my hand around the brass ring and put her hand on my shoulder.

"Hush now. You're not alone, Patrick. Listen to your heart; your family will always be there," she said, quietly. Nodding to her, she gave me a pen to sign for the items.

Standing in the Library of The Dominion, I admire the certificates on the wall of the Dante family. Grandpa has all his kids' diplomas framed and hung proudly on the wall. It used to bother me when Mom and Dad would talk about me to their friends, feeling like I was being paraded around for show; but I wasn't. They were just proud of me. It took me a while, but I understand that now.

"Hey, lil' buddy! I been lookin' all over fer ya. Big day today...are ya ready?" Bryant asks me, patting my shoulder.

I stop for a minute, remember the letter, and the brass ring now hanging from a leather cord Eli gave me. Thinking about what Sheriff Blue said, there is no doubt in my mind where I stand with Mom and Dad...it was the same place I'd always been. Eli was right; I was always in their heart; and, for certain, they'll always be in mine.

A breeze blows across my face; and I quickly look to see where it's from, but there are no open doors or windows. I smile to myself as I feel my folks still cheering me on.

"I am now, Bry. I am now."

Bill

There are constants in the world that everyone has come to expect: twelve months in a year, seven days in a week, twenty-four hours to a day to name a few. Then there are my personal constants: my unruly hair will be unruly no matter what product my wife buys me, I will eat too much of whatever incredible edible my wife makes, and my daughter, Eli, will be late for any event, no matter how important it may be.

Where is that girl?

Standing in front of one of the mirrors in the portal hall, I prick my finger and tap the little spot of blood on the mirror…must remember to thank Patrick again for finding that out. The mirror ripples and rolls, then reveals the loft apartment above Circles.

It's quiet. Calling out Eli's name, I find I'm crying out in vain; no one is home.

Running down the stairs, I check the War Room, the Sports Room, and end up on the restaurant floor; still no sign of Eli. The kitchen door swings out, and at last I think I've found her.

"Well, it's about time, little miss…the ceremony is being held up because…," I start to say, but stop because Carlos shrieks at the sight of me and runs back in the kitchen.

Carefully opening the swinging door, I tiptoe in and peek around the corner. Carlos shrieks again and swings a metal soup ladle over his head.

"Stay away from me…you…you…ghost!"

"Carlos, I'm not a …just let me explain," I say, as the ladle comes flying at me unexpectedly and clocks me in the forehead. "Ouch! Damn it, Carlos. That hurt!"

"*You're not a ghost?* But…you died…then, you must be…Oh, my, God, you're a *Zombie!*"

"No. I'm not a Zombie. Do Zombies talk? No. Well…in some movies they do; but in reality, they don't; and besides, look, my clothes are clean, not dirty, like I crawled out of a grave; and my face isn't pale or pasty; or my eyes…look at my eyes, Carlos,…and…and…oh! Carlos, please put the cleaver down and let me explain?"

"Must cut off the head…only way to kill a Zombie…right?"

"Right. No! Wrong! No! I'm *not* a Zombie! Carlos, please let me explain!" I plead, backing away from the terrified cook as the swinging door starts to move, and I hear a familiar voice.

"Bill? Did you find Eli?"

"Chief?"

"Carlos, you put that cleaver down this minute!" Helen demands.

Carlos' eyes are giant, white pools; darting side to side taking both of us in at the same time.

"Sweetheart, Carlos thinks I'm a Zombie…"

"Oh, Carlos! Bill isn't a Zombie…look at how clean his suit is," Helen says, coming up behind me and putting her right arm around me. She looks up and notices the welt on my forehead, "Where did that come from?"

Carlos, standing like a statue with the cleaver held high, stutters, "Chief, y-you…y-y-you d-died!"

"Carlos, I said put that down!" Helen scolds; then sweeps her left hand in front of her, and the cleaver flies out of his hand, across the room and wedges the blade into the bulletin board where the restaurant notices are posted.

"Now, stand still and listen to me," Helen orders, and then proceeds to tell Carlos all about what happened: the car accident, who we really are, how we hid Eli, Corson, and brought it all up to now, and how we are looking for Eli to get to the Coronation.

Carlos listens carefully, changes his stance from left foot to right foot, and occasionally crosses his arms over his chest when he isn't sure if he should believe what Helen is saying. When she finishes, he takes a deep breath and scratches his head.

"You're…a Witch?"

Helen nods.

"And…you're a Demon?"

I nod, "My brothers, our dad, too."

"My sister, Peg, also a Witch…a White Witch; like Priestess level, or like…."

I stop Helen from going any further into detail because Carlos' eyes are starting to glaze over.

"Carlos, I know it's a lot to take in all at once…but…"

"No, no… it all makes sense. There were things that happened that I couldn't explain. Weird stuff. The kitchen, on our busiest nights…you cleaned up in minutes, and I could never figure out how…pounds of herbs would disappear. And here, Eli pours salt on the windows and doors…."

"It keeps *some* rogue Demons out…not all, but some."

"What about Captain Dave?"

"Human. All human…well, enhanced human. See, we…"

This time Helen stops *me* from going too far. When I turn back to Carlos, he's mere inches away from us. He puts his hand on my chest; I'm guessing, feeling my Royal Heart beating.

"There was a rumor that Uncle César died from a broken heart when he heard you died…truth is, he was dying. I saw a letter from his doctor on his desk; he made me promise not to say anything."

Helen places her hand on top of Carlos'; he smiles, moves in close between the two of us and hugs us tightly.

"I missed you guys. I came to work for Eli so I could keep an eye on her. It was my way of staying close to you; by protecting *her*, I was, in my way, protecting you."

"Speaking of Eli, have you seen her?" I ask, patting Carlos on the back.

"Earlier. I was coming in, and she was racing upstairs; asked me if I'd seen Consuelo. I told her 'No,' and then she said to keep an eye on the pot of Cioppino and that she had a big surprise for me later."

Helen and I look to each other, laugh lightly, and turn back to Carlos, "Surprise!"

Carlos laughs, "Never had such a nice surprise."

"Well, I hate to break up this happy reunion…but we need to find our daughter. We'll catch up later?" Helen says, heading for the door.

"Yes…I'll be here," Carlos says, with a wave. "Oh, Chief…by the way…the Cioppino? It needs a little more oregano."

"Oh, yeah? You don't say…"

"No…I don't say," Carlos says, as he takes a muslin bag from his pocket, opens the top and breaths deeply, "but, the rocks do."

Helen smiles and nods to him. "I'll explain on the way," she says, answering the puzzled look on my face.

Heading out the door, I pick up the ladle, place it on the counter and glance back at our old friend, already eagerly back to work adding the herb to the soup, just like old times.

The Vox

I gots me a secret! A secret ain't no one at Circles knows.

Maybe Eli do; I might've tipped my hand a bit. Well, maybe a might more than a bit; cuz when I thinks, I don't...my accent...it ain't...well, I ain't from Tennesse; I did live in Memphis for awhile but...

Well...Let me thinks this so I's clearer.

I'm actually from Encino; born in the back of a station wagon at the corner of Ventura and Balboa Boulevard. My mom, Willimena Dunesford Mayne, going by her stage name, Billie Dune, was on her way to a voice-over audition but never even made it to the freeway. Dad, Lester Mayne, was on the road again...as usual. A passerby called for help, and a cop by the name of 'Bryant' delivered me.

Dad was a truck driver and a lot older than Mom. She called it a May-December romance. Whatever it was, it worked well. Dad would be gone for long stretches of time, and Mom would go to auditions after she dropped me off at school. Dad would somehow come home just in time when Mom would get a part in a show or a commercial.

Sometimes, when she had a job and Dad wasn't home, she kept me out of school, and I went with her. The crew wouldn't mind because I could be quiet, and I was small and didn't really take up much space. Sometimes I'd even get to help if no one was looking.

I met all kinds of people waiting for Mom: directors, writers, actors from TV and movies...some from commercials. They would practice their lines on me, giving me their best rendition of whatever character they were doing; and I would give them thumbs up or thumbs down if I believed them. I started to get a reputation for this. One of the leads on a soap Mom was on would tell the others to 'Remember the Mayne' and nod to me. It was kind of intimidating but very flattering at the same time; especially when the younger actors would blow me off and then screw up. I mean, I was no expert! I just knew when they were being real. I could feel it all the way to my toes when they were really being the part. And if I didn't feel it, all I had to do was say one word.

"More."

After I said that one little word, no matter who it was or what part they were playing, they all just understood what I meant and did it.

One day, just after I turned thirteen, Mom told me she won a small role in a big-budget movie and had to go on location to Arizona for a couple of days. She asked our neighbor, Mrs. Benitez, to watch me until she returned.

Mrs. Benitez was a nice lady, a widow, whose kids were all grown and had moved away. She welcomed the company, and I entertained her with all my stories of Hollywood and the stars.

A few days passed and a phone call came. Mrs. "B" said Mom was going to be a couple more days; she said not to worry, and she'd see me by the weekend. That Saturday I woke to a man I barely recognized, patting my arm and calling my name.

"Bryant. Bry…Son, wake up. We need to talk," he said softly. His eyes were red and swollen, and he was a lot grayer than the last time I saw him. He sat on the edge of my bed, looking to the floor while he told me about Mom. She wasn't in a movie; she was at a hospice being treated for what they thought was some form of cancer. She wasn't coming home; I wouldn't see her ever again. She died, and he was there to gather me up to live with him in Memphis. I sprang from my bed and flew down the stairs to find Mrs. 'B'; she, too, had been crying. Wrapping my arms around her, I cried into her shoulder. Once I was more consolable, Mrs. 'B' walked me upstairs and helped me and Dad pack. Later that day, after I hugged Mrs. 'B' good-bye, Dad and me were heading out on Highway 101 in his big, black semi. After an hour on the road, the silence finally got to him.

"You don't talk much, do you?"

This was funny to me, even though I didn't outwardly laugh, because I was a talker. I was talked to in school about how much I liked to talk…but, suddenly, I had nothing to say. Another hour went by, as well as another highway sign. We were on Interstate 210 near Barstow when I finally spoke.

"Why didn't she tell me?"

Dad cleared his throat, checked his many mirrors, clutched and shifted gears, and avoided the question. We drove on through Arizona in silence.

We stopped for food in New Mexico, stayed the night in some cheesy motel on the border of North Texas, had breakfast in Oklahoma, lunch in Arkansas, and made it to Memphis for dinner.

Dad parked his truck in front of a tiny house: dark, no yard, only one, small window in the front. It resembled the bungalows they sold in Ventura, just big enough for an aspiring actor to rehearse or bring a date back to. This was similar, but not nearly as nice.

We walked in, and Dad turned on a single lamp. The light flickered like a black light on the two-bedroom house that was suited perfectly for a child of four: low ceiling, tiny room, an open kitchen with a bar instead of a dining room.

"This is your room," Dad said, as he opened the door closest to the kitchen. He flipped on the wall switch, and my six-legged roommates scattered for the dark. Some didn't make it there in time, and Dad stepped on them with a crunch. There was a mattress on the floor with blankets stacked at the end. Dad picked one up and opened it, shaking out more crawling free-loaders. Turning away, I ran...well, stepped quickly, from door to door, looking for a bathroom because my stomach was in my mouth.

"Bry...what are you looking for?" Dad asked, as I frantically grabbed a trash can beside the bar and let my stomach free itself of the disgust. I stood there clutching the can to my chest and leaned against the wall.

"Give me that," Dad said, motioning to the trash can. "Let's get you cleaned up." Putting his arm around me, Dad walked me outside and around the side of the house where another house, similar to ours, sat. It was brightly lit, and there were men sitting outside playing drums. People were sitting on the curb. A man came out the front door and yelled, "NEXT!" The people jumped up and argued loudly over who was there first, but Dad and I didn't stick around to see who won. We walked on to our destination.

Between the two houses sat a perfectly pristine, white house with a picket fence and a small porch. We walked up the steps, Dad rang the bell, and then, just like at some banks in Los Angeles, I heard the lock buzz its announcement to come in. Dad opened the door.

Inside was the most beautiful, immaculate bathroom I'd ever seen. Everything from the tiles to the towel racks were a pearly-white and clean. It smelled like laundry right out of the dryer; I was afraid to touch it.

"Well?"

"Well, what?" I answered, asking a question of my dad's question.

"I thought you were sick," Dad said, motioning towards the toilet.

"Um...no, I think I'm...I'm...all right."

Dad nodded, and we turned to leave. When he opened the door, he jumped; startled by the woman standing there.

"Good evening, Miss Louija," Dad said, with a slight bow of his head. "This is my son, Bryant."

"Mmm...so, dis her son? He thin; don't you eat, Boy?"

"Yes, ma'am, I do," I said, marveling at the beautiful, brown-skinned woman standing at the door. She wore a long, flowing dress with a tribal print; caftan, I think my mom used to call the shape. It was the color of fire, beaded and shiny with silk strings hanging. Her head, wrapped in the same cloth as her dress, brought the green in her eyes to a vivid and breathtaking hue.

"You like your new home, Boy?" Miss Louija asked quietly, her French-tinged speech becoming more pronounced.

"Um, well...I'm sure it will be fine," I said, gathering from the look on Dad's face that I'd better be polite.

"Why I no believe you? You lie to me, Boy?"

"No...ma'am...I..."

"No? You know how to mow a lawn, Boy? Wash a car? Hmm?...You know how to do dem tings, Boy?"

I nodded, suddenly scared to open my mouth.

"Tell you what ...you come tomorrow; after school. You mow my lawn; we see about making the house a little better. N'est-ce pas?" she said, almost in a whisper.

Silent still; I nodded again.

"Come now, Boy. No need to fear. You help me...I help you," Miss Louija said, as a broad smile spread across her face. "Smile for me, Boy. Dat will be your down payment."

Digging way down to remember all those times I'd listen to method actors trying to get the right emotions when they just weren't feeling the part, I put on my best happy face.

"Dat better, Boy. You and your poppa go to bed now. We talk again...tomorrow."

Miss Louija nodded to Dad, who again bowed slightly before she turned and glided away.

As Dad and me walked across the driveway, I looked back to the extraordinary outhouse; but my peripheral vision was distracted by a light in a back window of Miss Louija's house. A girl, maybe my age, maybe not, watching Dad and me walk away. I raised my hand and waved. She started to wave back, but stopped; and suddenly closed the curtains and shut off the light.

My head was a blur of questions when we returned to the house. I was about to ask Dad who that woman was; but as he turned on the lamp, something strange happened.

The house was clean; the light didn't flicker and the rooms were...brighter. Carefully, I entered my room and hesitantly flipped on the switch, expecting to see the floor crawl away...but nothing was there.

"Be careful what you say to Miss Louija, Bry. She...just be careful. Be polite. Don't do anything or say anything...bad. All right?

I nodded, suddenly scared again to speak. Dad said, "Good night," and went to his room.

Still uncertain about the six-legged beasties being gone for good, I left the light on and prepared for bed. Taking a glance out the small window in my room that I swear wasn't there before, I look across the driveway and see the girl in the window again. I wave; she waves back; but this time she stays there for awhile before closing the curtain and turning off the light.

This became the pattern of life for Dad and me for the next five years. Miss Louija and me became pretty good friends; as close as one can be a friend with a Voodoo High Priestess. My gift of gab and talent for acting became our greatest connection. I would pretend to be sickly, have a pronounced limp or a patch over my eye; and five minutes later I'd emerge from Miss Louija's parlour, healed.

This was an easy enough bit of show for me; tolerable even. It was the séances and conjuring events I was not so cool with.

Miss Louija would conjur ghosts. People would come and ask to speak to a loved one who had died, and Miss Louija would ask for a sacrifice; not like a chicken, or a goat, or anything, but more like an exchange; something of value that the spirits' would recognize and allow the loved one to pass over: jewelry, food, expensive clothing, and of course, cash always worked.

Most ghosts were nice; came to say their peace and then moved on. Others weren't so happy to be dead and were determined to take someone back with them. These angry spirits would cause total chaos that yours truly had to clean and somehow get the smell of rotten eggs out of the parlor before the next customer came in.

After she held a séance with a group of Vampires (real ones, not the wanna be's) who wanted to reach out to some fourteenth-century lord, I was done. Nice folks, very pleasant, but this lord didn't like the new Baby Vamps brought into the coven; and he insisted they be exterminated. So the elders did!

There's something most folks don't know about Vamps; when they are exterminated, they don't all go to dust. How they go all depends on how long they've been turned. When the elders cut the heads off those Baby Vamps, well...they must have been only a week or two old. Have you ever seen or smelled a dead body that's two weeks old? And here I thought the ghostly sulfur farts were bad.

The next time Miss Louija called for help with a séance, I said, "No."

"What?"

"Miss Louija, I just can't. I couldn't eat for a week after that last one. I'm just not cut out for that. I'm sorry. Please, forgive me?" I said, trying to be as pathetic and sorrowful as I could.

"All right, Boy. I understand," Miss Louija said, as she glided back to her front door and inside. Turning away I went home.

Home, now; since I was helping her; had grown much nicer. Dad had been lucky to find jobs that were closer to home and paid well. Things were just nice. The first time I said 'no', I noticed a change.

The walls were gray. When Dad came home that night, he said he had a job to drive to New Orleans, over three hundred miles away. He was leaving in the morning, which meant he would miss my High School Graduation. As Dad walked away, the lamp in the front room started to flicker again. Dad turned and looked at me sternly.

"Did something happen?"

"No...," I said, as a cockroach crawled up the wall behind him. Dad caught me watching it; he looked, and then looked back at me.

"What did you do?" Dad yelled.

"I...I...said 'No'."

Dad fell to his knees and started to cry. There was a knocking sound coming from somewhere in the house. Following the sound, it came from my room. I flipped on the switch and waited for the floor to clear.

It was the girl from the window of Miss Louija's house. All these years of just waving from afar; never before having been this close. Miss Louija would always tell me to mind my own business whenever I asked about her. Now, being this close to her was so unreal. I lifted the window and helped her inside.

"You have to go. Now! You and the man; leave, quickly!" she said, but I couldn't move. She was the most beautiful girl I'd ever seen. Her warm, brown skin glowed from the heat of the Memphis summer night; dark, wavy hair hung loosely on her shoulders; and her dark eyelashes emphasized her large, emerald eyes, with gold flecks that made her gaze penetrate my entire being.

"Why?"

"Momma is powerful; more powerful than you know."

"What will she do?"

"What she needs to do...wants to do."

"But..."

"Please?...Go!"

"I...Please, what is your name?"

"Alamea."

"Why are you helping me...us?"

"Because I can see your heart is pure. Even from a distance, I could tell," she said, as she placed her hand on my chest. Through the thin material of my cotton T-shirt I could feel the coolness of her hand. Reaching out to her, I was compelled to pull her closer to me; but she pushed me away.

"Please? No. You must go. I will occupy her," Alamea said. Turning away, she climbed out the window and strode across the yard, back to her window. She waved, crawled inside, shut the curtains, and turned off the light.

Running to the front room; crunching roaches with every step; I found Dad, sitting on the couch holding his head.

"Get your things, we're leaving!"

"What?" Dad asked, and then started coughing; his throat thick with fluid. His eyes were dark, glassy; fever riddled his body.

"Jesus," I said, touching his face and feeling the heat radiate. In the short time I was gone, talking to Alamea, how did he become so ill?

"What the hell have I done?"

Grabbing my jacket, I threw it in my school backpack along with whatever food I could find that wasn't crawling away, helped Dad up and quietly snuck him out to his truck. Walking him to the passenger side, Dad shook his head.

"You can't drive my rig!"

"I can if you teach me."

Dad agreed. After I belted him into his seat, I ran to the driver's side, threw the backpack behind the seat, and took the keys.

"All right, Dad. Tell me what to do."

Dad walked me through the basics: which for the most part wasn't too different from driving the little training sedan in school, just a whole lot bigger. We didn't own a car for me to practice in, so other than being a tad rusty, I didn't do too badly. Picking up Interstate Fifty-five, we headed south to New Orleans.

The further down the highway we went, Dad started to feel a little better; when we finally arrived in New Orleans, he was his old self. He was able to work and live a normal, every-day life. A week later, things began to change.

One day, while working as a waiter in a local restaurant, my boss came and told me the Sheriff was waiting to talk to me in the lobby. After talking to him, I learned that Dad had been in a bad accident. My boss said he'd cover my tables, and I left for the hospital.

When I arrived at Dad's room, I wasn't prepared for what I saw. His face, riddled with stitches resembling railroad ties to a horrific destination, swollen and disfigured, was nearly unrecognizable. His right arm, cast in plaster and bandages, lay across his stomach; while his left had tubes attached to it, feeding him fluids with a pain reliever cocktail. Drawing my eyes down the length of his bed, something seemed wrong. In the area where his legs should have been, there was space...empty space...just the hospital bed.

"Oh, my God, Daddy...," I cried, falling back into the chair by his bed. A doctor walked in and cleared his throat.

"Excuse me, are you...Bryant?" he asked, looking at the chart he had in his hands.

Nodding, I finally found my voice, "Yes. Yes, I am. What happened?"

"Your father was brought in earlier in a near fatal state. We were able to repair the right arm, but I'm afraid that both legs were devastated; the bones were crushed; we had no choice but remove them."

Dad had always been a good, safe driver. What the doctor was telling me was unbelievable. I couldn't fathom how this could happen.

"Bryant, there's something else I want to mention. The cuts on your dad's face...does your dad have a history of depression or mental illness? Self-mutilation?"

"What? No. No, of course not!"

"I'm sorry...I had to ask. Inside the cuts on his face...we found this," the doctor said, handing me a jar. Examining the little jar, the pieces looked familiar; but my focus was elsewhere, and nothing made sense.

"What is this, doctor?"

"Plastic chips, from an automobile headlight. The Sheriff said that the lights on his truck were intact."

All the air left my body, and I had no voice.

"One other thing; when your dad was brought in, he was briefly lucid. He kept repeating your name, and...he said, 'It's her. She wants me dead. Just like Willie.' Bryant, does any of this make sense?"

I felt the blood leave my face.

"No, I'm sorry...I don't know what any of that means," I lied to the doctor. He thanked me for my time, warned me that Dad was sedated and would be out for awhile. I sat by his side awhile longer; all the while I couldn't get the doctor's words out of my head.

"She wants me dead...Just like Willie."

Catching the bus at the stop just outside the hospital, I had a short ride home and an even shorter walk since the bus stop was close to home.

As I rounded the corner, there was someone on the front stoop. It was a girl in a white dress. As I got closer, her image was clearer; and I began to run. Reaching the stoop, I swept Alamea up in my arms and held her tightly and told her what had happened. Looking into her gold-flecked eyes, I lost my train of thought. She held my face in her cool hands, drew me close to her and kissed me. I pulled away and stared at her. She looked older somehow; weathered by the outdoors almost; not at all like she did that night when we ran. Her eyes were like rare gems and speaking to my heart. We entered my home; and I brought her to my bedroom where we made love and found comfort in each others arms.

For the next five days, I'd go to see my dad before work, after work, and then go home to Alamea. She had dinner ready every night and then slept by my side until morning. Dad was in a coma-like state according to the doctor; he had no time line for me as to when he would wake.

On day six, Dad woke. He was lucid and screaming for pain meds when I arrived.

"Where's that goddamn nurse?"

"She's coming, Dad. Hang in there."

"Hang in there? Hang in there? I've been hanging in there, Bryant! That's all I've been doing. Don't patronize me, Kid...it isn't attractive."

"Dad?"

"Bry, please? I don't want to talk. I don't feel like it. Okay? Just...don't."

Trying to be understanding, I kissed Dad on his forehead and left. When I went back to visit after work, Dad was sullen and staring out his window at the dark.

"I didn't try to kill myself."

"All right."

"And I'm not crazy."

Going to his side, I looked into Dad's eyes; he turned away quickly, not holding my gaze for more than a second. Angry and scared, I couldn't help but demand information.

"I'm not leaving until you tell me what happened?"

"A long time ago, your mom and I, just after we married, were on one of my long drives. I was headed to Los Angeles, so she tagged along to set up house for us there. We stayed at a motel in Memphis and on our way out of town, we had an accident. I hit someone; a young girl who was the daughter of the Voodoo High Priestess of the city. She died instantly. To make 'sacrifice' as she called it; to atone; we had to give something up. Your mom had just learned that she was pregnant; and the Priestess had originally said she wanted you, but we would have none of that. Someone had to atone; so, we agreed it would be me. I was allowed to visit as long as business took me there. Otherwise, I was basically a prisoner in that house; and a slave to her."

"After so many years of doing her bidding, I felt like you and said 'No'. She still wanted her 'sacrifice', needed atonement. I ran; left to get you and your mom, but when I arrived ...she was dead. Some strange disease that they thought was cancer, but...I had no choice but get you and bring you back."

"Had no choice? Of course you had a choice. You chose to use me...after you gave up Mom!"

"No, I didn't. I tried to protect you. Both of you. I just couldn't take her demands anymore. I couldn't. I didn't think she would still be so harsh. I'd hoped that time would have..."

"Made her forgive you for killing her daughter? Really? You think that time could heal a wound like that? Yes, I guess you would...seeing how much you valued us. Well, at least I can stop kicking myself for being weak. Guess this apple didn't fall far from the tree, did it?"

Dad didn't respond; he just lay there staring at the ceiling. His face was red from anger and the slowly, healing tissue. Tired of sitting there with him in an uncomfortable silence, I got up and headed to the door.

"Will you...will you come by, again, later, after work?" Dad asked, his voice tainted with worry.

"Yes...later. After I go home and talk to Alamea. Maybe if I offer my condolences for her sister, she can talk to..."

"What? Did you say Alamea?"

"Yes," I said sheepishly, "she's staying with me at the house. She..."

"You get her out of my house!"

"It's my house too, Dad...I can have..."

"You get that thing out of my house now! You hear me? Now!"

"That thing, is my friend; and she's staying as long as she wants."

"Damnit, Bryant! You listen to me!"

"Why? So you can tell me to kick her out again. Dad, for God's sake, you killed her sister, the least you could do is..."

"I didn't kill her sister," Dad said, clenching his teeth tightly.

"You just said you killed Miss Louija's daughter..."

"Miss Louija only had one daughter."

"Dad?"

"I killed Alamea. That crazy bitch of a Priestess brought her back to life. You've seen her do it before; she does it all the time."

"That's...It can't be. It's not true. You're wrong."

"Am I? Why do you think I crashed my rig? Huh? That fucking Zombie was in the middle of the road, and I slammed on my brakes to keep from hitting it and damning my soul to torture for all eternity. You get that thing out of my house!"

"You liar...I don't believe you."

"No son of mine would call me a liar; no son of mine would bring someone or something into my home that I didn't want. No son..."

"I got it, I got it. I can take a hint," I snarled, as I headed to the door and out. Walking down the hall, I could still hear Dad calling my name over and over. I ignored it. He made it clear I was no son of his.

When I arrived late at work, prepared to give my excuses about visiting Dad at the hospital and giving my greatest, humble, and dutiful-son performance; I tugged on the employee doors and found they were locked. Walking from window to window I look for other employees or some sign of life, but there was none. On the last window, closest to the front door, there was a sign that said the restaurant was closed by the Health Department. I saw something move in the corner of my eye and turned to once again find a dirty, six-legged monster crawling on the chain around the handles of the French doors. Running to the bus stop, I took the next bus that happend by just to get away.

The bus didn't drop me too far from home, so I ran the rest of the way. As I got closer, I started to smell something...something really foul that I knew I'd smelled before. Alamea opened the door and welcomed me home with a kiss on the cheek; her lips were scratchy, and the odor was stronger the closer she came.

"My love?" she said, peering into me, asking me what was wrong with her stare. Her eyes were suddenly old and cloudy. I backed away and hurt her feelings with my retreat.

"I...I'm sorry, but I need to ask you something."

Alamea sat on the couch; roaches scurried out of the cushions with her motion.

"Do you...did you...have a sister?"

Alamea shakes her head, "I'm an only child." She looks at me with innocent, yet aged eyes.

"Only?" Alamea nods yes to my question. "Did she send you here?"

Alamea sat silently.

"Did she send you here?"

Still, Alamea is silent.

"DID SHE SEND YOU HERE?" I yelled, as Alamea smiles an all too familiar smile. As she stands, her eyes roll back in her head.

"Of course I did, Boy. I've come to collect my sacrifice."

"What do you want?"

"Your only element of worth. Your voice."

"What?"

"Your voice, Boy! Don't be so surprised; it be your only attractive trait."

"So, then...what? I'll just be mute the rest of my life?"

"Oh, no no, no...I replace your voice wit anudder...and it won't even hurt."

"And my dad?"

"Your fadder's fate was sealed long ago...by your mudder. She chose the life of the baby she was carrying over him."

"But she died...she got sick; some disease they couldn't diagnose. You took your sacrifice."

Miss Louija makes a disgusted sound, "Boy! Twas not my doing. That just be fate giving me a helping hand. There is still a sacrifice to be paid."

"Let me speak to Alamea."

"What?"

"LET ME SPEAK TO ALAMEA!"

"What you want wit my dead baby? You leave her alone."

"Why? You don't leave her alone."

"Very well...," Miss Louija sighs; closing her eyes, she shivers slightly, and takes a deep breath. She exhales, and Alamea returns.

"Bryant...I'm..."

"Wait. Don't. Please, don't. I can't...what will she do if I don't do as she asks?"

Alamea walks towards me; her stench makes me gag, but I breathe quickly through my mouth and fend it off. She reaches in her pocket and hands me a card. It was a picture of a warrior with a sword in place of his left hand; one of Miss Louija's tarot cards.

"What does this mean?"

"If you don't do as Mambo, Miss Louija, wishes, she'll invoke the card."

"And I'll turn into a little, brown man with a sword for a hand?"

"No...this is, in a reading; you know, the cards; it means you will be found unworthy. Mambo will make you take your own life."

In a brief moment, I almost ran for the door and out into the street to allow 'Mambo' her atonement as ridiculous as it seemed. But, if I did, I'd have no chance to see Dad and apologize for the way I acted. Even if I couldn't save the man, I could at least atone myself to my father.

"Fine, take it."

"Bryant, are you..."

"Take it, damn you! Just take it, and let me get away from this sickening stench and go to my father's side!"

Tears fill Alamea's eyes; she sighs and shivers into Mambo...Miss Louija. She smiles broadly, blows some powder in my face that makes me cough. The dust rises and stings my eyes. I rub them, blink a few times, and find myself standing outside a diner in Somewhere, U.S.A.

In a panic, I look around for a pay phone and then head inside the diner to ask for help. "Pardon me, y'all gots a phone?" I asked, startled by the sound of my voice as the cook points to the back.

Reaching in my pocket, I find some change and ask the operator to get my dad's hospital on the line. When the switchboard operator patches me through, his nurse answers; and I somehow already know what she is going to say.

After the nurse informs me of my dad's passing, I run from the diner and find myself standing in the middle of the parking lot, unable to breathe and unable to see through the tears flooding my eyes. Hearing the blast of a horn, I wake from my hysteria and move out of the way of the semi coming into the diner parking lot too fast. Wishing I hadn't moved, I find myself drawn to the busy highway. Just as I am about to step off the curb, I hear someone call me.

"Excuse me. Excuse me! You left this on the pay phone."

Turning around, I found a tiny, grandmotherly-looking lady dressed in a bright-green flowered dress and running shoes, waving my wallet at me.

"Oh, well, yes...thank you kindly, ma'am. My mind is just not in a good way, right now."

"Forgive my forwardness; but it looked that way to me, too. The way you ran out of there, I thought to myself, 'Edna, that little cutie might need some help;' so, here I am. Is there anything I can do?"

"Thank you, ma'am. I wish there was, but I's afraid it's something only I can handle," I say, taking the wallet from her as a card falls out of it. Watching it, I gasp and realize the whole nightmare was really true.

"Oh, my stars!" the little lady cries out, as I refold the card and shove it in my pocket.

"Please, forgive me; but why are you carrying that card? Is someone after you, or just playing some kind of nasty joke?"

"What do you mean, ma'am?"

"Well, I've been around awhile; longer than you, that's for certain; I've seen things in my time...strange things. That card...well...it's not good.

And considering it looked to me like you were about to...well, I'm not one to judge, especially when I'm not certain of what I've seen; but is there something...anything, I can help you with?"

Looking into the wise and honest eyes of the elderly stranger, I suddenly felt compelled to tell her my whole story; I held back and fought the urge as the tears of my anger streamed down my face. She reached out and touched my arm.

"Do you like pie? I just remembered that I didn't have dessert. My late husband used to insist on having dessert as often as possible because you just never knew where life would take you next. Seeing as how life has brought me here to you, well...it seems to me it wouldn't be right to not invite you along and..."

Cutting her off in the middle of her invitation, I started telling her my life story; babbling on and on, even as she took my hand and walked me inside the diner and sat me down at a table. She ordered two slices of warm apple pie with ice cream and two cups of coffee. We sat and ate and talked until the daylight was gone, and I was finally all talked and cried out. Sitting in silence, I looked across at my dining companion; not quite a stranger anymore, but more like an unknown, long-time friend.

"Miss Edna, can I tell ya'll somethin'?"

Edna nods and smiles as I take a deep breath, and she again gives me her undivided attention.

"I ain't never felt so alone in all my life...I..."

"Oh, Bryant...hush now...you're not alone. Listen to your heart. Your family will always be there."

"But, my daddy..."

"You and your daddy just had a misunderstanding; nothing more. All family's do once in awhile...it's because you love each other so much; you hate to see each other hurt."

Miss Edna excused herself and went to the Ladies' Room while I sat and pondered her words. Truly wanting to believe her, but having trouble doing so, because I could still hear how angry my daddy was.

After awhile, the waitress came up and told me the check had been paid by Miss Edna; she left me an envelope, along with an apology for leaving so abruptly. Inside was a set of keys and a note that simply said, 'LISTEN'.

All my life, my voice had been my key that opened doors to experiences beyond my wildest dreams and sometimes my nightmares. That day, I heard a word that changed my way at looking at the nature of conversation and me.

The keys were to an old El Dorado in the parking lot that needed some help. Listening to a nearby discussion going on led me to a mechanic who needed someone to help him with his shop: organizing, cleaning, fixing up his storage area. We worked out a trade: he got a well-working shop, and I got wheels to take me places.

And it did.

I've lived in all fifty states and some parts of Canada; I've lived check to check and been reasonably comfortable; lived in expensive homes and even my car. I've bagged groceries, swept floors, cleaned bathrooms, worked a traveling carnival, read books to the elderly, dug graves, tended bar, bussed tables, recorded radio commercials and voice-overs, starred in a few local television advertisements and morning shows, and even sold peanuts at sporting events.

And through it all...I listened. And I learned.

Standin' on the balcony of the Royal Home, overlookin' the courtyard where citizens of The Dominion are alive with excitement of a new era bein' born for them, I listen as they chatter and banter away with each other. They's feelin' somethin' that they ain't never felt before.

Hope.

"Hey! There you are! Been looking all over for you, man...where ya been?" Robert asks, as he joins me on the balcony.

"I been all over this here place. Started down there in the Square, mosied on over to the Library, then took a stroll to the Main Hall, took a gander at all them pictures and awards, then came out here. Ain't it amazin', Rob?"

"Yeah, amazing. Going into a new job, with new duties, and dangerous circumstances facing God knows what. Just *amazing*," Rob replies, tryin' hard not to show his true fear.

"Don't be scared, little buddy," I say, pattin' him on the back. "This is just the next step on the road of our lives; our next big adventure."

"Scared? Who said anything about being scared?" Rob says, crossin' his arms over his body as he pulls away.

"Hmm...I'm shore sorry 'bout that, Rob. Could've sworn I heard you say...well, makes me no never mind. Shall we?" I say, givin' Rob an out for his overwhelmin' body language and motionin' to the door leadin' to the waitin' area.

"You better get those ears of yours looked at, Bry. I think you're starting to hear things…," Rob says, with a nervous laugh, as his eyes dart all over the room. He finally catches me watchin' him.

"What?"

"Nothin'," I say, "Just listenin'."

Galen

"*LARGATO!*"

Hoping to catch Peggilyn before she left for the Coronation, Tempus and I use my portal to pop over to Circles. Had I known she'd already left and that a high-strung chef would be here instead, I might have waited.

"Please, Sir, it's all right. Really! If you would just stop running and listen," I say, as we follow the little, nervous cook into the kitchen. "Perhaps we shouldn't follow him. Maybe if we back off, he'll come around."

"Nonsense. Fear is nothing more than a lack of knowledge. He simply needs to learn who and what you are, and then the fear will be erased," Tempus says, following the cook to the kitchen door.

"Your analogy is correct, but…"

"Please, Galen, let me handle this," Tempus says, as we turn the corner of the kitchen and find the little cook trying to pull a cleaver from the wall that appears to be deeply imbedded.

"Por favor, mi amigo; un momento de su tiempo?" Tempus asks; the cook looks at him incredulously, and then goes back to the task of prying the cleaver loose so exuberantly that he's walked up the wall while pulling at the handle with all his might.

"Buddy, I'm an American. Speak English!"

"Oh, I'm sorry. You screamed 'Largato,' and I assumed you spoke Spanish," Tempus replies, moving closer to the jittery man.

"Only when I get scared, or feel nervous," the cook says, still pulling on the cleaver. He eyes a sharpening steel and reaches for it while still scaling the wall. Reaching too far, he falls flat on his face. Asmodeus would compare it to the Three Stooges if he were here, but this was far funnier.

"May I assist you with that?" I ask, with a laugh as the cook jumps up and wields the sharpening steel like Zorro.

"You…talk? You speak English?"

"Yes, actually I speak seventeen human languages and one hundred thirteen Demon."

"Demon? Like *Demon*, Demon, or Demon from The Dominion?"

"How do *you* know about *The Dominion*?" Tempus asks, stepping in and appearing quite concerned.

"Bill Dante. He's an old friend, he was here earlier…"

"Asmodeus' oldest boy? Is he still here?"

"Tempus…," I say, trying to get his attention.

"Galen, we need to tell him about The Brotherhood as soon as possible. Today is the Coronation. They are all in mortal danger!"

"Tempus, I think…"

"The Dante's are in danger? Who is this Brotherhood?" the cook asks, suddenly more concerned about the family than my proximity. Trying for the third time to get his attention, I raise my voice.

"Tempus!"

"What?"

"Shhh…" I say, placing a finger to my lips. Tapping my ear to indicate I needed the two men to listen, they both fall silent. Then, we all hear the sound of the unwelcomed guests.

Click-click-clickety-click

Following the sound, we turn in unison as they move across the vents in the ceiling.

But there is a series of clicks that seem to get closer the longer we stand there. A prickly feeling comes over me. Tempus whispers my name, and I know what he's trying to tell me.

Whipping around, I find a pestilent Spec hanging from a heat lamp over the order window. Digging down deep, I pull a guttural roar up and out as I unfurl my wings and swing my talons, splitting the Spec in half with a snarl. I toss the two halves of the dirty, little demon into the garbage disposal as Tempus flips the power on and opens the faucet to wash it away. Looking to the floor, I see the cook: out cold, flat on his back.

"Was it the wings? The teeth and talons? The roar?" I ask Tempus.

"Wings. Definitely the wings," Tempus says, with a laugh. He looks at me, and slaps himself in the face with a fwap.

"Oops!" I say, lifting the cook's limp body, "we should get him somewhere safe." Tempus nods, and then walks ahead of me.

"Next time you do that," Tempus says, still laughing and flapping his arms to depict my rapid unfurl before opening the office door for me, "you might want to consider a warning."

The Sentry

If I promise not to beat the crap out of anyone or sever any limbs or heads for at least a week, can we start this day over?

Please?

Should have known this day would be tough; it was destined to be. It started off with that weird nightmare. Note to self: the next time you dream about a graveyard and a spooky old dude in a trench coat with white cloudy eyes, *stay in bed.*

Looked for Connie in her four favorite malls, six local boutiques, and a consignment shop where her grandmother made her get rid of some of her more trendy clothes; cut Mom and Aunt Peg loose after two malls because I kept losing them every time we passed one of those herbal bath and body or candle stores. I think I used up all my allotment of minutes calling them on my cell phone to track them down. Came back to our apartment thinking; hoping really; that she came back home to change into something more appropriate than pink sweats and water socks. When I walked in, it looked like an explosion at a bubble gum factory. Pink, pink, and more pink everywhere. The place looks like my room did the night I killed Corson and she tried to dress me in my entire closet. The only time she acts this way is when she's upset, scared, angry, or all of the above. I just hope she can move beyond it. If she can't, I can easily see it bringing an ugly and bitter end to our friendship...and I don't want that.

Giving myself a once-over in my mirror portal, I also notice the clock on the wall, spew a couple of obscenities when I see I am thirty minutes late, but sigh a little when I remember it's really only fifteen minutes in The Dominion. Pricking my finger, I try to remember where we were supposed to meet.

Sapphire Square? No, that's where the ceremony takes place. Ruby Hall? No. Emerald Room is where we were to wait for the procession; by now they should all have gone to the Topaz Foyer, just before they make their entrance, so...

"Elizabeth Dante! Get yourself here! Now! Your father is sick with worry!"

"On my way!" I reply to Mom's warning thought.

Touching my pricked finger to the mirror, I envision the Royal Hall just outside the Emerald Room. Walking through the portal, I see the door to the room is open. A man is speaking, but I don't recognize the voice. Suddenly, an old, familiar feeling comes over me as my opal necklace starts to vibrate. Looking down I see it is glowing brightly, and I tuck it under my shirt. The man is speaking in a low whisper that I can barely hear. Needing to be closer, but not be seen; I call on my powers.

Wiping away the droplet of blood on the portal mirror, it swirls back to the mirror image of my entire body becoming invisible; I jump up and down, make funny faces and see nothing in the mirror, even though I feel my body doing it. Taking a deep breath, I walk into the Emerald Room.

As I enter, a tall male with a slim build wearing jeans, black boots, and a navy-blue, hooded peacoat is whispering to two young Demons dressed in Dominion Army uniforms. Whether they are real enlisted or imposters; if either of them is involved in anything illicit or treasonous, the act is punishable by death; and The Void is the executioner. When I approach them, they disburse and then open a closed, closet door on the right side of the room. Each soldier returns from the closet escorting a hooded being; Demon or human I don't know; moving slowly and feebly.

The tall Demon turns, and I see his face; he has white blonde hair, blue daggers for eyes, and is strikingly attractive...*and familiar*; I feel as if I have seen him somewhere before.

"You know what I want you both to do, right?" the hooded man asks the two captives, as he pushes their hoods back from their heads; one, a woman about Sean's age, wearing a Cal Bears sweatshirt and the the elderly man from my dream in his trench coat. Both have similar features and the same big, warm, brown eyes. The two look at each other lovingly and tell each other everything will be all right with a glance. Their ability to speak to each other without words clearly tells me they are family, a close one. They remind me of...

"Well?" the man asks, as the two continue looking at each other. The man sighs impatiently and places his hands gently on either side of the two victims' heads. "You know what I will do to you if you do not do as you are told...yes?"

As he says this, I feel the two victims' eyes on me, like they can see me. Their eyes plead with me; begging for help. The man turns briefly to see who or what they are staring at so intently, but he looks through me.

"Am I boring you? Or are you trying to *will* someone here to help you? Or perhaps you just need a reminder of who you are dealing with," the man said, as electrical tendrils flowed from his fingers through the two victims; their mouths open in a scream but there is no sound. The elderly man's eyes become cloudy and white, while the young girl's body folds in pain as her spine hunches over, forcing her to appear years older.

Knowing I can't possibly take on all three rogues alone, I move to the door leading to the Square to get help; but as I do, he dismisses them all.

"Go. Now. Don't force me to reach out to you," he says, tapping on the right side of his neck. As the two victims and their escorts turn to leave, I see what he's referring to.

A tattoo.

An unfamiliar symbol that looks to be a mix of something Gaelic or Norse, but its shape is similar to an hour glass. Damn, I wish Sean and Galen were here! After the quartet exits into the hall of the Royal home, the hooded man stands at the door alone.

He lowers his hood; his hands are delicate, with long fingers and perfectly manicured nails. His hair and skin are perfect and belong on the pages of a magazine. A hint of an unidentifiable tattoo peeks from under the cuff of his coat. A jagged, shiny piece of stone, marble or granite, hangs from his neck. He takes a deep breath through his nose, and then licks his lips.

"I like your perfume…*Sentry*," he says, with a cynical laugh as he turns and exits into the hall.

Shocked and poised to run and open the door to call for backup; my mind is a furious blur of information as I breathe deep, return to my visible form, and then open the door.

Waiting for me there is Hawthorne, Grandpa's new assistant and closest, long-time friend. His regret for hiring Nina prompted him to ask Hawthorne to come on board; needing someone he could trust implicitly, he saw no other option. He's dressed in a sharp, grey suit, black shirt, and plum tie. He's almost completely bald now and chooses to shave the remaining hair from the back of his head, leaving just a shadow of its jet-black hue. Speaking into his headphone, he informs the staff on stage that I am here. Looking up at the group standing there, I smile as I see Dad sigh heavily and wipe his brow.

"So good of you to join us, Sentry; your father has been *anxiously* awaiting your arrival," Hawthorne says haughtily.

"Let me guess, he's been pacing?"

"Need you ask?" Hawthorne replies, with a grin and wink. "Where were you?"

"Something weird was going on in the Emerald Room…you didn't happen to see a tall, strikingly-handsome man, with piercing, blue eyes wearing a hooded peacoat, did you?"

Hawthorne's face turns white and his eyes widen; concern and fear are radiating from every fiber of his being. "What…did you say?"

"Judging by your reaction, *I think you heard me clearly.* Let's continue this conversation after, all right?" I say calmly, touching his arm to reassure him that everything was *really* going to be fine.

Hawthorne nods and smiles tentatively. He waves his arm in the direction of the long, blue-carpeted walkway that welcomes me to my next, new journey; and speaks into his two-way radio to notify the Royal Guard to be on alert for anything unusual.

Suddenly…I get that same, old, weird feeling again.

Bill

A more than obvious sigh of exasperation mixed with relief escapes me when I finally see Eli arrive; Helen chides my actions, but I'm distracted by Hawthorne's reaction to something Eli says to him. His regular jovial disposition is completely shaken to his core as he sends her on. He immediately speaks into his two-way, sending a message to every member of the Royal Guard in the Square and on the platform.

"Be on alert! Investigate and report anything unusual immediately! I REPEAT, *ANYTHING* UNUSUAL!"

Looking to Dave to garner his attention, I see he's holstering his radio while trying to console and calm Connie who is reacting to the nervous energy flowing all around her. Dad's announcement of the Sentry brings the crowd to its feet, and Eli on her long walk up to the platform.

No more than a third of the way up the carpet, Eli slows down and grabs at her throat. Pulling her opal free of her collar, she and everyone else on the platform sees it is glowing brightly and pulsing. Eli looks at me with her mother's eyes, and my instincts read her meaning.

"Connie," I call out. "How many?"

"Two. Just two…or…," she says, breathing hard. She reaches out with a trembling hand, "Robert?"

Eli stands perfectly still, listening with her soul as well as her ears.

Robert takes Connie's hand. "Can you feel them?" she asks.

Robert closes his eyes and sniffs the air like an animal hunting prey. He hits Marco in the chest and shouts, "Arrows at ten and two. Run, Eli, run!"

Eli runs full-speed up the runway, then leaps into the air and spins like a top, catching an arrow in each hand before landing on the stage directly in front of Dad and Sage. Robert and Marco have the two assassins on the ground, and I give the guards the signal to take them to the holding cell. Turning my attention back to the group, I see Eli staring intently at the crowd as if trying to make eye contact with each and every citizen in attendance.

Sean, also watching every movement of the crowd, approaches Eli and lifts her left hand. Pierced by the arrow, Zach reaches his hand in and cradles the wound as Sean snaps the arrow in half and quickly pulls the bare end through. Zach heals it while Eli grits her teeth and guts out the pain.

Patrick uses some lazer gizmo that he shines over the crowd, determining the trajectory of the arrows and ultimately confirming the targets: The Emperor and the newly-crowned King. While Sean takes the arrow pieces over to Dave, Bryant steps up front and center.

"Now, now. Come on y'all...everything's fine. Just relax...y'all just gettin' a lil' sample of what we's here ta do. We's here to protect y'all," Bryant says, as he plays to the entire crowd.

"See, we knows what'cha wants; and we couldn't be happier. We," Bryant says, indicating the group on the stage, "we want the same thing for y'all, but there are some folks here that don't want cha to have that... ya know...freedom. Where we come from, freedom can't be taken away unless you give it away! While I stand here, lookin' at y'all...I shorely don't see any of y'all who are gonna let that happen,...but...I want y'all to look around you... take account of who's here *...and who ain't.*"

The crowd grows jumpy. Citizens point to each other, calling out others' names. Some are answered; others are not.

"Now! See there? That's what we's talkin' 'bout. You watch. We watch. We protect. We're here to *help you*; not *hinder you*."

Bryant steps back and watches the crowd; tears flow from the eyes of some while others can't stop smiling. And then there are those that are either unsure, or worried.

Worried perhaps, as Bryant said, about those that are part of the missing.

Dave

"Peanut, I have to ask; how did you do that thing you did, when you did the...you know...that *thing*?"

Eli looks at me like I've lost my marbles, "What?"

"You know?" I ask, using my finger to draw a curlicue in the air.

"Oh...that...," Eli replies. She thinks hard then says, "I've no earthly idea, Uncle Dave." She shakes her head, "All I knew was I could hear Hawthorne's frantic call to the guards and Connie's thoughts racing at me saying how scared he was. Then when Robert told me to run, my necklace got *hot*. Not warm and glowy like always, but like a potato out of a soup pot hot. Then, I heard the pings."

"The pings?"

"I heard the pings, and then felt the arrow leave the bow. I jumped. It was all instinct. And the...," Eli says, twirling her finger in the air like I did, "that only happened because I heard the scratch of another bow being pulled. There was a third assassin."

"She's right," Patrick says, walking in with Robert, Connie, and Marco close behind. Robert carries another bow; bigger, yet similar to the other previously confiscated.

"*Who* was the target?" Eli asks casually, her tone is slightly comical like she already knows the punch line to a very bad joke.

"That depends," Robert says. "Who can tell us about the set-up of the stage?"

"I can," Hawthorne says, joining the conversation. He stands and walks over to where we are all gathered and opens a brown-leather notebook to a schematic.

"This was the planned layout. Guards at sixteen visible key points, Emperor here, King here, and the Marshall with his team in front."

"Was there a particular order The Kindred were to take?" Patrick asks, taking his PDA from a pocket on the side of his backpack.

"Yes, from the audience view, alphabetically starting with the Empath and ending with the Vox," Hawthorne answers, reading from his notes.

Patrick taps the screen of his PDA hard and looks at the diagram sternly. Taking off his backpack, he reaches inside and takes out a sheet of transparent material like plastic, graph paper. Laying it over the diagram, he looks at his PDA and writes some numbers and dots on the plastic in various different places with a dry-erase pen, and then draws three lines to the stage connecting the dots.

"Bryant? Why would they want to kill Bryant?" Marco asks, pointing to the last line.

"It isn't Bryant," Patrick says, "It's"…

"Me," Eli says, already knowing deep down it was her all along.

"No. Hawthorne said The Kindred were to stand in alphabetical order. This last is Bryant," Marco insists.

"The Kindred are only eight: Empath, Healer, Hunter, Inventor, Peacemaker, Scholar, Soldier, Vox. The Sentry is not technically part of The Kindred. This dot is number *nine*…It's *me*, Marco."

A painful silence comes over the group when Bill storms in and breaks it.

"Um…we need to have a team meeting in the Great Hall. We need to discuss…well…let's go in there. I'll explain everything."

"Bill, what's wrong," I ask, concerned by his demeanor. In all our years together, I can't remember ever seeing him this confused and nervous.

"The interrogation…it didn't go well," Bill says, wiping the sweat from his brow as we leave the Emerald Room and turn the corner past the interrogation room. The door is open; two soldiers are sweeping up two piles of ashes. Bryant, designated to assist with the questioning because of his gift, squats against the wall outside the Great Hall; ashes in his hair and all over his face and clothes. His eyes are red and swollen, and his face full of remorse. Zach kneels next to him as he checks his vitals and makes him drink tea from a cup. Patrick runs up and starts brushing off his buddy.

"Bill, where are the…"

"Dead. They're dead! Damndest thing…we were just talking. They wouldn't divulge anything. Bryant went into one of his long-winded speeches, stopped half-way through and started telling us what he was hearing in their heads. How scared they were and how they and their families were in danger if they didn't succeed. They didn't want to do it, but *he* had control over them," Bill stops, shakes his head, "the two said *nothing*. Then…their eyes…they were…*more than terrified*…and then the tattoo…"

"Tattoo?"

"On their neck; some sort of Gaelic symbol that looks like an hour glass…it opened up into a straight line and stretched across their necks…and …its like the line cut their head off from inside…one minute they're there and the next…"

"Do you know who this *'he'* is, Bill?"

Bill shrugs, "Only one Demon I know with that kind of twisted mind and the power to make it happen. I'd no idea he was still…"

"Is that what we're going to discuss in there?"

"Yes," Bill says. "I need to talk to Sage first. We're going to need a little more help. We need to reactivate The Eternals."

Helen

Heading back to Circles to finish dinner as Bill and his team investigate the happenings today, Peg decides to come with me; and I've no idea why.

"You hate cooking."

"I don't *hate* it; it's just not my *favorite* thing to do," Peg says, activating the portal and taking us back to Eli's apartment.

"Yeah, I know. Your favorite thing to do is order at the drive through," I snap, as we head downstairs to the kitchen.

"Keep it up, Missy, and I won't help you at all."

I sigh, "Fine. What *exactly* are you going to do?"

"I'll provide witty conversation and play your favorite tunes on the juke box and...," Peg abruptly stops listing all her helpful handiwork because, as we turn the corner, neither of us is prepared for what we see.

The restaurant is crawling with crustaceous-looking, spidery critters with tails like scorpions whipping around. There's a tall, good-looking, black man that I don't know trying to fend them off with our old friends, Galen and Carlos, with Carlos now sporting a bandage on his head that makes him look like Gunga Din.

"Watch out!" Galen roars, whipping his right wing over our heads as we duck down.

"See! Didn't I tell you?" the black man scolds.

"Not the best time for I-told-you-so's,...but point taken," Galen says.

Peg and I sneak behind Galen, and then make our way to the bar where Carlos and the stranger hide, each holding one of the hoses that dispenses soda and water. They are spraying the mechanical spiders as they approach. Most scamper back. Some don't and become gooey slime. A thought occurs to me, and I grab my sister's hand.

"Brilliant!" Peg says as she receives my message; and together we focus on the puddles of water and soda on the floor and create a misty fog that floats just slightly above the floor. Being out of practice, the fog dissipates quickly and barely gives the critters a rash.

"See what happens when you don't practice?" Peg scolds.

"What was it that Galen just said? Oh, yeah…not the best time for I-told-you-so's…but …"

"Yeah, yeah, yeah…we need a little help," Peg says, as she focuses on Eli and calls to her mind.

"What *are* these things? And why are they here?" I ask, grabbing cups of ice cubes and pouring them on the bar so I can 'fire' them at the pests with a wave of my hand.

"They are called Speculari; lowest of the lower-level Demons in The Dominion and just a half-step above the top echelon of the Underworld," Galen says, eyeing the largest bug sitting atop one of the pipes in the ceiling. "They are here to keep this man from meeting *The Sentry*."

"Eli? Why? What do you want with my daughter?"

The man looks to Galen with much surprise; and then takes a moment away from spraying the bugs with water to throw his head back and laugh, "*Your daughter*, did you say? Well, I'll be…we never figured on that."

"What's so funny?" Peg asks, clearly annoyed by the man's reaction; she always was a bit of a feminist.

"Nothing, Madame, I assure you. My apologies if I offend; it's just that…well, The Erudite…"

"How do you know *The Erudite*?" I ask.

"Stolas told me."

"You *knew* Stolas?" Peg interrupts.

"Yes. And The Erudite…"

"Let me guess; they told you about a prophecy in some sort of twisted, incomprehensive, gobbledee-goop way that you spent weeks trying to decipher?" Peg answers.

"Try *years*, Madame," the man says, showing just a touch of the anger and frustration we had twelve years ago.

"Seems to be a lot of that going around," I snicker. Remembering the past, I angrily grab a pitcher of ice and *wave* it over towards one of the beasts and turn it into slimy Swiss cheese.

Asmodeus

While Helen and Peg return to Circles to work on our family celebration dinner, The Kindred, the Marshall, and the newly-crowned King convene in the Great Hall to discuss what happened; my coordinator, Hawthorne, insisted I go into seclusion following the assassination attempt.

"Nonsense!" I bark, "I'm safer here amongst my family. Besides, I think you can offer some insight on who is behind this."

"Asmodeus,…I don't know if I can…"

"Thorney, you have to. You know first hand how…"

"Please? Asmo, don't push me. Besides, we're not even certain it is…"

Hawthorne stops speaking as we hear yelling in the hallway.

"Connie, please? It isn't that I don't understand. More than anyone here, *I understand…and I'm sorry*…but there are other things going on; others lives who are on the line that I have to consider. I can't dwell on past events that I have no control over."

"So, that's it. I'm supposed to just forget that my parents died because of *your* family's plan. If it wasn't for them…"

"If it wasn't for *them*, I wouldn't be here; and we would never have met. I'm sorry you feel cheated. I'm sorry you feel misled. If there were anything I could do to fix this and bring them back to you, I would; but I can't. I am here for you. I always will be. But if you can't get beyond this…"

The silence in the room was almost as deafening as it was in the hall. When Eli walks in alone, all eyes turn away but mine; my grandbaby is in pain, and all I want to do is go to her and hold her; soothe away her fear. But that's the Grandpa in me talking. Right now, I must be the Emperor; and she, The Sentry. She fights past the discomfort and moves on.

"What's first on the agenda, Marshall?"

"Well, first, we need to have the whole team here. Where's Con…?"

"Connie won't be joining us today. In fact, I may need to look for another Empath," Eli says, looking at the floor.

"She'll come around. Just give her time to realize that there was nothing anyone could do. It was an accident from a deliberate act on Corson's part, and your family had to keep it quiet or…"

"Damnit, Marco, why couldn't you take her side?"

"What?" Marco replies, shocked at her outburst.

"She feels completely abandoned right now; from all of us; because you are all on my side…but you, *you* should be on her side. Yes, you are my best friend; and I appreciate the support; but you are the man she is planning on spending the rest of her life with, your future wife and the mother of your children. You hurt her. I hurt her. We all hurt her."

"Eli, there was absolutely nothing anyone could have done to change things. In my vision, The Erudite showed me only the lives that could be saved. There was no life there. I'm sorry, but my focus was the family," Sage says dejectedly.

"No, Uncle Sage, I know," Eli sighs, "It's so hard…I'm in this spot where I totally see both sides, but I'm smart enough and old enough to know better than to let either side of the argument get the best of me."

"Sometimes," Hawthorne says quietly, "when it involves the ones we love, our emotions don't allow for the most intelligent of actions."

Eli and Sage look to each other and snicker and nod.

"Very true, but if we listen to our heart," a familiar voice interrupts.

The group's attention snaps to the door of the hall as a special guest appears. Dressed in a pink and purple, flowered-pantsuit, running shoes, and carrying her rather large, denim bag; she is obviously very familiar to them based on the expressions on their faces. The first one up and running over is Bryant.

"Miss Edna? Oh, my Lord, look at you! How you been, Darlin'?"

"Just grand, Bryant. I hear you have a new job, as well as some new friends, who just happen to be old friends of mine…My stars! Just look at how you've grown, Zach!

"Hello, Edna," Zach says shyly, as he hugs her and lifts her off the ground making her shriek like a little girl and drop her bag on the floor.

"Hiya, Handsome!" Edna says, peering over Zach's shoulder at Sean as he picks up her bag and puts it on an empty chair.

"Mrs. Davies," Sean says, as Zach gently sets Edna down. Sean takes Edna's hand, lifts it to his lips and kisses it, making her blush and sigh like a school girl. She turns away shyly and catches Marco's attention.

"Ma'am," Marco says, nodding courteously.

"Sergeant," Edna responds, with just a little salute.

"Remember me?"

"Of course, David. How *are* you?" Edna asks, as Dave leans down to hug her and she tenderly pats his back.

As she pulls away, her attention is drawn to Robert and Patrick. She reaches up and places a hand on each of their faces; Rob and Pat both lean down and kiss Edna on the cheek. After Edna has made the rounds, she turns and finds Eli; she looks at Edna with a grin and the Dante twinkle in her eye.

"Mrs. Davies?" Eli asks.

"Stan and I kept our work life separate from our home life. It allowed Peter to have a somewhat normal life…as normal as one can, being half Demon," Edna answers, with a wink. Robert looks to Eli with surprise; Eli just shakes her head and smiles at this new information.

"Well, it seems many of you already know Edna. What you probably don't know is who she *is*, or who her family is. Edna is an *Eternal*. She comes from a family of *Eternals* that have been around for centuries," Bill says, before he waves Edna on to finish her story.

"Yes, I come from the 'Blue' family. Some of you know my cousin, Galen."

Sean nods as he looks to Bill, who acknowledges him with a smile.

"Edna, what *is* an 'Eternal'?" Patrick asks.

Edna smiles; her nose crinkles with delight as she winks at Hawthorne. She takes a deep breath; holds it and becomes a little cherub statuary that you find in most cemeteries or elaborate gardens; then she shivers and returns to her animate form

"Wow!" Patrick sighs.

"You think that's trippy, you should see Declan and Darius," Edna says proudly.

"Who?" Robert asks, joining in.

"My brothers. Declan is the Royal Cleaner; when one of the rogues leaves any trace of something humans won't understand or like, he cleans it up. Darius is the Royal Procurer; he organizes and obtains all the surplus here in the Dominion. On occasion, we pick up side work with the Royals."

"*Side* work?" Dave asks. "what is it you *do* exactly, Edna?"

"We're spies," Edna says, taking a wintergreen candy out of her pocket, unwrapping it and putting it in her mouth. "Not spies like in the movies or in the way of mercenaries…you know…Specs."

"Specs?" Bryant asks, taking the cellophane wrapper from her and getting up to throw it in the garbage by the door.

"Specs, yes, Speculari…lower-level Demons…do anything for anybody for the right price…look like giant spiders made from an erector set…No? Don't know of them or never heard of them?" Edna asks, as the group sits dumbfounded and over-whelmed. Edna sighs angrily, "Bill Dante, you're the Marshall. What have you been teaching these kids?"

"Well, Edna, we've been dealing with a few things…Corson for one…"

"Bill, Eli condemned Corson to The Void on Christmas Eve…what have you been teaching them since then? It's been seven days! My stars, Bill! You can't send them out untrained."

"Yes, Edna, I know but…"

"Oh! Do I have to do *everything*?" Edna fusses, pulling her cell phone out of her giant bag.

The group sits uncomfortably looking at each other; Bill especially. Eli is tilting her head like she's trying to hear something in another room; she's listening, carefully, and wrinkling her brow. Zach touches her shoulder; she pats it, and shakes her head as if its nothing.

"Well, Dec and Dari are on their way. I just realized…we're missing someone…Eli, where is Connie?"

"Um…there's a problem there…my mom and my aunt…"

"Yes, I know…they waited far too long to tell her about her parents," Edna says, as she turns to Bill. "They should have told her before Corson was condemned. It would have given her *closure* to know the person at fault was gone…but, no…of course, they waited for the busiest day. No matter…I'll take care of it, *as usual*…," Edna says, taking a notebook out of her bag and making a note.

"Take care of it? Edna, I thought you just said you were a spy?" Zach asks, looking completely confused.

"As well as my *espionage work*, I'm the P.O.C. or Point of Contact for the team. My new title is *The Orbis*. I was appointed to the position after the tragedy. I *was* The Historian, but Galen was promoted to that post."

"Tragedy?" Eli asks.

"Yes... our little sister, Lisette, was caught off guard; and...The Sandman destroyed her,...we couldn't put her back together."

"What?" Patrick asks, glued to Edna's every word.

"Eternals can't be killed, but we can be kept from *animating* if a piece of us is taken. Lisette was...crushed, and The Sandman took a piece of her. Her remains, the dust, are in an urn in our family crypt next to my husband. One day we'll catch him and resurrect her...I know we will."

Hawthorne stands, wipes his face, and excuses himself as he walks out of the room.

"Oh, Thorney, please?...I didn't mean to...It's just that they ...," Edna turns to me, "Emperor, I'm sorry. I didn't mean to upset him, but we *will* get her back!"

"Folks, what the hell's going on here?" Robert asks, annoyed by all the abrupt changes.

"Lisette was, *is*, Hawthorne's fiancé. They were to be married the day after she was doing surveillance for me to see if my brother, Stolas, was all right because I hadn't seen him in weeks; and The Sandman caught her off guard. She was hiding in her stone form; an angel in the graveyard. He used one of his borrowed powers and blew her up. He keeps a piece of her on a chain around his neck...without all of *her,* we can't bring her back," I say, as the group stares at each other; blown away by the new information. Eli has an interesting, pensive look in her eyes. The wheels of her mind are spinning wildly.

"All right; if I may speak for the group and ask, WHAT?" Marco says, as he looks around at the rest for help.

"I think someone better start at the beginning, please? I'm starting to get that feeling again. All this talk of this 'Sandman'. Does he have something to do with the events today?"

"We think he does, Dave. That's why I activated The Eternals. You're going to need all the help you can get," Sage says.

"Edna, if your stone form is a Cherub, and Lisette is an angel; what are your brothers?" Patrick asks, always wondering about the unobvious.

"Darius isn't a stone Eternal; he takes after our father and becomes metal. In procurement, he has to find the right vehicles to obtain so he usually turns himself into a hood ornament. His favorite is the little bull dog on those semis, or a jaguar. Declan is the outdoorsman…you can usually find him in a garden as a gnome, or a frog or a mushroom…whatever the décor calls for."

Stunned, the group sits silent.

"Well, shall we get on with the discussion about The Sand…"

"Um…no…," Eli says, standing up and grabbing at the chain under her collar. "I think we need to postpone and…"

"Oh, my stars! Why is that flashing like that?" Edna asks.

"It tells me when evil is near and…OW!" Eli yells, dropping the amulet as she runs to the door and then out into the hallway; Bill and The Kindred follow. Ash gets up and runs out after them. Sage, Edna, and I stare at each other, not knowing what to do. Ash comes back in, out of breath.

"Well, it's something really bad going on at Circles. Eli says Helen, Peg and Galen are in danger."

"Galen!" Edna exclaims, as Ash turns and heads back out the door. "In danger from what, Ash?" she yells.

"Speculari!" Ash yells.

"Hmph! We'll just see about *that*!" Edna barks as she straightens her outfit, smoothes her hair, and takes off running for the hall in her sneakers, tossing her big, denim bag over her shoulder.

Eli

As we arrive through the portal, I don't see Mom or Aunt Peg anywhere. What I *do* see is my restaurant crawling from top to bottom with grayish, rock formations with legs and tails; clicking and clacking from one corner to the next, scratching my newly-polished dance floor, and destroying my tables and chairs; some swinging from the lights, while others are limping out of puddles of melted ice and soda. Drawing on my powers, I listen carefully and find I understand their clickety-clacks. Snapping my jaws, I pop and crack a warning. The little bugs stop momentarily, and then laugh while they continue. Drawing a knife from my back pocket, I open it, and throw it at a critter crawling up the wall, and pin it there; then I focus on a full glass of water on the bar and slam it into the pinned critter, and watch it melt down my cherry-wood trim.

"Who's next?" I click, stepping out of the portal and drawing my machete. The critters; which, I guess and guess correctly; are Speculari. Being the cowards they are, they have scampered to the other side of the room. Quickly, we exit the portal; Marco closes it after Uncle Sage and Grandpa join us. I call out for Mom.

"Here, Sweetie!"

"You all right?" I ask as she, Aunt Peg, Carlos, Galen and some man I've never met cautiously stand up from behind the bar. The stranger looks at me curiously then clutches at his chest. Mom nods to my question as I do a double-take of the stranger. "Friend of yours?" I ask Galen, but he doesn't get time to answer the question. The Specs have found Uncle Sage and Grandpa and are mounting an attack.

"Get them out of here! They are in grave danger!" the stranger yells, as Uncle Ash, Bryant, Marco, and Dad draw weapons and surround them, guarding them from all angles. Sean, Dave, and Robert form a line in front of the group, ready for action. Patrick has retreated to a corner, taking photos of a melted Spec and a live one that is chasing him. Zach and Edna somehow zip behind the bar; Zach is looking at Carlos' head, and Edna is hugging Galen's knees. I hear the biggest of the Specs as he jumps to the ground with a thud, from a speaker up high and lands too close to us. As a group, we move quickly to the bar and stand in front. The big bug makes some lewd remarks, and I stop him.

"Hey! You *watch* your mouth! That's my mom you're referring to!" I click, but the Spec is relentless; he goes on. "Go ahead; keep it up, Bud...I dare you to say something about the King, or the Emperor...or *me!*"

The Spec pops and clicks an answer, and then poses a nasty question.

"Not in a million years, you over-grown roach...," I click, catching Aunt Peg placing a dishpan full of water on the floor; she pushes it next to me with her mind. Hearing Mom's message in my head, I understand completely what they plan to do. I back up, lean against the bar and stretch my arms out along the wet wood. "On second thought, *General*, how about a drink?"

Mom and Aunt Peg grab my hands the moment I say 'drink', and together we turned the tub of water into a roving sauna; quickly directing the thick, wet mist over each and every one of the Spec army, and cornering the General with nowhere to run.

"Maybe we should question him first," Aunt Peg asks; but before either of us can answer, Mom slams the warm, wet cloud into him melting any chance of an interrogation.

"Well, I think that answers *that*," I say, letting go of their hands as I turn to look at them.

"*That*...was impressive," Zach says, with his impish grin.

"Thanks," I say, "but just a side note, don't mess with my mom." Zach nods and agrees with a wink.

Turning back around, I view my bar.

"Aw, shit!"

"Hmm...no, no, not to worry. I'm on it. Declan will be here in...," Edna says, looking at her watch but is interrupted by an odd, little man.

"I know, I know...I'm late, I'm late. I was cleaning up a mess Galen left up in Piedmont..."

"I had no choice, Dec...the Specs..."

"Oh! *I know*, Galen! Trust me! Don't know what those creepy, little bastards have been eating; but boy, oh boy, what a stain! The smell? And sticky? Yeesh!"

Looking at Edna, she smiles, "Don't fret, Eli. My little brother is the best. He'll have this place looking like new in no time."

Catching my reflection in the portal mirror, I see the stranger stepping up directly behind me. "Galen, is this guy an old friend of yours?" I ask, becoming just a little wary of how close he is. I turn, call upon my powers, and then push him away slightly. He cocks his head and smiles at this.

"No, Eli, he's a new friend; but an old friend of your Uncle Stolas."

Grandpa moves in close upon hearing Galen mention his brother.

"Elizabeth," Zach says, pulling me to him and away from the stranger, "why is *that* pointing at you?"

Leaning closer I see what Zach is referring to. A brass skeleton key, hanging on a burgundy satin ribbon, is pointing straight at me. Moving to the left and then to the right, the key follows me. Robert and Bryant step in and try to grab it, but it moves away from their touch. The stranger takes it off and hands it to me.

"This is *yours*. That is, if you *are* who I *think* you are."

Looking closely at the man, I recall him from my dream. Reaching out to accept his offering, the key jumps from the stranger's hand into mine. He laughs; relief comes over his face, and he seems a few years younger if that's possible.

"Eli Dante," Galen says, "may I introduce, Tempus Raleigh."

"Tempus?" Uncle Ash asks; he hasn't hardly said a word all morning. "Tempus is latin…."

"For *time*," Uncle Dave finishes Uncle Ash's thought.

"*Time* will tell you all you need to know," Uncle Sage mutters to himself, but he also repeats what we are all thinking.

"Yes," Tempus says, "my name means time. My father was a watchmaker. I guess my mother…"

"And did you follow in your father's footsteps?" Grandpa interrupts.

"No," Tempus replies.

"No?" Dad snaps, curiously.

"I studied to become a teacher, but Dad did teach me all he knew. As did Stolas."

"And this key…what's it for?" Sean asks, just as direct as the rest.

"A lock."

"What lock?"

"I don't know?"

"*You don't know?*" Marco inquires sarcastically.

"I thought it was for the safe, but when Liz…"

"Liz? You know Liz? How do you know Liz?" Grandpa barks, bristled and alarmed.

"Yes. She helped me store the project."

"What *project?*" Patrick asks, taking notes of all the previous conversation.

"The Master Watch…*The Sentry's Watch*. The Watch The Brotherhood has been chasing after me for all these years that…," Tempus backs away, clearly feeling attacked by us all. "Hold on just a minute! I have some questions, too! What is *this* place, and who *are* you people?"

Smiling, I brush my cohorts back to allow some breathing room.

"Well, Tempus,…this is 'Circles,' my restaurant. And they," I say, motioning to the guys, "are The Kindred."

"And *you?*" Tempus asks, offering me his hand which I gladly accept and answer his question.

"I'm Eli…*Elizabeth*…I am The Sentry. Welcome to the family."

Tempus

After rounds of formal introductions to the entire Dante family, The Kindred and friends, Bill's lovely wife, Helen, asks me to join them for dinner; a celebratory feed to commemorate the Coronation of the new King and the presentation of The Kindred to the citizens of The Dominion.

"It would be my honor," I reply, bringing a glowing smile to Helen's lovely face. She turns and walks to the kitchen with Carlos, bubbling with excitement as she rattles off a list of orders for him.

Giving my attention back to the group, I half expected to find a firing squad waiting for me; instead I find each member diligently working on some task they are assigned: measuring the melted Specs for size, jumping trajectory, taking samples of the venom. When they are finished in one area, Declan moves in and scrubs the area clean like a germicidal twister.

"Amazing, aren't they?" Edna asks, coming to my side with Galen.

"Stolas told me one day this team would be formed but," I sigh, and choke back an emotional flood, "oh, if he could only see this. He'd be so pleased."

"Well, aren't *you* a sight for sore eyes!"

"Darius?" I exclaim, greeting my old friend with a hug.

"It's been too long, Tempus."

"Twenty-plus years," I say, catching a peripheral glimpse of Edna looking at Darius, then at Patrick, and then at Darius again. She is not pleased. "Something wrong, Edna?"

Edna looks at Darius with a furrowed brow and turns on the heel of her sneaker with a squeak and storms off.

"What?" Darius asks irritably; Edna turns back and shakes her head at him disappointedly.

Curious as to what she saw, I take my own comparative look at the two and catch on to what Edna saw; the two could be brothers...or father and son...

"What!" Darius says, beyond irritated now.

Deciding it's just a coincidence, I shake my head and say, "Nothing, it's nothing."

Just as Declan finishes cleaning the General's remains and the place is shiny clean, Helen calls us to dinner.

Seated between Hawthorne and Bryant, I look across at Galen and smile as we both enjoy piping-hot bowls of Cioppino with crusty, San Francisco-style, sourdough, French bread.

"Helen, this meal is magnificent. I haven't had such fine Cioppino since my friend, César, opened his bistro in Hayward."

Helen's mouth opens in shock. She looks at Carlos, who is also surprised.

"You knew Uncle César?" Carlos asked, curiously

"Well, I used to bus tables at a restaurant where he was a young Sous Chef, just starting off in Piedmont."

"Jet-black hair, always dressed to the nines?" Helen asks, describing the very same César I knew.

"Yes...what a coincidence! How did you know him, Helen?'

"I was his Head Chef at The Faultline, his Bistro in Hayward. And Carlos is his nephew. He was Head Chef at his other bistro...in Piedmont."

"Yes; but, he passed away twelve years ago," Carlos answers, blessing himself as he hangs his head. The silence that follows is deafening. Looking up at Galen, he smiles gently and tries to help me overcome my obvious uncomfortable situation.

"Tempus and his father used to occupy my store. They were the original owners there," Galen tells the group. Galen goes on, telling the group a condensed resume of my life. Then The Emperor, Asmodeus, clears his throat, holds up his hand, and commands our attention.

"How...How did you come to know my brother?"

All eyes are on me; not just looking at me, but through to the very core of my being. Feeling the need to be heard and understood, I push my chair back and stand.

"Stolas saved my life. I was attacked: beaten and shot because of the color of my skin. Your brother came to my aid. He said he'd known I was coming; The Erudite told him. He said they told him of a prophecy and kept repeating a phrase to him."

"*Time will tell you all you need to know?*" Sage asks, with a hint of sarcasm.

Looking to him, amazed that he knew it verbatim, I nod, "Yes, yes…that's it exactly. How…?"

"The Erudite told me, too…*told us*…the very same thing," Sage answers, with eyes of a man far older than his years. He is suddenly tired, and the discussion is difficult for him.

"What else did Uncle Stolas tell you?" Bill asks, as he pats his younger brother, the King, on the back; and then looks to his youngest sibling who is seated across from the two as he blows a kiss to his newly crowned, more serious, older brother. With a roll of his eyes, King Sage calls him a 'stupid ass' and the three share a jovial, fraternal moment.

"Stolas asked me to teach him about humans and our way of life. In turn, he taught me about Demons and The Dominion. He asked me to show him how a clock works; so I'd take him to Dad's shop when it was closed, and let him look around and ask questions. We discussed history, sports, philosophy, political science, theology…but mostly, he wanted my help understanding the Prophecies."

Again, all eyes turn to me.

"Do you remember them?" Sean asks, taking a notebook from his inside, jacket pocket.

Thinking back to the days when Stolas would meet me on campus, looking like a caricature of a mad scientist, frantic to discuss another piece of the puzzle, I reply, "As if it were yesterday."

> "*Danger awaits the Royal Crown and the branches of the familial tree must risk sacrifice, or face cleansing by fire. A marriage, though necessary, holds dire consequences if disregarded. A birth of two, nets a battle with three. Three become many if left to their own. Attention paid is a small price for eternity. A keeper of history and a teacher of life will align to prepare the tools and ready the Sentry for a battle with the one.*"

"Holy crap! What does all *that* mean?" Robert barks.

"The one?" Eli asks, before she is distracted and waves and smiles at a group of men who enter and take seats near Zach. One of the men looks very familiar; it's been a long time, but it appears to be Raffa. He leans in and whispers something to Zach, making him smile broadly; and he looks just like Nate, Raffa's old partner. I wonder if he is…?

"Tempus?" Sean says, bringing me back to the present.

"Yes, 'The One'? Stolas and I spent hours trying to figure that out," I say, watching Asmodeus shake his head in amazement. "Emperor?"

"He married *her* because they told him to."

"Emperor, he had to. He did it to protect you," I reply, getting up from my chair and going to him.

"He should have told me."

"Perhaps, yes; but I think he loved you *too* much to get you involved. Here," I say, taking the letter from my back pocket "see," I say, pointing to the phrase Stolas wrote about him; a single tear falls from his left eye.

"May I borrow this?" the Emperor asks. "I have a meeting with the Board of Trustees of The Brotherhood about…"

"Emperor…You can't!"

"Tempus, I need to speak to them and shut them down…"

"Stay away from them, *please*?"

"I'll do whatever is necessary to protect my family."

"Your brother gave his life to protect you…to protect them…You…"

"I am aware of that, Tempus, but…"

"Stay away!" I snap, snatching my letter back from him.

"Tempus…"

"Stay away from them, Emperor," I say, holding my anger in my jaw as I slowly walk back to my seat and sit down, collecting my thoughts and blowing off my fury.

"I'll take extra guards with me and I'll…"

"STAY AWAY FROM THE BROTHERHOOD, DAMN YOU!"

Standing abruptly, I knock my chair over and startle the group; me, the stranger, barking at the Emperor.

"*You watch your tongue, Tempus!*"

"No, Emperor, *you watch yours.* For if you go to them, they will surely cut it out…and then send it, along with the rest of you, piece by piece to your family."

The room is silent as I calm myself. Pacing, I find the words to say.

"Emperor," going to his side, I take a knee, "The Brotherhood is not what it used to be. It's a collection of the corrupt; rogue Demons hiding behind the guise of a long-treasured, Royal-approved faction with all of the benefits and none of the moral or ethical values. Stolas loved you more than anything in this world. I beg you. Please don't let them turn his life, or any of the other lives they have taken, into just another checkmark on their list of things to do before they acquire control."

The Emperor is quiet; pensive. I feel a rush of heat rise from my feet to the top of my head and dissipate; my anger finally extinguished, and my point made. He looks to his sons, his granddaughter, and the rest of his extended family. Hesitantly, he looks at me; and I see the familiar twinkle in his eyes as he nods in agreement to my impassioned plea.

"That key," the Emperor asks, pointing to his granddaughter. "What does it open?"

"Well, in anyone else's hands…nothing. In the hands' of The Sentry, only one lock until the Master Watch is in her hands," I answer, piquing the interest of all at the table.

"And…then?" Eli asks, leading me to my answer.

"This world, as well as any other, is yours to open."

"No time like the present…let's go, Tempus. Eli? Bill?" Asmodeus says.

Eli excuses herself and goes to Zach to kiss him goodnight. Bill gives the team the night off and promises to fill them in on all that they learn tonight. They exit hesitantly but with stretches and yawns that tell me the time off is welcome; we head to the mirror portal in the main restaurant. Stepping up to the mirror, Bill is already readying to prick his finger. I stop him.

"No, Bill, I don't believe that is necessary. Eli, if you would, please, try using the key like you are opening any other door."

Eli is puzzled; she grins, looks to the key and then to me as she lifts it off and over her head. Then she stops.

"Should I be envisioning somewhere specific?" she asks, slightly hesitant to proceed.

"No. Not until you have the Watch. Right now it will only open one lock. Go ahead," I say, as I watch her approach the mirror.

The key, as it gets closer to the mirror, begins to glow blue. When Eli taps against the mirror lightly, an antique key hole appears. She pushes the key in and turns it to the left to open the door that has magically appeared.

As the door opens to gasps and muttered cursing, Eli steps through and turns in circles, looking at the secret workroom Stolas built inside the Royal Safe. Stepping in behind her, my mind drifts back to the first time I came here.

"Wow!" is the only word that escapes her.

"Those are my thoughts exactly, Sentry…my thoughts exactly."

Marco

Feeling a little pissed off when Bill *dismissed* us, I was actually more than grateful after I stood up. Stiffness had set in on one side of my body from when I tackled the bowman at the Coronation. Putting my jacket on, I let out a small grunt, followed by a long, welcomed yawn.

"Jeez, old man, leave some air for the rest of us," Robert says, as he playfully punches me in my gut; and I mumble 'shit head' in his direction as he walks away. Following him out to the main floor, I flip off the lights.

"Hey! The ladies are still here…leave them on!" Patrick scolds, as he opens the door.

"No, no…it's all right. I'll lock up behind you. Helen and I are raiding the herb bins with Carlos. We'll take the portal home," Peg says, as she kisses Dave and pats his butt.

"Really didn't need to see that; thanks for burning that image into my retinas," Patrick says to Aunt Peg, before stepping outside. Then suddenly his attention is drawn elsewhere. "Hey, Mister, are you all right?"

"What's wrong, Pat?" Zach asks, as Raffa follows him quickly outside.

Parading outside, our merry, but tired group, grow concerned as Patrick tries to talk to an old man sitting on the ground in the middle of the parking lot, rocking himself, and singing a song in a foreign language. His arms are mimicking the actions of holding a baby; he fixes an imaginary blanket, and gently touches the cheeks of the invisible infant. A chill runs down my back as Raffa and Zach reach out to help the man up. He stands and suddenly shrieks.

"No! Leave her alone! Don't take her!"

The man, dressed in a beige, hooded, trench coat and bedroom slippers turns to face us; his eyes are milky white and sightless, yet I feel his eyes on me just the same.

He begins to weep and sob; suddenly he takes off, pushing his way through us one by one, apologizing for every touch he makes. With each apology he makes to us, the air grows colder; our breathing, heavy from the excitement, hangs in the air like clouds. Stunned, we stand motionless just staring at each other.

"What the bloody hell was that?" Michael asks, rubbing the area on his arm where the man touched him. Overwhelmed by sadness, I feel my chest grow tight where he touched me; looking to Bryant, as he clutches his throat and tries to swallow, I shiver and somehow know that this is only the beginning of something very wrong.

"It's been a long day. Let's all go home," Dave says, rotating his ankle before we head off to our vehicles and then home in a murky mist of confusion.

Connie

When I'm really angry, I shop. When I'm hurt, I come to a BART station. Any BART station; they all have their own special ambience.

My favorites are the underground stations with their tiled walls and acoustic ceilings, where silence is the loudest sound there. As the trains leave, the hushed trail of wind whistles gently out of the tube like a parent whispering goodnight to a sleeping child. I used to pretend the trains were saying goodbye as they left; comforting my loneliness until the next train arrived with its horn blowing a happy hello. The best part of the BART stations and the real reason I go, is the people; watching them come and go and making up stories about them...Russian spies planning their next mission, jewel thieves planning their next heist, and all the torrid love affairs....countless hours of entertainment to take my mind off my troubles and clear my thoughts.

Today...was just too much, too soon and...well, some of it, all too late. But...when would have been a good time to tell me how my parents really died. And if they had told me, would Eli be here now...would I have met her. Would she be...? And I met Marco through Eli. I wonder if I still would if she...if she weren't....

A sudden chill comes over my body, and I shiver uncontrollably. Looking down at my hands as they tremble, I shriek and pull away from the cold, white hand that touches me.

Backing away from the elderly man, I see my horrified reflection in his cloudy, white eyes. Cold, clammy hands reach out to me as his bottom lip quivers near tears. "Please! Help her? Make him stop...I don't...I don't want to...Please?"

The man speaks with such sincerity; I'm compelled to go to him.

"Sir, who is she? Who needs help?"

The man begins to cry, then suddenly screams in terror, *"No!"*

Grabbing at his chest he doubles over in pain and falls to the floor. Laying on his side, I see a strange mark on his neck; some kind of tattooing. His mouth is moving like a fish out of water, he tries to speak. Looking for my cell phone in my purse I remember I left it at home.

"I'm going to get you some help, all right? Just stay…"

Finding his voice, he whispers something but I can't hear him. Kneeling down, closer to him, I hear him softly say, "Run…She's coming. I'm sorry."

Just before he disappears in the blink of an eye.

Patrick

It was a quiet ride home with my roommates; Ash chose to ride shotgun so he could become more familiar with the streets around town. Bryant, unusually silent, sits in the back looking through his wallet like he's lost something very important. Unable to shake the chill from the encounter with the old man has me feeling…anxious, tense…about to pee my pants scared…maybe all of the above.

Remembering something Bill and Dave told me about their days together at the Police Station, I say, "Sure is quiet."

My words fall on deaf ears. A minute later Ash awakens from his gaze out the window, "What? Sorry, Pat, did you say something?"

"He said, 'sure is quiet', like he's a waitin' on somethin' bad to happen," Bryant said, cutting me off to the quick of the breath I took to answer. "He's feelin' a might anxious; just like you, ain't cha, Pat? I know. I's feelin' it, too. Like there's somethin' comin' that we ain't gots no control over and no idea how to deal wit it. Somethin' ugly…and *real bad*."

The car is silent again, and I'm sorry I said anything. Bryant's words should have given me comfort in knowing I'm not alone, but now I'm actually more scared than before.

Pulling into the long driveway that stretches around the back of my home, I park under the carport. Entering the house, we all breathe a sigh of relief at feeling the safety of the walls. With the nagging fear that pounds at the back of my head, the comfort is welcomed; even if it's short lived.

Zach

Half-way home to the ranch, I left the band in the dust and arrived long before Michael's old, blue Suburban even got out of second gear. The eerie coldness from the strange man in the parking lot left me so weirded-out that even riding my Harley fast down the highway didn't clear my head. Sitting down on the front stoop of the ranch house, I wait for the guys to get home.

And I can't get them out of my head; my parents' faces in the car, lifeless and cold. I try to remember them alive and happy; but when I do, all I see is his face…the man I killed.

Michael's car turns up the drive; his left headlight is burned out; and as I try to remember if we have a spare bulb for 'Old Bertha,' something knocks me to the ground.

My lip is cut and already swelling; the taste of iron fills my mouth. Trying to sit up, I feel something hit me in the middle of my back; several ribs crack, and I have trouble breathing. Michael is calling my name, asking if I'm all right…I think…but, all I can hear is *him*.

"How's that feel, *Heathen*?"

A blinding pain shoots through my left eye as I'm hit again. Rolling over to get away, I see him with my one good eye.

"Spawn of the devil; back to hell where you belong!"

Again and again, the man, the ghost, whatever he is, delivers what I believe to be my long-overdue, expected penance.

The band is calling to me. They try to help, but he shoves them away with great force. Gabe is on his cell phone calling for help, I think. Garnering enough strength to pick myself up, I lift my body and try to crawl away; but another kick to my mid-section knocks the wind out of me.

As the light dims, I think of the one regret I have in my young life...
I never told Elizabeth how much I love her.

Ash

The ride home was way too long. I swear we went down more streets getting home than we did going there. Finally arriving at my room, I flip on the light and close the door.

Having my choice of the many different bedrooms in Pat's boyhood home, I picked the one furthest away from the rest; mainly because I didn't want to disturb anyone with my bass if I stayed up late practicing. Putting my headphones on, I plug into my amp, open the newest chord sheets Zach gave me and try to play; my hand is so cold that I can't grip the neck firmly enough to create the correct chord.

"Let me help you with that."

Letting go of my bass, I rip off my head phones to see where the voice is coming from; but there's no one there. The room grows incredibly and painfully cold, and I see my breath in front of me. Placing my bass down on my bed, I get up to check the windows; but they're all shut tight. Turning around, a shiver overcomes my entire body as Nina is standing before me holding my bass.

"How?" is all I can muster to say; the room is so cold my teeth chatter.

"Where were you, Ash? I called you so many times, but you never called me back."

Taking the bass from Nina, I lay it on the floor and move to the door; but she blocks me.

"All my girlfriends said I should give up on you...*make a change*, they said. So I did. I changed my hair, but you...you weren't there to see me...you weren't there for me...you forgot about me...didn't you?"

As Nina, or the spectre of what she was, speaks, her image changes. Twitching and twisting she morphs into the Vorax she later became in life;

lifting me off the ground, she shoves me into the wall and claws my face. Making a break for it, I open the door and run.

Marco

After driving around town to all our old, favorite haunts, I head back to *Circles* and head up the outside stairwell; still unable to shake the cold ache in my chest from where the old man touched me, an icier shiver runs up and down my spine when I see the door to Conn and Eli's apartment ajar.

Trying hard to keep it together and not freak-out completely, I gently push the door open; it opens all the way, proving to me that there's no one behind the door waiting to gut me. Knowing that didn't make me feel any better when I stepped inside…it was freezing there; and I was breathing so hard and fast, I was creating a fog in front of me.

I call out Connie's name. A small, child-like whimper comes from the living room; and I creep along quietly towards the sound coming from the darkness. Reaching for the wall behind me, I feel the switch and flip it up.

"Turn off that light, you fool! That costs me money, and I need every cent I can save to raise this brat my son dumped here. He and that wet-back bitch of his just left her here!"

The voice is familiar; I'd heard it before. The acidic tongue is well known.

"Mrs. Gutierrez, please…?" I say, as the ghost of Connie's grandmother shoves me to the wall; unable to move, the angry spirit has its frosty grip on my throat.

"No, Abuelita, please?" Connie whimpers.

"Speak English, mutt!" the ghost yells, as I fall to the floor when she lets me go.

In the darkness I can hear Connie screaming, pleading with her grandmother to let her go. Reaching for a light switch that no longer works, I hear Connie's heels as she is dragged across the hardwood floor.

Bryant

Takin' me a hot shower as soon as we git home didn't do a lick a good to warm me up. Pulled on muh sweat pants and a sweatshirt, and I's still cold. Wrappin' myself up in a big, fluffy comforter that was on a nearby oak rocker, I sits on muh bed and tries to relax.

Then the rocker starts a movin'.

Muh room gits colder with each to and fro of the rocker, and I hold the comforter real tight.

"Hmm...I like dis place, Boy. Why you no tell me you live here?"

"Miss Louija?"

"Of course, Boy! Who else you tink it tis? Santa Claus?" she say, reachin' out and smackin' me in the head hard enough that I falls off the bed.

"But, you ain't really here. I mean… you died. I read it in the paper. An angry widow done shot you in yer head."

Miss Louija waves me off, "Just stories. You know me, Boy. Even death can't keep *me*, down. Do it, now?"

Crawlin' away, I tries to reach the doorknob, but she strong. She shoves me away and pins me to the wall with a wave of her cold, bony hand.

"Why you scared of me, Boy? You and me…we know tings 'bout each udder. Don't we, now?" Miss Louija say, as she changes into Alamea.

"Oh, my love…"

"Oh, my God!" I screams, and push away her cold, pleadin', dead hands as theys come close to muh face. She falls away and rolls on the floor.

"Oh, my, look what you've gone and done…," Alamea say, holdin the left side of her face in her hands. "Help me put it back on, Bryant baby. I wants to be beautiful for ya."

Screamin' at the top of my lungs, I lunge at the door, fling it open, and then run; never lookin' back at what's behind me, but feelin' a might more scared at the screams of my roommates closin' in.

Patrick

Even though I live with two rather noisy roommates, tonight the house is quiet. On any other night, Ash is either playing music or listening to it; and Bryant is talking to the television or in his sleep.

Tonight is unusually quiet; uncomfortably quiet and cold.

Deciding to fix some hot chocolate with cinnamon schnapps, I head to the kitchen but stop because there is a knock at the door. Peeking through the one-way glass on the sides of the front door, I see its Robert and unlock the latch.

"Hey, Dude…Couldn't sleep?" I ask, as Rob walks in with a shrug of his shoulders. "Can I get you something? Beer, wine…? I was just about to get…"

Rob holds his hand up to stop me, shaking his head no. He coughs, clears his throat and really struggles to speak. "Ash? Bry?"

"In their rooms. Quiet, so I'm guessing asleep," I reply, watching him walk around, looking at the living room like it was all new to him, even though he's been here before; even crashed here for a few days. "Rob, are you all right?" I ask, feeling more than a little tweaked by the strange behavior of my old friend.

"I'm j-j-just f-fine, Pat. How are y-y-you? S-s-still mourn-n-ning your p-parents?"

"What?"

"Shall I t-tell you h-how your m-m-mommy b-begged for her life as s-s-she was eaten alive? Or how y-y-your f-f-father's s-s-s-creams c-c-came to an a-a-abrupt halt when his h-h-head was r-r-ripped f-f-from his b-body?"

Feeling a fury in me like I'd only felt once before; the night we fought the Vorax army; I tried to keep my head clear while I figured out what to do with Corson as he walked around in Robert's body.

"Your f-folks w-were aged to p-p-perfection."

"Shut-up, Corson!"

"M-m-make me, c-c-college b-boy!"

Somehow, when I envisioned Robert; Corson; slamming into the glass patio doors…it really happened, but I don't know how.

Getting up and brushing himself off, "Oh, b-b-boy…I a-a-always knew you'd b-b-be f-f-fun. *Let's play!*"

Dave

It's funny the things a man will do when he loves a woman.

It's late and I'm tired after a really long and strange day; but we are still moving in, and I promised to wash and put away the heavy boxes of dishes. Turning on the radio, I luckily catch an old tune I haven't heard since high school. I start unpacking the box.

Still feeling the chill in my shoulder where the old man grabbed me, it seems to be moving down my arm and throughout my body. Even having my hands in the hot, soapy dishwater doesn't help. Turning the hot water on only, I try to warm it up. As I wait for the water to get hot, something kicks me in the shin and knocks me to the ground. A cold, bulky weight on my chest holds me down and knocks the wind out of me. Stacked dishes, waiting to be cleaned and dried, fly across the room and crash to the floor in pieces.

"Remember *me*, Pendajo?"

"Jesse? You're…?"

"Dead? Yes. A little slow in your old age, eh, Pendajo?" Jesse says, slapping my face playfully but hard.

Feeling the pressure release from my chest, I roll over and then try to get up. As I get up on my knees, my body is lifted and shoved against the wall, hanging suspended above the floor. A large, broken piece of plate floats up to my face; and the hand holding it finally becomes visible.

"Know how I died? Hmm? I died because of you and that bitch, Vera. Told the cops I raped her…repeatedly."

"Didn't you?" I ask, stalling for time.

"Sure…but only because she didn't love me. She loved you. Did you know that? So, I got thrown in prison. And in prison, they don't much like rapists. This is what they gave me," he says, lifting his shirt and showing me a Coroner's crude stitch line where he was gutted. "Here, let me show you how they did it…"

Sean

I don't believe in accidents; I believe everything happens in our lives for a reason.

Everything.

From my hunting abalone poachers, to my three failed marriages, and then my unorthodox transfusion…everything had its purpose.

So, why did Bill tell us about Helen's discovery that she's a Necromancer, and why did I happen upon Connie researching a Nahuali,… and Eli is finally getting the Master Watch and it's untold powers?

Why?

Why *today*?

…Then as we left, we run into, literally, a strange, little man who tells his personal spectral demons to *'leave her alone'* and *'don't take her'* and then apologizes to us as he leaves, touching each of us on the way?

My arm is cold where he touched me. Ice cold. *Like the dead, cold.* Like any good biologist would, I put all the pieces together and a shiver runs up my spine. Picking up the phone, I start calling the team one by one…from 'A' to 'Z'. When I get no answer from Zach, I panic and call Galen to run my theory across his brain.

"Oh, my!…Sean, call Peg! I'll grab some supplies and meet you. Go to Dave and Peg's house first. Peg will need some things from there before we move on, I've no doubt. Go! Now!"

Calling Peg, as we discussed, I turn my cell phone on speaker and set it down on a table beside my mirror portal, pick up a few items; and then tell her what I've discovered. Pricking my finger, I envision Peg's home and touch the mirror. As the portal swirls and sways, I pray that I'm wrong but somehow know I'm not; my concerns are confirmed as the portal stills. I fire my shotgun loaded with rock salt and yell, "Get here, Peg! Get here, now!"

Peg

Leaving Carlos behind to lockup, Helen and I high-tail it out of Circles; bags of herbs in hand; hitting the mirror portal on the run and using the blood from a cut I received when I took Sean's call. Feeling his intense fear through the phone, I accidently cut my hand with kitchen shears clipping the tie on a bag of dry beans.

"Are you sure you heard a shotgun?" Helen asks, juggling multiple grocery sacks full of zip-locked bags of herbs. "It could have been a car backfire, or kids tossing firecrackers in garbage bins, or…"

Helen stops speaking as my ransacked home comes into view; Sean is thrown down and slides across the kitchen floor to the living room doorway. He stops as he runs into Galen, the two topple into a box labeled 'bedroom,' and then look up at us as we step through the portal.

"Dave's in your workroom. He's beat up pretty badly, but he crawled under your table. Said he'd be safe there, and he's right; the ghost can't touch him," Sean says, breathlessly.

"Iron legs?" Galen asks.

"Yep…," I reply, digging in my bags and dumping several into the bottom of the larger, grocery bag. "Helen, do you have…?"

My voice trails off into the air as I watch my little sister walk purposefully into my kitchen, towards my workroom. She stops just at the doorway, breathes deeply, shuts her eyes, and holds her locket in her left hand.

From somewhere near an icy breeze blows, lifting her chestnut curls off of her shoulders. The breeze grows until it finally blows her hair back away from her. Her brow furrows just like it does when she is annoyed with me, and she sucks her bottom lip for a moment. She holds her right hand out in front of her like a crossing guard and repeats a commanding phrase three times in a language I've heard before but have no clue what it is or what she is saying…or maybe? It's so familiar…I think she's saying…

"Helen!" Galen cries out, shaking me from my momentary memory lapse to see my sister shoved into the wall behind her, nicking her forehead on a low hanging cabinet.

We start to move in, but she stops us and again focuses on her work. She repeats the phrase and holds up her hand…then waves it away, dismissing the spectral invader. We listen as the entity curses and wails as he is ushered away into the space between life and death.

Running into the kitchen, Sean catches her before she falls; I catch her eye, and she gives me a playful wink to tell me she's all right. Going to Dave, I kneel down beside my antique work table and help him out.

"You remembered," I say, kissing his forehead and feeling the cold, clamminess of his fear. Dave's lip is cut badly and both eyes are swollen and bruised. He grimaces as he crawls out and up on all fours; he hesitates to stand because breathing is difficult.

"Damn it, Cap, you've got cracked ribs…I know that dance all too well," Sean says, coming to Dave's side and helping him up.

"We need to go," Helen says, grabbing the grocery bags from the floor in front of the portal.

As we approach the mirror, Dave touches his bloody, split lip and then touches the mirror; it swirls and sways continuously but never goes anywhere.

"Does anyone know where Zach lives?" I ask, as we all stare blindly at each other.

"Maybe if we just think of Zach, like Bill and I used to do to see Eli," Helen suggests. We turn and focus on Zach, and the mirror portal finally knows where to go.

Entering a warm, country-style farm house, we hear yelling coming from the porch. Sitting Dave down on a nearby couch, Sean, Helen, and I follow the sound and exit the front door; Galen stays behind to keep an eye on Dave.

"What the…?" Sean mumbles, as he crawls beneath a flurry of wings and loose feathers, floating and falling to the ground.

"Watch out!" Gabe yells, as he swoops in and brushes the floating entity away. Helen watches it move, never taking her eyes off of it for a moment.

"Peg?"

"What?"

"Ash."

"Where?"

"There! Ash!" Helen says, pointing to her left.

Looking at the porch, I see Zach being tended to by Sean and Raffa; Zach is out cold, but Raffa is still holding him and diligently healing his badly broken body. Ash isn't anywhere in sight.

"PEG!"

"WHAT!"

"Ash!"

"He's not here! What...?"

Helen, still watching the spectre trying to get past Gabe, Michael, and Uri, points to the left again. "Ash," she snaps, pointing to a tree on the far left; then to the right in three different areas, "Birch, Bay, and Juniper."

"Uri!" I call out, but he was already way ahead of me; obviously listening to my one-sided conversation with Helen; he lands in front of us with a branch of each tree.

"Is this what you need?" he asks.

"Yes, Uri, thank you. Just put them down right here. I'll do the rest."

Uri does as Helen asks, and again she is holding her locket. Waving to the branches, she lays them in a square on the ground. Focusing on the angry spirit, Helen tries and tries to draw him into the sacred space; but he fights; kicking, and screaming the entire time.

Seeing she is weakening, I grab my little sister's hand. Focusing my energy with hers, the ghostie has no choice but give in. Holding up her hand and repeating the foreign phrase, the spirit fizzles and sparkes and then disappears into the darkness.

"He was strong," I whisper to Helen, feeling my knees give slightly with the onset of dizziness; she puts her arm around me and holds me up. Licking my lips, trying to fend off an awful dry mouth, I ask, "What's that taste?"

"Sulfur," Dave answers, limping through the front door, assisted by Galen, joining us on the porch. "Right, Galen?" Galen nods, somberly.

"Yeah...I smelled it at your house, too. I thought it was another Vorax. They had that smell when we killed them," Sean states.

Dave winces and staggers, "No...that, was Jesse Santos...kid I knew in high school; blamed my brother for his dad's death. I nearly killed him at graduation."

"Mine was a total stranger. A Preacher, I think; he killed my parents," Zach says, his voice is haggard and dry and his face still bruised like Dave's.

"He was so strong...still harbors so much anger. He was angry in life as well as death," Helen says, kneeling beside Zach.

"He's angry...at *me*...because...I killed him...with my bare hands...my powers to heal can...if I don't control it," Zach says, tears filling his swollen eyes. "Please, don't tell Elizabeth. Let *me* tell her. She doesn't know."

Helen places her hand on Zach's face gently and kisses his cheek; whispering something in his ear, he tries to smile but winces, making the collection of tears flow.

"Why isn't he healing, Raffa? You spent all that time and he..."

"Helen, I'm a healer but not of the physical nature. I'm more psychological; matters of the mind and heart. Little brother here has been carrying so much guilt with him, that ghost nearly took him away from us for good. I healed his mind and his soul; brought him back to his senses. The rest is up to him now."

Helen puts her arm around Zach at hearing this and gently pulls him close, she again whispers a secret to him. He smiles gingerly, and then lifts his arm to hug her back. She pulls away and looks at him, then quietly asks, "All right?" Zach nods, and tries to stand up. Once vertical, Helen walks Zach inside the house.

"Well, where to next?" Galen asks, holding Dave up with one arm.

"I think we should find Marco. *This one* will be no help to us at all for awhile," Sean replies, referring to Dave as he helps Galen walk him across the floor.

"Shut up, *Kid*! I still outrank you...," Dave snarls, grimacing all the way.

"He's right, *Captain*...I think you should stay here until I can proof the house better," I say, guiding Dave back onto the couch as the band stack the four tree branches by the fireplace.

"Do you mind, guys? We'll come get him after we find the rest of The Kindred."

"Don't worry, *Pet*. He's in good hands here," Michael says with a nod.

Helen comes downstairs, "Zach's asleep. Already looks much better. Uri, I noticed out Zach's window an old cedar tree. Do you know which one I mean?"

"Sure…what do you need, Beautiful?"

Helen blushes, "A few small twigs; just enough for a Talisman for each member of the family."

"Just five? I can grab that for you now…"

"No, no, no, Uri," Helen says, stopping him, "The *whole family*: the Dante's, the Young's, The Kindred…and Stealth."

Helen

When the mirror finally stops swirling, the room it takes us to is at first unfamiliar; but the overwhelming smell of Connie's perfume tells us it is her bedroom. Stepping in; Peg, Sean, and I, look back to Gabe, who wipes the portal clean of the droplet of blood and closes off the only source of light there was; other than the glow from under the door leading to the hallway and the other from the bathroom door.

Walking forward, we can't help but announce our presence; glass shards and; my guess; Connie's collection of porcelain ballerinas in pieces on the floor; as we approach the bedroom door, the room becomes colder; and we hear a thumping from the other room, like a person walking slowly, assisted by a walker or a cane.

Sean, readying his shotgun with a rock salt canister as quietly as one *can* ready a shotgun with a rock salt canister, takes the lead.

"Shh…let me go out fir…,"Sean starts to say, but is again thrown to the wall across the room, taking us with him for padding.

"I HEAR YOU IN THERE, CONSUELO. YOU HAVE A BOY IN THERE WITH YOU, DON'T YOU? YOU DIRTY, LITTLE HARLOT! FILTHY, FREE-LOADING WET BACK!"

"Who the *hell* is that?" I whisper.

"Lorraine Meyer-Gutierrez, Connie's lovely grandmother," Peg says, disgustedly.

"YOU'RE JUST LIKE YOUR MOTHER! LAY ON YOUR BACK AND OPEN YOUR LEGS FOR ANYTHING WITH A PENIS!"

"Jesus H. Christ! Her grandmother? What grandmother has a mouth like that?" Sean retorts.

"CONSUELO!" bellows from the hall and rattles the walls, shaking what's left on the shelves to the floor.

"Cool it, Granny! We're sending you home soon!" Sean yells, as Connie and Marco burst forth from the bathroom.

"No, no, no!...Shhh!...No!..." Connie says, coming towards us with her arms waving, ushering us into the silhouette of light behind her coming from the brightly-lit, pink bathroom.

No sooner do we see the petite, scared child emerge, the door to the hallway flies open, and there is Lorraine in all her glory: perfectly coiffed, dressed in a crisp, white-linen suit, pounding her cane into the ground with every limp across the room.

"Aha! *Two* men! I knew it; salacious, immigrant whore!" Lorraine yells, as she lunges her cane outward and hooks Connie around the neck.

"Marco! Astringent!" Peg yells, as I grab onto my locket and ready for her to act. "Marco?" Peg yells again.

"What? You want...what?" he asks, lost as can be in a young woman's bathroom. Sean steps in, grabs the giant bottle of gold liquid, and then soft tosses it to Peg.

"Ready?" Peg asks, as I refocus my energy. Nodding once, Peg pops the lid and squirts the contents all over the entity as she is just about to shove Connie into the wall.

Lorraine's specter screams and tosses Connie away to use both her hands to wipe her eyes and face as she retreats towards the hall. Holding my hand up as I had before, I feel the hot vibration of the locket radiate in the cold fear gripping my body. Saying the phrase I remember Poppa saying; using my best Bulgarian; I tell Lorraine Meyer-Gutierrez that she is not welcome here; three times. The angry apparition swirls and sways and dissipates into the air as the lights come back on; the rancid sulfur air clears, and calm is restored.

"Astringent?" Sean asks, holding up the empty bottle and waving it at Peg.

She nods, "Camphor, clove, eucalyptus, and witch hazel. All the ingredients needed to shrink large pores and..."

"Helps clear up pimples...no matter how large and nasty they are," Connie says, rubbing her head and neck as she makes her way to her bathroom, slams the door, and sobs uncontrollably while we wait in the hall not knowing what to do.

Dave

When the group returns to the farmhouse, they are quiet and a little more than reflective. Connie and Marco have joined them, but they may as well have been a million miles away. Marco, looking like he's been bed-ridden with flu, makes a feeble effort to talk to me.

"You look like hell."

"Thanks. That's just the look I was going for," "I reply, looking to his fiancé quietly cowering behind him. Nodding in her general direction, Marco looks to me with disgust and rolls his eyes.

"Don't ask…," he answers, going to Zach who is still badly bruised but looks far better than before. Marco helps Zach down the last few stairs, and assists him to the portal where the rest of the group has assembled and is ready to go.

"Hold on, guys. I want each one of you to keep these on you," Helen says, as she hands out muslin bags tied to the small cedar twigs that Uri went out and gathered while we waited. Peg follows behind with zip-lock bags full of vanilla-wafer-size discs of brown, smelly shit.

"What's this brown, smelly shit?" Gabe asks, as I snicker.

"I'm giving you each a bag of, well, for lack of a better description…wiccan cherry bombs. Since our local baseball hero appears to be on the disabled list, we're all going to have to help out. Any ghost, spectre, evil entity, poltergeist, or Casper himself…you toss these beauties at them, and you'll be safe to get away."

"Aunt Peg…I'm all right. I can throw anything you give me," Zach says, tightening the bandage around his ribs; Raffa assists and clips the end in place for him.

"Helen, what's in this little bag? It smells like …like…I don't know, but it smells," Marco says, starting to untie the string.

"No, no, leave it tied! Peg and I bound it with a spell to make the herbs active. It's your own personal Talisman. You need to keep it with you. In a pocket is best so that it takes on your personal magic; your aura. It needs to become a part of you."

"All right…but what's in it?" Sean asks, wrinkling his brow as he takes in another good, long whiff.

"Anise, basil, organic black beans, wild rice, cinnamon sticks, cumin, curry, fennel seed, dry mustard, parsley, sage, rosemary, and…"

"Thyme?" the entire group answers in unison, shaking their heads and amazed at how that word; in all its forms; has come to play in everything we do.

"Yes, thyme. Well, has anyone tried calling the boys?" Helen asks, pulling on a letterman's jacket Zach loaned her. The chill she gets fighting off the spirits still hasn't left her, and I'm more than a bit concerned.

"Been calling all night, and not an answer on any cell phone, or the house phone," Michael says.

"Me neither," Raffa says, showing us his cell phone.

"We better go," I say, activating the mirror with a drop of my blood and thinking about the brilliant young man who discovered that million dollar nugget of information.

The mirror focuses quickly; not taking the usual sway and swirl to get to where we need to be. One by one, we step through to Pat's house. His portal mirror, just like the rest of us; was installed by Michael and crew in a safe space.

We walk down the large hallway and look in each room carefully. Coming to the cross of the three large and long corridors of Pat's family *mansion,* we stop, uncertain where to go. Taking a breath, I fight the familiar need to call out their names and instead turn to the group and tap my forehead, choosing instead to listen to our internal voices. Quietly we stand; listening with our hearts, souls, and minds.

"Oh, God, please? Where are you guys, already? We need help! He's back! He's back! He's…!"

Receiving the message together, we turn as one and aim for the living room. Reaching the doorway we slow down, and I count the number of voices I hear.

Five.

But, is that Robert…or…is that…?

"S-s-so angry! Why s-so angry, little b-b-boy? I'm just g-giving you w-w-what you w-want. A g-g-glimpse of your p-parents' last moments of their p-privileged lives."

Helen sighs angrily, pushes up the sleeves of Zach's oversized jacket and starts taking down the still hanging Christmas decorations: oranges spiked with cloves, holly wreaths, bay sprigs tied with cinnamon, and every piece of mistletoe over all the doorways.

"What is she doing?" I whisper to Peg, watching Helen assemble the pieces and *us* into some sort of line of precision. Peg shakes her head and looks proctectively concerned at her little sister. Helen places her hand over her heart and turns to us. Using her thoughts only, she sighs.

"I need to perform a sort of...exorcism. Robert is...Listen. Close your mind to anything else but what is in that room. Listen here," she thinks and pats her chest over her heart.

Closing my eyes, I carefully listen to nothing but the people in that room and then finally hear exactly what she is talking about.

"Oh! My! God! Why can't anyone hear me? Somebody get this mother fucker out of me! Look what's he's doing to my little buddy. Oh, God, no, no, leave him alone, God damn you, leave him alone! Wait! Hey! How did you do that? Did you do that, Pat? You did! You did do that! Do it again! Do it again! Do it again! Don't worry about me...KILL THE BASTARD!"

"Holy shit! What do we do? What is Patrick doing?" I think, as I see the sisters deep in concentration. They smile simultaneously, and I somehow know everything will be all right; but at the same time, I sort of don't want to know how.

"Everyone have their Talisman? The defense pellets? All right. There is something different in Patrick that we never knew. His biological father may have been Demon. He is radiating energy like Eli. He is able to move things with his mind when he's angry...and right now, he's pissed! Anything spectral, throw the pellets. If they defend, Patrick will pick up the charge, and one more thing,...do not be shocked by what you see. Do not give these spirits anything to fuel their uninvited existence. Are we clear?" Helen thinks, as Peg wipes a tear from her cheek.

"We need to hurry!" Helen thinks, grabbing a firm hold on her new necklace. *"Go! I'll follow behind and clean up...Go!"*

Walking cautiously to the doorway of the lavish living room, we enter, two-by-two, and see the physical damage done to Patrick's home and to our three friends, who are being tortured by the personal Demons released on them.

Bryant, bound by a wicker chair that has been undone and wound around his body from head to toe, tethered by the other end to a ghostly floating figure of a woman dressed in a fiery caftan. She speaks aloud to herself and cackles at her own joke. She turns and sees us; hisses like an old, angry, feral cat as she holds her hand out, reciting something in French. She blows across the palm of her hand, and a cloud of black grows large, headed right for us. Sean takes the cue and throws a handful of pellets at the cloud, and they become suspended within it. The cloud lurches and then flies at the ghost of the woman, holding her in a grip of her own magic. Helen steps in and says the phrase I heard her utter before, three times over; and then waves her hand to erase the entity from our sight. Bryant falls to the ground as the wicker bindings disappear, and the chair returns to its functional shape.

Sean and Michael stay behind to see to Bryant as the rest of us press on and enter the next area of destruction, a home theatre where Ash is pinned to the white screen by the talons of a Vorax with a Demon's face; stark white, even for a ghost, but her body is that of the beast she became. It is clearly Nina, Ash's former girlfriend. She has clawed and ripped at Ash's body mercilessly. The screen is sprayed and splattered with his blood, bringing to mind the wall of The Void when Eli sliced off Corson's arm.

Marco charges at her and throws the pellets from his bag one-by-one, waiting as each pellet sizzles and smokes when they hit her body. She releases Ash from the wall, wailing in pain.

Helen turns to Peg with a knowing glance, speaking to each other's minds privately as they sometimes do. Helen turns back, looks at the burning spirit, claps her hands, and blows up what's left of Nina back into dust.

"Rogue Demon; they give up their soul when they go rogue. No soul, no power. So far, all the others were human," Helen says, filling us in on her secret conversation with Peg.

"So, can we do that with Corson? Once you get him out of Robert?" I ask quietly.

"Let's hope so," she says, without a shred of confidence as she turns to move on.

"Wait a minute! What do you mean *hope so*? What could happen?" I ask, as Zach and Connie go to Ash and tend to his wounds.

"From what I remember, exorcisms of this kind can be tricky. If the host is weak or gives in to the intruder, the host...the host may not..."

"That ain't acceptable," Bryant says sternly, joining the group from the other room. He is pale, but walking on his own beside Michael and Sean.

"I know...I know...I...Peg, how did you help Sage transfer the virus to Corson. Do you remember the spell?"

Peg nods at Helen's question, "Yes, I do. What are you thinking?"

"How many pellets do we have left?" Helen asks, as all but two of us hold up our full bags. Helen smiles and looks at Peg, "Do it!"

"Do *what?*" I ask angrily.

"Change the spell…We'll change the spell in half the pellets to empower Robert with a booster shot of confidence; then when Helen extracts Corson, hit him with the others," Peg says, as Raffa pushes his way forward.

"I believe you are going to need me," he says, with his patented thousand-kilowatt smile.

"Take my hand, my friend," Peg says, as she closes her eyes and then casts her spell on the pellets; enforced by Raffa's happy and self-assured disposition, turning them a bright pink.

"Oh! Look how cute mine are now!" Connie says. First thing she's said all night.

Opening the bag I sniff them. "They may be cute, but they still smell like shit," I say, garnering a nervous chuckle from the gallery.

Pressing on into the next room, we see a trail of blood amidst overturned furniture, broken lamps, fallen pictures, and shattered crystal. We enter the adjoining dining room where we finally find Robert and Patrick.

Patrick is suspended from the arch that divides the two rooms; his face is bloodied and looks like mine felt earlier. Blood pools on the floor from his hands and arms that are held in place by sterling-silver cutlery from a china hutch that is all but destroyed. Other pieces of silverware are imbedded in the wall opposite Patrick, obviously deflected out of anger.

Robert; *Corson*; is stoking a fire in the fireplace. He retrieves the red-hot poker from the flames and throws it like a javelin at Patrick. Defending himself, he sends it flying out the window, shattering the pane on impact.

"Oh! B-b-boy! That was a g-g-good one…let's t-try this one." Corson throws a lead-crystal sculpture at Patrick; and he again deflects it; but this time at Corson, hitting him in the head, knocking him to the ground.

Laughing uncontrollably as he staggers to stand, "Your f-f-friend R-R-Robert says, Ow!"

Unable to see any way clear of getting to Robert without Corson knowing, I turn to ask Peg what her thoughts are; and I see Helen giving all the pink pellets to the band, with the exception of Zach, who gets all the original brown ones.

"Ready, gentlemen?" Helen asks, as Michael, Uri, Gabe, and Raffa all nod. "Zacharias, I'll need a direct hit. All right?"

"Consider it done," he whispers, with a stern and determined look in his eyes.

With a quick wink from Helen, Michael, Uri, Gabe, and Raffa use their lightening speed to pummel Robert's body with the pink pellets. He staggers and coughs, then collapses to the floor, out cold from the spell. Helen moves in quickly with her supplies, and the rest of us, too, wrapping Robert up in the Christmas decorations. She stations herself nearby, grabs hold of her necklace, and goes to work. Speaking once again in the unknown, but beautiful language, she speaks in verse; poetic in nature, her spell is spoken with intensity and strength that I personally would never want to cross.

Within seconds, Corson is awake, "Oh, Helen…I knew it w-w-was you. You w-w-wanted me f-f-from the f-f-first t-t-t-time we m-met, I could tell. M-M-Maybe we c-can g-g-go somewhere p-private and b-become better aquain…"

Never stopping her oration but unable to listen to anymore, Helen grabs an asparagus fern laying nearby and shoves it in Robert's mouth before Corson can say anymore.

Robert's body begins to twitch as Corson fights to stay, but he has no choice as Helen's recitation draws him forth from his safe new *living* home.

"Now!" Helen yells, as Zach stands and fires a strike with all of the brown pellets at once, and Corson's entity flames and then sputters into a smoldering cloud that dissipates into nothing.

Bill

Being Demon, and having seen the weird shit I've seen and done the weird shit I've done, it takes a lot to surprise me. The depth of the mind of my Uncle Stolas was by far one of the most underrated, modern miracles of our time. From the moment Eli took off the key and allowed it to lead her to the invisible door in the portal that lead us to and opened the Safe Room of the vault; to all the miraculous wonders and inventions he created that we found there; I don't think I will ever again be made so speechless.

"Ready?" Tempus asks Eli

"For what?" she replies cautiously.

"The grand finale…," Tempus says, showing Eli an old, cedar box with the name '*Elizabeth*' burned in the top.

"So, that's where it went. I made this for your grandmother when we were in high school. Remember the amber jewelry I gave you? She used to keep it in here; and after she died, I looked high and low for it," Dad says, admiring it as if it were the woman herself.

"Stolas told me to hide the watch, but Liz was concerned about the magics here. She said I should use a box that nothing magical could penetrate," Tempus says, as he hands the box to Eli.

"There's no hinge or lock…or…oh, wait," Eli says, as she takes the brass skeleton key in hand and points it towards the box. It shakes slightly; like a shiver of excitement comes over it just before a shiny, glittering key-hole appears. Eli giggles quietly to herself and inserts the key. Without turning it the box opens, and the key jumps out and back to the safety of its owner. The Watch, nestled lovingly amidst an emerald green, velvet lining, appears to need some attention.

"It isn't ticking. Is it broken?" Eli asks

"No, my friend, it doesn't need batteries or winding. It simply needs *you*," Tempus says, encouraging Eli to pick it up.

Looking to Tempus like it's some kind of practical joke, she does a double-take and then reaches in and picks it up...and it does nothing. She opens the gold cover, brings it to her ear to listen for gear movement, pops the pin and sets the time with her cell phone, shines the face, and then sighs.

"It's broken. Look it's not...oh, hold on...what the...?"

No sooner does my baby girl declare the Watch broken, the Watch bathes her in bright, white light; and she can't stop staring at the Watch.

"Eli?"

She holds a hand up to me, "Just a second, Dad."

"What's happening, Baby?"

"Daddy, I'm reading."

"What are you reading?"

Laughing like her mother, Eli says, *"Everything!"*

Looking to Dad and Sage, I nod to call them over to join me.

"Tempus, what the hell is going on? First the Watch doesn't work, now it does, and now, she's reading? That's all this *Master Watch is,* an electronic reader? She already has one of those. What about...?"

Sage interrupts me because he has realized something I haven't. Tempus is radiating the same white glow that Eli is drenched in. He's breathing hard, just like Eli; Eli laughs and so does Tempus; Eli grimaces at reading something she doesn't like and so does Tempus. The two appear to be somehow connected by the Watch.

Sage, in his own way, is glowing himself.

"What's got him so happy?" Dad asks, as he tickles the side of Sage's face.

"You guys don't get it?" he asks, amazed that we haven't picked up on his inner joy.

"Spit it out, Sage. What's the punch line?" I say, play punching my brother, the King.

"Its Tempus...*Uncle Stolas* figured it out. *He did it.*"

Looking to Tempus and then to Eli, still both glowing, smiling, laughing, learning, and truly tuned-in to each other; I finally get it.

Time is finally telling us all we need to know!

Eli

After the glow dissipates, and the novelty of my new toy ebbs; it was time, *no pun intended*, to learn the business and get down to it.

"All right, there are three things you need to know right away about the Watch: one: it functions on the borrowed magics of the Elders, therefore like any other magic, every action has a similar reaction; two: the Watch will not work for personal gain, so forget about using it to get tomorrow's lottery numbers or a weekend in Las Vegas; and third: never let anyone, human or Demon, touch it or take it from you. Other than that, anything; and I mean anything; you need to help, save, protect, defend; whatever and whomever; is now possible with this Watch."

"Wow! No wonder The Brotherhood wants it…and *you*. You are as much the key as the key. This is way too much to handle all at once," I say, carefully placing the Watch back in the box.

Tempus looks at me; at first he's surprised, then suddenly very sad; both emotions disappear when he finally understands what I'm saying.

"The decisions you make to use the Watch will not be easy, but I'm certain they will be without doubt."

"But, Tempus, what if I make a wrong decision? What if I lose it? What if something happens? I'm not the most *graceful* thing ya know…I fall. I'm a clutz, I…"

Using the box like a baseball mitt, Tempus soft tosses the Watch to me and I miss it. It falls with a clang and bounces under the table that Uncle Sage, Dad, and Grandpa are gathered around looking at old projects and notebooks belonging to Uncle Stolas. Dad kneels down and picks up the Watch, and it starts to screech a deafening, uncontrollable alarm. Taking the Watch from Dad, it quiets; but my ears are stunned, like when I attended a heavy-metal concert with Uncle Sage and had to sit near a floor speaker.

When my hearing returns, I still have a lot of questions; and I try to ask them all at once.

"Eli...we are linked by that Watch. I don't know how Stolas did it, but he did. I'm not going anywhere. I'll be here to answer anything you want or need to know. My friend, your uncle, saw to that."

"You two were close?"

"He was family to me. If I'd ever had a brother, I'd have wished for Stolas," Tempus says, as Grandpa comes up from behind and pats him on the shoulder.

"I think that makes us brothers, as well. I think you should stay here, in the Royal Home, with us," Grandpa says, acknowledging Uncle Sage who nods eagerly.

"Emperor, I can't impose; it wouldn't be right. I'll find a hotel nearby."

"Nonsense, I won't hear of any member of *my family* staying in a hotel. You can have Stolas' old room. I think he'd want that," Grandpa says, with that twinkle in his eye. "I would, too,...and stop calling me Emperor. My friends call me Asmo....All right?"

Tempus is tentative and quite shy; I nudge him and nod, encouraging him to stay. He takes the hint and agrees. We lock the workroom, exit the portal, and find ourselves back at Circles. It's dark, quiet, and locked up for the night.

As I place the Master Watch in my inside, jacket pocket, another of my nifty tools starts to act up; the opal is working overtime, once again. Dad sees me with it and immediately opens his cell phone and starts tapping numbers frantically.

"Dad, I think she's all right. I would have received a message by now if not," I say, tapping *my* forehead.

"Um, actually, no, you wouldn't. Stolas reinforced the walls of the vault and his shop to outside magics coming in. You won't get any type of signal there. Even cell phone," Tempus says, as Dad and I suddenly panic.

"Eli! Bill! Sage! Grandpa! Anybody! Please? Help Us?"

"Whoa! *What* was *that*? *Did you hear that?* That was...that was in my head...Eli, tell me you heard that?"

Even though I am very concerned about my family, and in a hurry to get there, I have to stop for a second and laugh. Tempus' reaction to our *mind messaging* is just precious.

"You're going to need to get used to that if we're going to be 'connected'," I say, as I pat him on the back. He nods, still a little stunned. *"Welcome to my world."*

Patrick

"What do you *mean* I can't touch it?"

Eli is walking quickly from teammate to teammate, checking on the aftermath of the night; I'm following her trying to get more information and a closer look at the Watch.

"Pat, you're still limping. We better find Zach," Eli says, turning me around to go find the big, red head.

"Why *can't* I touch it? All I want to do is play with it for a little while…"

Zach catches us in the middle of the conversation, does a double take, and then shakes his head. "I don't even want to know," Zach says, leaning over to kiss Eli; she playfully hits him for the snide remark.

"He's talking about *my Watch.*"

"Oh, yeah, I heard. Tempus said no one but you could touch it. Didn't say *why;* but if it's magical and someone tells me not to touch it, I don't," Zach says, grabbing Eli around the waist and holding her close as she gently kisses his bruises.

"Eli's magical; you touch her!" I say, and instantly regret it the minute it's out. "What I meant was…"

"Zach, fix his leg, please? I don't want a reputation for pummeling the handicapped," Eli says, flicking my head like a marble before moving on to another teammate.

"Why do you think no one can touch it? Is it alarmed? What will it do if someone else *does* touch it?"

"Are you talking to me or to yourself?" Zach asks, as he runs his cold hands over my knee cap and I gasp.

"A little of both," I reply, trying out my newly-healed leg.

"Well, I always think of the old saying 'curiosity killed the cat'."

"All right, but what if the cat has nine lives?"

"Then he dies painfully eight times because the dumb shit didn't learn the first time," Zach says, turning away.

"Yeah, sure. Thanks for your support, Zach," I mumble, as I walk away.

Sitting by the fireplace, I see Rob wrapped in a blanket and looking like he just wants to crawl into a hole and stay there. His eyes meet mine, and he turns away quickly.

"Hey! None of that, you hear me? Don't you turn away from me! You have nothing to feel bad about," I say, sitting down beside him. His cuts and bruises are healed; no doubt by Zach; but his internal wounds are going to take awhile to heal, I'm sure.

"Pat...the things I did...what I said..."

You did *nothing. You* said *nothing.* It was Corson. And just like Helen explained about the old man in the parking lot, we all came in contact with a Necromancer. He tapped into our biggest fears and weakness: I never realized how scared you were of Corson. You marched right up to him and stared him down..."

"He's my brother."

"You...What?"

"Half. Corson. He's my half-brother. Well...he was..."

"How? When? How? Are you sure?"

"Yes. *Fuck me!* If you tell anyone, Pat, I'll..."

"Hey, did you see me limping earlier? Corson or no Corson, you kicked the shit out of me already. Believe me, your secret's safe."

Rob nods, clearly still not comfortable in his skin. Considering who was just in it *with him*, I don't blame him.

"My dad was assaulted by Lilith. She used him. She got pregnant..."

"Your dad was raped by Lilith!"

"Shh...Shut up! Keep your voice down! And...yes. He always told me stories about her, but I never believed them. Then I faced him...Corson. He had my dad's eyes."

Listening to Rob's incredible story, I understand even more why he feels so bad. Looking away from Rob so he doesn't feel like I'm staring at him, I see Eli's jacket draped over a chair at the dining-room table where

Aunt Peg has left a pot of tea for us to drink. There is a silver chain hanging out of the inside pocket.

"I'm going to get you some of that tea Aunt Peg made; supposed to calm your nerves, make you strong," I say, standing up.

Rob shakes his head, "I've had three cups already; hasn't done a goddamned thing."

"Well, after *that* story, maybe it'll help me…," I reply, walking to the table.

Pouring myself a piping-hot cup, I take a sip, and check to see if anyone is watching. Seeing that the coast is clear, I pull the cuff of my sweatshirt down over my hand and use it like a potholder as I *borrow* Eli's Master Watch for a look-see. Leaving the cup behind, I make my way to the upstairs bathroom.

The master bathroom upstairs is made for two: two sinks, dual shower heads, two dressing areas, each with adjoining doors to his and hers walk-in closets. Pulling Dad's valet chair up to his dresser, I grab a towel to cover the surface before putting the Watch down. Using the only tools I could find: cotton swabs, dental floss pick, nail file; I pop the cover open and look at the face; nothing remarkable, just a pocket watch like the others. Then I notice the latch on the back. Flipping the Watch over with my crude tools, the latch pops open on its own; and I see the inside workings of its mechanics. Again, nothing spectacular; it must be one of the decoys Tempus carried. Convinced it's nothing but a fake, I decide to head back down to the group and grab it with my hand.

And then the alarm goes off.

The shriek is deafening and painful; my head is throbbing and my eyes water because the lights hurt them. Tripping, I fall to the floor and drop the Watch; but the alarm goes on and on as it rolls away.

And then the Watch opens.

The covers on both sides and another set from somewhere inside, twist and turn to create a cube. The cube lights up. The lights are a holographic digital clock that shows thirty seconds. The clock is counting down.

The bathroom door bursts open at five seconds. It's Eli. She's pissed. She grabs the Watch from the floor with two seconds left, folds it all back together, puts it back in her pocket, and then the alarm stops. My vision is still a little blurry, but it's clear enough to see the daggers Eli's eyes are firing at me.

"Sorry," I whisper to her. She turns and walks out without a word, taking the rest of the team with her.

All but one.

Zach stands there with his arms crossed and shaking his head. Sighing, I shrug my shoulders at my faux pas. Still unable to hear from the ear-splitting alarm, Zach sends a thought to my mind.

"Meow," is all he thinks, as he holds up a single finger.

Zach

After I was sure that everyone was healed, and I'd consumed more than my share of tea and water; I said my good nights and headed home to the ranch with the band. Heading upstairs, Raffa calls to me before I turn the corner.

"You can't carry that guilt forever. *Tell her.*"

I nod and wave to him. Entering my dark room, I flop on my bed, hope to finally relax and maybe even sleep. Far too wired, I go downstairs, grab a glass, fill it to the top with ice-cold chocolate milk, and grab the phone. Sitting at the kitchen table I make two calls: one to Ash, to ask if he felt up to covering for me tomorrow night; the second to Elizabeth, asking her out on a date. Both agreed, but it didn't make me feel any better. Draining my glass, I wash it out and put it away; Gabe hates finding dirty dishes in the sink first thing in the morning, and I don't need anymore bad feelings on my plate.

Daylight peeks through a gap between the shade and the window frame and warms me awake before my alarm goes off; I take it as a good sign to the start of a new day.

Driving around with Raffa, taking a call here and there, the day flows quickly and Raffa; being Raffa; keeps the conversation lively and bright, enabling me not to think about my mission tonight for a full eight hours. After I shower and change, I decide to head out to Circles early; my nerves are wreaking havoc with my head and stomach; best to get the worst over with and deal with the consequences before I have to call Raffa to come get me.

When I arrive, Connie greets me with a weird, standard-issue, fake smile she gives customers when her heart isn't in it; I guess she still hasn't come to grips with everything yet. Asking her where Elizabeth is, she questions me with attitude.

"Where's the band? Aren't you guys playing tonight?"

"They're on their way. Ash is sitting in for me. Elizabeth and I have a date night."

"Oh…," she says, "I didn't know."

"She didn't tell you?" I ask curiously.

"No…I mean…she probably did, I just haven't been listening…," she answers, so distressed she fidgets like a young child.

Nodding, "I see. Do you know where she…"

"Office," she says, cutting me off quick before storming off with a bin of dishes as if she's mad that I didn't ask why she's angry. How can I condone her childish behavior while dealing with my own; time for her to grow up, just as it is for me

Making my way to the kitchen, I take a deep breath before opening the door. Waving to Carlos and Helen as they work together in the kitchen, I knock on the door of the office and hear a muffled and mumbled 'come in' from the other side. Opening the door, I find the object of my affection sitting behind her desk, gripping a pen in her teeth, and cradling a phone in her neck as she types on her keyboard like a mad woman.

She looks up with surprise, glances at the clock on the wall; but I hold my hand up and say, "I'm early."

Elizabeth nods, holds up two fingers, and tells me, "I'll just be…"

"Don't worry…I'll wait."

Two minutes comes and goes, and Elizabeth bounces out from behind her desk and jumps into my arms, "I was worried I was late…I was half-asleep last night when you called me."

"I know," I say, getting lost in her eyes, "I'm sorry, but I couldn't wait to ask you."

"That's all right…I like hearing your voice before I fall asleep," she replies, suddenly blushing.

Wanting desperately to kiss her, I fight hard not to; afraid to lose myself in her completely and not be able to tell her what I need to say. Instead I hold her close to me; tighter than I should out of a need for her support.

What am I going to do if she doesn't understand?

Elizabeth pulls away and looks in my eyes; tilting her head as she does when she feels something out of the norm. Pulling me in close, she leans her forehead to mine and whispers.

"Talk to me. What's wrong?"

"How do you do that?"

Sighing, "I may not have known you for a long time, Zacharias Neason," she says, placing her hand over my heart, "but, *I know you*...talk to me."

Reluctantly, I set her down; and we sit on the leather couch, facing each other. Taking a deep breath, I prepare to tell her of the terror in my past; but looking in her eyes, I lose my nerve and all ability to speak in the same moment. I sigh angrily at myself, and Elizabeth immediately takes my hand, reaches out with the other, and then touches the side of my head.

"Show me," she says gently, as she closes her eyes and focuses on my mind. Rewinding my memory to my thirteen-year-old self, I show Elizabeth the past that haunts me every day of my life.

Traveling through time with her, I watch as she goes through a series of emotions; at the moment I feared revealing the most, her reaction is not at all what I had expected.

Opening her eyes wide, she gasps and looks at me with the exact emotions I felt at the time; moving from moment to moment, she was reliving my life through me. When I arrive at the end of the ugly scene, Elizabeth can't catch her breath and tears are flowing freely from her eyes. Taking her hand from my face, I wait for her to speak.

"Zach, I..."

"I didn't know how to tell you. I was afraid you would...feel differently...see me as a...*I killed a man, Elizabeth.*"

Swiftly moving closer, Elizabeth wraps her arms around me, holds me tightly and tries to whisper through her sobs, "You. Did. Nothing. Wrong. You tried...to save them.... You were so young; no child should have to...you saw them...oh, Zach!"

"I'm sorry, Elizabeth. I didn't know I could do anything...like, *that*. I..."

"You have *nothing* to apologize for. You did what anyone would do in your place. How could you know that your powers...I'm sorry you had to experience that...I just wish there was something I could do...I..."

"Elizabeth," I say, pulling away to see her face: her big, brown eyes puffy from crying. "You *are* doing something...you're still here," I say, as she smiles gently, still feeling the emotions from the memory. Leaning in, I kiss her; and feel her body give in to me, responding intensely. Changing speeds abruptly, she stops kissing me and pushes me away.

"Ow!"

"What?"

"Ow!" she says, as she yanks her opal out from under her shirt; it's glowing with a reddish tint and getting redder by the second.

"Wow, I've never seen it do that! Is this going to be a *thing* with us? We never seem to be able to get our dates off the ground."

Holding the opal in her hand, Elizabeth smiles and kisses me again; building in intensity until she suddenly stops again and yells, "Ow!" as she drops the stone.

"What the hell…?" I start to say, but stop when we both hear screaming coming from the restaurant floor.

Jumping up and out the door, we meet Carlos and Helen at the doorway; both are wide-eyed and answering the call of the troubled. As we quickly approach the swinging door, Connie comes abruptly stumbling through as if pushed.

Carlos helps her up; her lip is cut and her arms bruised.

"What happened?" Elizabeth asks.

"The ghosts are back! I thought *your mother* said these bags would repel them? Real good spell there, *Helen!*" Connie snaps, tossing the muslin bag at her.

"Watch it, Connie! Friend or not, I will not tolerate you speaking to or about my mom that way. Are we clear?" Elizabeth says. Touching her arm, I feel the tension in her body; and I know there is no calming her down, even if I wanted to. Connie is out of line and has been for a while.

"Yes, Eli. We are clear. I'm so sick of this shit…," Connie barks, as she turns on her heels and pushes open the swinging door; but something on the other side pushes back; and the door hits Connie in the head, knocking her out cold.

"I'll take care of her. You guys go on and see what's happening," I say, picking Connie up and carrying her back to Elizabeth's office. Placing her on the couch, I check her vitals but get distracted by Patrick yelling from the restaurant floor, "Eli! Look out! Behind you!"

Patrick

Twisting and turning, being carried by an evil, shapeless mist, I watch from behind the bar as Eli is carried from wall to wall; her face clawed and cut, she tries to defend herself but can't. Little by little, the longer they are allowed to exist, the clearer their form becomes.

Vorax.

Their angry ghosts seek vengeance for the war they lost with us, and ultimately, with The Void. Helen tries to control them; but every time she raises her hand, a Vorax jumps to her side and pushes or claws her away. Peg joins her, and they unite forces. The longer I stand by and wait for the sisters to control the ghosts, the angrier I get.

Helen tries again; focusing together with Peg, they struggle to move the spectral army off of Eli in a misty lump. Eli falls to the ground; but just as she tries to stand, the front doors of Circles burst open; and the ghosts of our pasts float in, each looking for their token, personal haunt. Following close behind the mass of angry spirits, is the old man. The Necromancer waves his hands to the front doors. At first I thought it was to close them; but instead, he calls another ghost: tall, lean, well-dressed with cold, ice-blue eyes.

Corson.

Floating in, he looks around, finds his target, and goes in for the kill.

"Eli! Look out! Behind you!" I cry; but Corson hits her hard from behind, shoving her face first into the back of the stage with a clatter like all the change in her pockets fell out.

Or was it…?

"Oh, my, God!" Zach yells, suddenly at my side. "Patrick! Let's go…"

"Go? Where?" I ask, but Zach is already gone.

He swoops in, grabs Eli, and yells to me, "*Get it!*"

Frustrated as all hell, I throw my hands out in front of me and yell, "Get what?" and see the Watch fly up from the ground and into Eli's extended hand, as Zach brings her back behind the bar where we started.

Placing his hand on her stomach, Eli moans; Zach's touch to her face heals the cuts and scrapes instantly. She sits up, keeping a tight grip on the Watch; she's breathing hard and pissed...again.

"Someday, you and me, we're going to figure out a way for you to do *that* without getting angry. All right?" Eli says, patting me on the head.

I nod approvingly as Eli walks out in front of the bar; calling to Zach, she points to her mom and Peg who are cut badly. Holding the Watch in front of her, Eli focuses on the ghosts destroying her business.

"Eli, what are you going to do?" I ask, peeking over her shoulder, finally getting a glimpse of the Watch at work.

"Every action has a reaction, and I have to control the ghosts. If I freeze the ghosts, I freeze the Necro; ultimately killing him, then no more ghosts...or; I hold the ghosts behind a wall of some kind, containing them until Mom and Aunt Peg come up with a way to break the Necro's spell. I vote freeze 'em'!"

"No!" Peg yells.

"No?" I ask, unable to believe my ears.

"No!" Helen agrees, as Zach tries to finish healing her cuts but she breaks away. "You can't kill him!"

"Mom, he's calling up ghosts by the butt load. You saw what happened the other night. How can you...?"

"He's your great-grandfather."

"What did she say?" Eli asks me.

Helen comes to Eli's side, "Your great-grandfather. His name is Valko Ivanova. He's a Traveler...a Gypsy. He's a very powerful Necromancer and Shuvani. We have to help him."

Looking back at the mass of ghosts; who are decidedly bored with the destruction of the bar; they start to follow the voices and head straight for us.

"Eli!" I yell, as she turns, pops the Watch open, and focuses on the floating evil and angry cloud, containing them behind some sort of wall with the Necromancer, her great-grandfather, inside with them. One by one, the rest of the team crawls out from where they were hiding.

"Oh, no, no, no. They'll kill him, Eli!"

"Mom, he's one with them. We have to break his spell, or the spell he's under, and separate them."

"I can't."

"You can't? Why? What if the three of you try together?" I suggest.

"We can't...He's strong. Stronger than all three of us combined; and the spell he's *under,* it's also strong and very angry. It would take the dark arts to break it...or..."

"Or?" I ask, wanting to be included in the conversation; I hate being left out. Sean steps in, listening to the conversation. He has that determined look on his face that scares the hell out of me.

"We need a Nahuali," Sean says. " A Shaman. We need Connie."

Connie

Sitting in the BART station again; unable to figure out how I got here and why I have my work apron on; I sit on the bench nearest the escalator and wait.

For what? I've no flippin' clue, but I'm waiting for it.

There are no trains.

There are no people.

Just me...*and* Edna.

"What are *you* doing here?"

"Well, hello to you, too, Kiddo. Aren't you just a bucket of sunshine," Edna says, coming off the escalator, carrying my suitcase.

"Are you going somewhere?" I ask, cooling my tone down.

"No. You are. This is for *you*."

"Where am I going?"

"I don't know. Where *are* you going?"

Confused by it all, and not knowing what to say; I shrug my shoulders.

"Oh?" Edna says, "I thought I heard you say you were tired of this poop, and you were going to leave?"

"I...? I only thought that last part...."

"You? Think? Ha! That's a laugh."

"Excuse me?"

"No, there is no *excusing* you, you little *brat*!"

"Hey!"

"Oh, pardon me…I made *a mistake*. I forgot. No one can make a *mistake* around Miss *Perfect*.

Having had enough of this weirdness, I get up and walk away. No sooner do I make it to the next bench, Edna is there again. She looks me up and down and shakes her head.

"What *now*?" I ask, completely exasperated.

"You can't even run away right. Look! You leave and you're right back where you started."

"What are you talking about?" I ask, standing up and turning around…and find that she's right; I *am* right back at the same bench by the escalator.

"Oops! Connie made a mistake. Shh, don't tell anyone," Edna says, sitting at the other end of the bench with her back to me.

"What did you do with my suitcase?"

"You mean *that* suitcase?" Edna says, pointing to my bag as it sits on the train tracks and explodes.

"*Why* did you *do* that?" I yell.

"Do what?"

"Blow up *my* bag?"

"I didn't blow it up. I simply moved it away from you because it was dangerous; keeping it away from you, kept you safe."

"But it was *mine*!"

"It was dangerous."

"*IT WAS MINE!*"

"Mine, mine, mine…that's all you ever worry about. Keeping everything perfectly in line and just so because *it's yours*. Someone moved something dangerous from your reach to protect you, and you can't even say thank you. All you can say is '*It's Mine*'…well, boo-hoo, little girl. I didn't do it to hurt you. I did it because I care. I guess that's just too hard a concept for you to understand, especially growing up with that ogre of a granny. It's no wonder you're so much like her."

"What?"

"My stars, that woman never did a nice thing for you: took your clothes, took your dolls, took away the privilege of being a child,…and then there are your parents."

"My parents?"

"Oh, yes. You mean, you don't know?" Edna says, keeping her back to me. "Your grandmother hated your mother, you know? Who do you think called the Seguidors? They were supposed to take her away; but she was stronger than anyone thought, and then eventually things went too far and; well, it was only supposed to be your mother. Just goes to show if you want something done right," Edna says, standing up and straightening her white-linen dress, "you do it yourself."

"Grandmother?" I say, shocked at the transformation

"Who did you think it was? The Easter Bunny?"

"But?"

"Stupid, selfish child; you still don't get it? I made you *who* you are."

"What?"

"Well, of course. You expect perfection in all you do; no exceptions, including the people around you. No room for mistakes in our world; and bottom line, *we control everything.* Right?"

"No! No, I'm not like you."

"No?"

"No," I say, incredibly confused but trying to stand my ground. "People make mistakes, even when they mean well; sometimes things don't turn out quite the way they meant, but that's no reason to...to..."

"To, what? Turn your back on them? Stop being their friend because they don't agree with you? Leave them in their hour of need?" Grandmother says, sitting down at the end of the bench again. "They aren't important. What's important is staying true to ourselves and making sure *we get what we want.*"

"I'm *nothing* like you!" I say, as my grandmother turns her back to me and waves me on like I'm bothering her.

"People make mistakes. I make mistakes. It's all right to make mistakes because it means you're normal and not some bigoted, old bitch whose own son didn't love her. People love me. They care about me. And I...I..."

"Connie."

"I...?"

"Connie?"

Sitting up, I suddenly get dizzy; Edna grabs my shoulders to steady me.

"Honey, are you all right? Zach said I'd find you in here; he was right about that nasty bump," she says, looking at my forehead with forlorn. Reaching up I touch it gingerly and wince.

"Poor little thing…I feel bad coming to ask for your help?"

"Help with what?"

"The sisters have tried everything; Eli can only hold the Necromancer off for short amounts of time, seeing as how she's still learning about the Watch and all…Sean says they need you. They need your powers. The shaman powers"

"The Nahuali?"

"Yes; but, if you don't feel up to it, I can…"

""No…I…I think I can…I just don't know how to. What do I do?"

"Well, what do you know about being a Nahuali?" Edna asks.

"Just what I've read: ability to break spells of other practitioners, control the elements of the earth, powers are dictated by their character."

"How so?"

"Well, if I was dark and mean, my powers would be dark and mean."

"Like your grandmother?"

"Yes."

"So, someone as cute, kind, and perky as you…"

"Not of late, I haven't been."

"Connie, you made a mistake. People make mistakes. It's all right, it means they're normal," Edna says, with a wink; and I see that twinkle in her eye that Eli says all domesticated Demons have.

Was it really all a dream or some kind of magical soul-seeking adventure? Whatever it was, I'm ready to face the new world before me and embrace whatever obstacles…and mistakes…I may make.

Bill

Watching my daughter learn to use that damn Watch on the fly makes me wish Uncle Stolas had made training wheels for it. Seeing the ghosts break through for the umpteenth time just burns me up.

"Damn it!" Eli yells. "What the hell am I doing wrong, Tempus?"

"Focus, Eli. Remember what we read in the guide Stolas wrote: heart, mind, and soul all in alignment and then go."

Eli brings the power wall back in line and holds it steady like she's deep sea fishing with a bite on the line. Wanting to show his support, Robert pats her on the back and the wall breaks, sending everyone scrambling for cover.

"Eli, what's wrong? Why can't you...?" Ash asks sincerely, but she cuts him off.

"Every damn action has a flippin' reaction. I'm afraid to hurt him. He's..."

"Your great-grandfather...we know. We heard. Keep trying," I say, listening to the ghosts destroy the building behind the wall as she harnesses the power once again.

Helen returns from the kitchen with Peg and gives Zach a handful of spell-enhanced, herbal pellets; and he sends a few escaped Vorax ghosts away; but for every few he destroys, the old man calls twice as many. As we hear the stage being torn apart, the band, Sean, Patrick, Marco, and Bryant scramble and make a run for it before Eli enacts the power wall. Some of the ghosts have escaped and have the band and Patrick pinned against the wall. Sean uses his last rock salt round and frees the band; he then finds himself cornered with Patrick. As Helen holds on to her locket, she grabs Peg's hand and tries one more time to contact her grandfather when we hear a familiar voice of a long-time, very lost friend.

"Get away from my family," Connie says, looking a little more than scared. Edna stands behind her and nudges her. Looking at Connie sternly, she nods and pounds her fist in her hand as if to tell her to fight harder. Taking a deep breath, Connie turns around and faces the ghosts with that old feisty, fiery attitude we know and love.

"Hey! Retirate de mi familia!" she commands, and the Vorax cornering Sean and Patrick fly away without control to the power wall instantly. A few other Vorax ghosts hover around the bar above us; Connie takes care of them promptly.

"Détente! Vete ya!" Connie yells, sending the specters soaring back behind the wall. "Eli, where's the Necromancer?"

Eli points to the corner of the wall, and the two look back at each other without a clue of what to do; but after a moment, they both seem to remember something.

"Zach, you know that thing you do when you move fast?" Eli asks, as he instantly appears at her side in a blink.

"You mean *that*?" he asks, with that patented goofy grin.

"Yeah, *that*. If I drop the wall, can you go get my great-grandfather before I bring it back up?"

Zach cracks his knuckles and his neck and is back with the Necromancer before he finishes the word 'Go'.

Still entranced, Valko raises his hands to command more spirits, but Helen stops him. "Poppa? No, Poppa, please? Bryant, talk to him. See if you can get through," Helen pleads, as Bryant calmly steps in and talks to the Necromancer.

"Howdy, I'm Bryant; how y'all doin'? I see…ya brought some friends with ya…uh, is there a reason?"

"*He* want's them," Valko says, his voice dry and hoarse.

"And…*he* is?" Bryant asks, trying to lead more information out but an answer comes from a different source.

"Uncle John," Robert says.

"Yes, It's Uncle John," Ash concurs. "Corson's Uncle John…He's…"

"Sandman," Valko says. "The leader of The Brotherhood; he is evil incarnate. *He* has my, my granddaughter, Claudia. *He* has marked us both," Valko says, as he turns his head and reveals a tattoo just like the ones on the two assassins.

"How do you two know this?" I ask Ash and Rob. They look at each other then reply together in perfect synchronization.

"Possession."

"I think I've actually met him. He's very creative. He likes to take pictures," Ash says, looking to me as I recall our conversation yesterday; suddenly ill, Ash grabs his stomach and breathes through his mouth.

"He's *her* brother. He's a soul stealer," Robert adds, falling ill, too.

"*Her?* Who's *her?*" Bryant asks, backing away as if needing to view the big picture or in fear of falling ill as well.

"Lilith," Valko whispers, then starts to choke as if being internally strangled. The Gaelic looking tattoo separates into six pieces of thorny vine that join ends and stretch across and around his neck.

Connie pushes her way through with a growl and grabs Valko by the neck yelling, "No mas! No mas! No mas!"

Valko falls to the floor; Connie shakes and trembles from the spell as the tattoo moves across her hand, heading towards her arm. Angrily she shakes her hand like she is flinging filthy water from it. The tattoo flies from her fingers and breaches the surface of the wall; shoots Eli like a bullet into the group standing behind her.

Evil and angry spirits fly everywhere as Helen and Peg go to the side of Zach, who is trying to help Valko. He appears like used, tissue paper. Zach hands the last of his pellets to the team as they try to defend themselves.

"Poppa? Poppa, can you hear me? We need your help. I'm not strong enough to send this many ghosts back. Even if I were to borrow power from Peggilyn, Eli *and* Connie, it won't be enough. I need your help."

"I can't...I can't help. Can't send back. *He* will know. *He* will *kill* her," Valko cries like a lost child and takes Helen's hands in his. "You must call them."

"Call who, Poppa?"

"Call the families. Use the good souls here. Call to their loved ones. Only they can help you now."

As the rest of us take turns throwing the herb pellets at the spectral barrage, Helen stands, holds onto her pendant, and sends us a message.

"Think, now, all of you...think hard and concentrate...bring to me visions of your loved ones; all those we have lost but will forever live on in our hearts, minds and souls."

The ground quakes and the building crumbles a little more as a bluish mist rolls in from under the front doors. Slowly they open in the billowy fog that glows as it glides across the floor, creating a barrier between the evil spirits and us.

Then the barrier grows.

Taller and higher than even the tallest of us, protecting us from view of the apparitions called to do us harm. Helen speaks to them with her mind; no incantations or magical charms; just her words from the bottom of her heart.

"Please, we call to you today, taking you from your place of rest because we need you…we need your protection. We need your love. These lost spirits aim to harm your loved ones. We need your help sending them back where they belong so they will do no harm no longer."

The mist becomes agitated, swirling and swaying until one by one…they appear. From Marco's father to Zach's parents, no circle of family is incomplete. Every member of The Kindred walks amongst the spirits and finds their loved ones; even our new friend, Tempus, finds his father, and Carlos locates his Uncle César.

At the far end of the mist, Peg recognizes someone. Grabbing Helen's hand, they help Valko up and hurry to be near their mother. Helen turns back and calls to Eli and me; I think; to meet her mother…but when I arrive there, it isn't her mother she is calling me to…it's my own.

Bewildered by what I am seeing, I take Eli's hand and walk to Mom's side. Eli says something to me, but I am too lost in the vision before me. Dad walks up behind us, tears flowing and lost in his own trance. He's followed by Sage as he brings our baby brother to meet Mom; and I have to choke back tears when I see the look in his eyes, seeing the mother he has never known. He reaches out to touch her; his hand combs through the thin, empty, blue mist; and my heart breaks like the dam behind my eyes.

Eli

My Mother...is amazing!

Standing amongst the spirits of all our loved ones, I can't help but notice that even in death these people all have the same twinkle in their eye that domesticated Demons do; a sparkle of life that apparently only appears in those with a good heart and soul.

The spirits look to Mom for direction; and with one nod from her, they sweep through the mass of evil sent to eradicate us and send them back to their place of eternal slumber, leaving behind only the destruction and the smell of rotten eggs. When the room is completely swept clean, the good spirits return to their family members and marvel at each other; parents reach out to their children to touch them, but can't. Children look lovingly at their parents, and the longing to be held is visible on each. Their tired faces and weary bodies ache for just the touch of a hand or a loving word from their family, lost long ago, or in some cases, taken away too soon; some, without a chance to say goodbye, or worse,...I love you.

Thinking back over all that's happened coming to this point, I still haven't found any way of really thanking my family, new and old, for all they have done and sacrificed. I've toasted them, thanked them more times than I can count, cooked for them, and cared for them...but, it's never been enough.

Seeing Uncle Ash busting at his seams with joy; Patrick trying to talk to the parents he lost; and my Zach, fighting tears at seeing the people he loved, who were taken away from him.

Every action has a reaction...

Mom announces to the good spirits that it's time to go, but I stop her.

"Wait, Mom. Not yet," I say, stepping away from the group. Looking at all their tired but happy faces, I take a deep breath, remove the Watch from my pocket, open it, and focus on my command. A warm wind blows from somewhere in the building; melting away the cool, blue mist from the spirits, rolling it away until suddenly…they are corporial.

Standing tall and strong, I fight the power of the Watch that is feeding the spirits and giving them tangible form; it pulls at me, but I bend my knees to gain balance and hold the Watch steady to allow the spirits and their loved ones to have what they most want and need right now. *A touch; a feel;* a chance to *say* what they have longed to say and *hear* what needs to be heard. Watching my Uncle Ash connect with the mother he has never known, tells me in a glance that whatever sacrifice of my time on this plane I give up is well worth the expense.

Finally in control of my breathing, I 'tune-in' to my brethren and feel the love flowing through the room; one by one, I eavesdrop on conversations and emotional interludes happening all around me. Looking around the room, I don't know where to direct my attention first because I simply don't want to miss a single moment.

Marco, Sean, and Uncle Dave all talk together with their parents; Uncle Dave jokes with his brother, Drew, picking up right where they left off. Uncle Carlos, at the age he is now, bears an even stronger resemblance to Uncle César than before. The two join my family for a long-awaited reunion of old friends with those they'd only known by tales told over time.

Bryant, more animated than ever, is performing for his mother, father, a family friend who cared for him as a child, and a beautiful girl with green-gold eyes he loved, even though he never really knew her.

Patrick, usually the quiet one, has not stopped talking. His father laughs at a story he tells; he amazingly resembles Patrick even though he is adopted. When Patrick finally stops to breathe, he reaches out and hugs his mom and dad with everything in his body; not wanting to ever let go, knowing that he will have to for good very soon.

Robert, speaks very seriously with his father, listens intently to every word he says; but then smiles broadly and reaches out for a hug. His mother wraps her arms around both of her men, and they stay in a huddled mass for a long while.

My grandpa, still so enamored with his first and only love, looks at Grandma as if it's the first time he's seen her… and to his brother, Uncle Stolas, he still sees the hero and best friend he always was.

The Gutierrez family resemblance is uncanny. Connie looks equally like her mom and her dad and their connection to one another is seamless; when one speaks, another finishes the sentence. She's crying. She's been an emotional bumper car for two days now. I hope this encounter will heal what needs healing and allow her to move on.

In the far corner of the room, Zach and the band are beside themselves with Zach's parents, laughing and telling stories of past and present. Zach sits on what's left of the stage between his mother and father, arms stretched wide around them both, not letting go until he absolutely has to.

And then there's Tempus.

He makes the rounds from group to group with his father, re-acquainting himself with members in each: Patrick's mom, Zach's dad, Uncle César and Uncle Stolas. He introduces them all to his father, the man who made him who he is today.

Marco starts heading in my direction, eagerly bringing a familiar face my way. Calling my name, he reaches out to touch me; but I stop him.

"Marco, no…I can't. As much as I would love to hug you, Mr. Conti, I can't. I must remain one with the Watch alone. This is my gift to you for raising such an incredible young man."

Marco's father smiles at me and reaches out to touch my cheek but stops just short of doing it. Feeling the emotion from the intent of the touch, my breathing becomes rapid; energy flows through me as if Mr. Conti's spirit is giving me back what I'm spending.

"Thank you, Eli. It was a joy knowing you," Mr. Conti says.

"It was my honor, Mr. Conti."

Tears well in my eyes as I watch my best friend walk away with his hero, and I fight to hold them back in fear of weakening my grip. As I regroup, each member of The Kindred brings their loved ones to me to say hello, thank you, and good-bye. I was doing pretty well fighting the tears until Patrick arrives.

"Eli…you were right. They did know, but I told them anyway."

Patrick's Dad, Kevin, places his hand near my cheek just as the others and asks, "Take good care of my son?"

"Count on it," I promise, tears flowing when I hear him call Patrick his son. Thinking and hoping this is the worst of an emotional evening, I'm not ready for what comes next.

"Elizabeth," Zach says, bringing his parents in front of me. "I'd like you to meet my mom and dad…Mom, Dad, this is…this is *my…My Elizabeth.*"

My heart races; it's the first time Zach has referred to me as anything other than just my name in public….and it's to the two people he holds dearest in his heart.

"Elizabeth, it's a pleasure to meet you. We've heard a lot about you in a very short time. Be happy, little one, for you have made many very happy and at peace tonight," Zach's dad says, leaving me feeling like I was given a glimpse of what Zach will look like in thirty years. Zach's Mom looks to him and nods; answering a previous, private conversation between the two. Zach looks at me and smiles; making me nervous and excited all in one glance.

After Zach and his folks walk away, I realize that everyone has formed a circle around me. Feeling a wee bit unnerved by this, I can't help myself and ask, "What?"

Marco winks at me and points over my shoulder at someone behind me. Carefully turning around, I find three people who have been waiting to speak to me.

"Hola, M'ija!"

"I miss you, Uncle César," I say, almost reaching out to hug him. Instead he reaches out and places his hand near my face like the others. He motions to the person next to him, encouraging me to move on to the next person.

"You are even more beautiful in person than in your pictures, Grandma."

"Must be something about the name," she says, with a sassy wink as she makes her namesake blush.

"So, this is what you're using my Watch for? All that work for a parlour trick?"

Looking at Uncle Stolas, not knowing his sense of humor, I try to figure out if he is serious or joking; then I see the twinkle and I smile.

"Well, I was going to do a big musical number guaranteed to bring the house down, but the ghosts did a pretty good job of that themselves," I say as the back wall behind the stage falls, punctuating my joke's punch line perfectly.

My hand starts to shake, and I suddenly grow very warm; the power of the Watch is draining my strength, and I am tired.

"Times almost up," Uncle Stolas says, "you were right. Fifty minutes is the max."

"That's not bad compared to the earlier trials," Tempus replies, "I'll change the notes on the addendum."

"Notes? Addendum?"

"Yes, Eli...there are more notes. Stolas told me where they are. I'll get them tomorrow, and we'll review them. There were some things *we* couldn't test in the Watch, but tonight *you* confirmed them. Like a Shaman breaching the magics," Tempus says, making a note to himself in a small, leather-bound notebook.

Losing my balance briefly brings a sad smile to Uncle Stolas' face.

"When did you start this, Eli? What time was it?"

"Right on the hour," I reply.

"And how much time has passed?"

"Forty-nine minutes," I say, sadly.

"Helen?" Stolas says.

Mom nods and turns to the families, "We're down to the last minute of power. Please prepare to return."

There are tears, lots of hugs and handshakes, and no one really wants to go; but there is, also, a general understanding of what must be.

Stumbling again, Uncle Stolas reaches out and stops me from falling, momentarily holding me until he fades away into the blue mist he arrived in.

With a tear in her eye, Mom holds her locket, focuses on the energy in the room, and sends the joyful spirits back with a single word.

"Rest."

Peg

Walking with Helen and Poppa along the Berkeley Pier, we talk about our dad, our mom, where Poppa's been, and what happened to him over the last couple of days.

"Poppa, are you cold? You should have on a jacket".

"Done be a ridiculous. I fine, it brisk…Refreshing. After where I been the last few days…it welcome."

"What happened, Poppa? Who is Claudia? How did this 'Sandman' get her?"

"Claudia is you cousin. You father, Julian…he have brother…my son, Niko. We were on picnic on Mt. Tamalpais. Julian want nothing to do with our way of life, so he leave. When he learn you mother a witch and his girls, too…he come, find us, accuse me of having something to do wit it. His brother gets mad. They fight…they fall off mountain. Julian…he supposed to be next Shuvani. His mother, Clara, give her locket to him before she die. Then he die; powers pass to you. My Niko die; he next Shuvani; his powers pass to Claudia, his daughter. Niko's wife kill herself when she hear he dead. I get Claudia to raise."

"And The Sandman?"

"He come to our house in Oakland…charming, handsome…flirt with my Claudia and talk her into reading for him. I have bad feeling about him, walk into parlor where they are, he touch my neck…then I wake up in Dominion. Then…I don't remember…and I wake up somewhere else."

Poppa slows down, suddenly weak; he appears tired.

"Helen, maybe you better get your car and take him home. I think you need to rest, Poppa."

"I think you right. I like the football. I want to be awake to watch Super Bowl. It tonight, yes?'

"Yes, tonight. There's a party at Circles. Would you like to come?"

"Big screen television?"

"Yes, Poppa…"

"And Hot Wings?"

Laughing, Helen stops looking in her purse for her car keys and answers, "Yes, Poppa, and pulled-pork sandwiches."

Poppa wrinkles his forehead, "What is this pull pork…"

As Helen describes how she makes the stewed meat, Poppa's eyes grow large until she mentions the cole slaw.

"Mmm…No. I no eat cole slaw. Give me gas."

"Oh…okay…we can leave it off. I don't suppose you drink beer then?" Helen asks.

"Oh, yes…I drink beer. I like beer. Beer good."

Stifling a laugh as I share a look with Helen, I take Poppa's arm and help him off the pier as Helen runs ahead to get her car.

Hawthorne

Finally agreeing to talk about the past, I request to talk to the team all together so it won't feel like an interrogation. It didn't matter; it still does.

"As you know, Lisette was on a mission. I didn't want her to go, but it was her job and important to her. We were to be married the next day… He was a menace to The Dominion, and he had to be stopped. While his sister was wreaking havoc on earth, he was a cancer to us."

"When you say 'he,' you're referring to The Sandman?" Eli asks.

"Yes."

"And just for clarification, his sister is?"

"Lilith. They're twins…well, more than twins. Best friends. Co-conspirators…Lovers," I explain, and see more than half of the group squirm at my description. The others shake their heads in disbelief.

"Can you describe him?" Sean asks, taking out a notebook and pen from a brown, messenger bag.

"He's tall, white-blonde hair, blue eyes…handsome; always wears a hooded, blue-wool peacoat." I laugh. "I'm a man that's not at all attracted to men…but this guy is handsome. He looks like a runway model."

"Just like Lilith," Eli says. "She's flawless."

Robert squirms in his chair, clearly uncomfortable with the subject. He rubs his face, clears his throat, and then asks, "Why is he called *'The Sandman'*? How did he get that name?"

"He used to sneak into his victim's homes and watch them; sometimes photograph them as they slept. The Dominion Guard has found his encampments numerous times and has photo albums in evidence, filled with photos of the Demons and humans he's killed. He's a different sort…like Corson. Carried the Succubae trait like him, but he steals souls. He leaves his victims in a coma; vegetative state; uses their powers to his benefit until they are gone. When the power is gone, the victim dies. I was working the case at the time. Then after Lisette…apparently, you've found his latest modus operandi with the tattooing."

"Hawthorne, I know it's difficult; but I have to ask…please tell the group about that night? The night you lost Lisette," Bill asks cautiously.

Sighing, I grab hold of my bearings and relive my greatest nightmare.

"I was on a leave that weekend; Sergeant in The Dominion Army then, training with the guard in the Criminal Justice Department; Lisette told me that she needed to go on a mission. The Eternals had a lead on The Sandman. He was encamped in the cemetery and apparently learned through a Speculari General who was working with him, that he was under surveillance. The Sandman became enraged and used one of his more destructive borrowed powers and started destroying anything made of stone. Lisette was caught off guard and turned to her inanimate state too late…he saw her; crushed her with one blow. The army guard has it all on video if you would like to see it."

"That's when the dirty varmint took a piece of her, right?"

"Yes, Bryant. We need the piece to bring her back."

The group grows quiet and pensive. Zach reaches out and places his hand on Eli's. She looks at him, smiles, and then turns her hand over and takes his in hers.

"Is there anything else you can tell us about this 'Sandman'?" Dave asks, as he turns the page of his notepad. I clear my throat and try to recall the details of the case.

"He came from a strained home. His mother didn't want a boy; she wanted all girls, so he had no relationship with her. She placed a wedge between him and his sisters, especially Lilith, which was devastating to him. He started acting up and getting into trouble in his teens. The first time he was arrested was the real turn in his life."

"What happened?" Patrick asks, lifting an orange-plastic stick off his little electronic pad thingy.

"He killed a hell hound puppy and left it on the doorstep of the then King," I reply, acknowledging Asmodeus sitting in the back. "He confessed to the crime, was arrested, arraigned in a court of law, and sentenced. Two hours later, he escaped on his way to prison. When the Royal Guard went to his home to find him, he wasn't there. His father was so upset, a domestic situation took place in front of us; and we had to arrest him."

"Sandman's father?" Zach asks, trying to keep up.

"Yes. His name is Ethan; an Incubus. He was so upset and blamed his wife for all the problems in the family that he destroyed her right in front of us. Grabbed her by her ears and just twisted her head off. It was horrible. Second most horrible thing I've ever witnessed."

"Where is Ethan now? The Void?" Sean asks.

"No. Asmodeus couldn't bring himself to destroy an already broken man. He's in prison, and the Succubae were exiled to the Underworld."

"Hold on there…If them Succubae are exiled, how did Lilith get…?

"I was kind to her," Asmodeus says, hanging his head in regret. "I felt sorry for her and her family. I gave her a job and a place to stay. She took it to mean…more."

Dave sighs loudly, "Shit! Long ago when I first heard you were *kind* to her, I thought, I don't know maybe you gave her a scarf, or stationery, or something…I didn't think it was…?"

Everyone sits; quietly and patiently waiting on each other for more questions.

Eli thumbs furiously through a handout I brought and then switches to her notebook. Sitting with a puzzled look on her face, she realizes something and my curiosity piques.

"Eli?" I ask, smiling at The Sentry at work. "What is it?"

"He was president of The Brotherhood wasn't he?"

"Who, Eli?" Sean asks, trying to jump onto the freight train of her racing thoughts.

"Ethan. He was president of The Brotherhood. This report shows the dates he was arrested, and the dates that Uncle Stolas was appointed," Eli says, thumbing through the pages again.

"Appointed? Who gave Uncle Stolas the seat?" Bill asks, as he leans over Eli's shoulder and reads what she is pointing at.

"At that time, The Brotherhood's Board of Trustees," I reply, as again I watch one-by-one the members of The Kindred jump on board.

"Who made up the Board? What do you know about them?" Dave asks, turning to another clean page of his notepad.

"Long-existing members of The Brotherhood, who were at one time candidates from their clans for Emperor…Kings of each family: Vampires, Werewolves, Ghouls, Wendigos, Speculari…," I stop short to open the old file I brought with me.

"What is that, Hawthorne?" Patrick asks.

"This file is old. It was passed on to me just as it had been passed on to the soldier who worked this case before me. The Brotherhood is ancient; centuries old. It was built in the spirit of camaraderie; a place where Demons of all breeds and levels could embrace their individuality and bury their differences and form...well, a brotherhood. It helped to build The Dominion into what it is today. Over time, things changed. According to my notes, the Board appointed Stolas to clean things up and get The Brotherhood back to what it once was...and not what it had become in the hands of Ethan."

"What had it become?" Sean asks, never looking up from his own notebook.

"A den of thieves and Rogues," I say, "who wanted nothing more than to create mayhem and take what they wanted, when they wanted it, in an attempt to raise themselves up to a place of power. The Board lost all control. Ethan was not a strong leader; he's an Incubus, they're more lovers than fighters. Then he was arrested; Stolas took control and things improved for awhile. Then Stolas was killed; and Lilith's brother secretly took over. Many of the Board escaped and went into hiding. Others weren't so lucky and were killed. It's a *secret society* now, but it's still under Royal sanction."

"What will happen if we pull their charter and shut them down?" Sage asks, with a determined look in his eye as he directs his question to his father as well as me. Asmodeus looks to me for an answer.

"I don't know. In all these notes, there is nothing that says it's ever been done," I answer.

"How do we pull their charter?" Eli asks, with the same look as her uncle.

Asmodeus stands, walks to Sage's side, extends his hand and says, "The Brotherhood is officially..."

"Wait, Grandpa! What y'all doin'? Think 'bout this a flea-bitten minute. If you just up an pull the charter like that, you're liable to piss 'em off and maybe even flush 'em out into the open!"

Zach leans over to Bryant, "I think that's the whole idea, Bry."

"Oh," Bryant says, thinking it over to himself until the light bulb finally goes on, "Oh! Yeah, I see...well okay then. Carry on!"

"Thank you, Bryant," Asmodeus says, with a chuckle. "As I was saying, The Brotherhood is officially dissolved. All privileges are hereby revoked, effective immediately."

"I concur," Sage answers. "Hawthorne?"

"Duly noted, my King. Emperor," I acknowledge. Taking an official form from my black-leather secretary, I fill out the appropriate squares and prepare the document for signature.

"That's it? That's all you need to do? You don't need to confer with officers of the court or have an attorney present? Or a notary?" Zach asks, on behalf of The Kindred, who all sit with the same incredulous look on their faces.

"I *am* an attorney," Sage answers.

"And I'm *a notary*," I add, taking out my ledger and pre-inked stamp.

"And I did confer with officers; *seven of them*," Asmodeus says, indicating The Kindred, "as well as their senior officer." Eli smiles when she realizes he is talking about her.

Presenting the documents to Asmodeus and Sage to sign, Asmodeus turns to Bill, "You know what needs to be done, Son."

Bill nods to his father and takes his cell phone from his belt clip, but stops briefly before making the call to the Royal Army Guard.

"Well, if no one has any more questions for Hawthorne...," Bill says, but he is cut off by the one member who has been quiet for quite some time.

"What's his name?"

"What?"

"His name. The Sandman is a nickname...a moniker, right? What's his real name? Who is he *really*?" Marco asks, angrily.

"Ethan named him Adam because he was the first male child in his family....but he prefers to go by John. *John Smith* to be exact, after the explorer."

Sean

Finishing some notes I made during our staff meeting, I glance around the room and find I'm not alone; Marco is finishing up on notes of his own.

"Interesting stuff, huh?" I say, trying to engage him in a conversation. He hasn't been too talkative of late. "I'm glad at least that we finally had our meeting; long overdue if you ask me…"

Marco looks up and nods; his voice still obviously caught in his throat by a ring left on the sink of the Ladies' Room with no note to explain why, and a fiancé that is MIA.

"Look, Marco…I'm not going to tell you that I know what you are going through because I don't. What I do want you to know is…I'm here for you. Anytime you want to talk, or just hang out and get shitfaced…"

"Eli gave us one of the greatest gifts…and it changed my life in ways that I will never understand," Marco says, coming over to my side of the room. Pulling a chair out, he sits down. "That night, my pop, God love him, dares to tell Connie how he really feels about her. All along, he thought she was a witch. Told me he thought she had some kind of spell on me. That night, she proved him partly right. We told him about our plans and he …he refused us his blessing."

"I've been writing this letter to Connie since that night, explaining how I feel and how Dad's feelings are not mine. Normally, during one of our meetings, if she and I are fighting, my mind can still be drawn away, worrying about her. This time…*I am all about the mission.* I haven't given Connie a second thought. I'm beginning to feel that I'm writing this letter to convince myself more than Connie."

"Marco, I will be the first to tell you that when it comes to these issues, I am no expert. I do, however, believe that everything happens for a reason. It's been three weeks since you found the ring, and no one has heard from her. I think it's time you let go, and let yourself heal. The anger…"

"I'm not angry, Sean. *I'm relieved.* Is that wrong?"

Thinking back on my three failures makes me wish I had someone who told me not to do it…but then again, would I be who I am now if they had?

"No. It's not wrong. It's right, for right now."

Patting my brother on the back, I offer to buy him a beer and he accepts. Leaving our stuff in the War Room, we head out through the Sports Room, grabbing a sandwich on the way and grab two stools at the end of the bar.

"What'r you fellers havin' tonight?" Bryant asks, with a stressed grin.

"Whatever is coldest, Bry," Marco says, as Byant looks at him with a smile.

Bryant glances at me and nods in Marco's direction as if to ask if he's okay…I nod, but it doesn't de-stress the wiry man. Looking around I see Patrick at the other end of the bar talking Tempus' ear off; Dave and Zach in the corner closest to the taped-off construction zone in front of what used to be the stage. Bryant gives us two, cold bottles from a new local brewery, and I stop him briefly.

"Seen Robert?"

"Yep," Bryant says; no smile and the concern on his face was wearing thin, but now I think I know why.

"I take it he isn't well?"

"He's in Eli's office; he's gettin' loud and spoilin' for a fight. Bill and Eli just took him back there to sleep it off. Ever since that night with the ghosts in Pat's house, and then again here…he ain't been the same. He's drinkin'. *Drunk everyday this week!* I's worried. He's mumblin' somethin' 'bout his daddy and what he said to him. Told me he still loved him, but he could *never forgive him.*"

"You talking about Robert?" Pat asks, pulling up a stool beside Marco.

"Yeah…What's with the binge? Do you know?" I ask, and then watch Patrick's eyes. He knows something; but knowing Rob, he asked Pat not to tell. Patrick, being the good little brother he is, isn't about to snitch on his older, more grizzled sibling. Shrugging his shoulders, he lets his body lie for him so his voice can remain true.

Eli walks out of the kitchen with Helen and Ash, followed closely by Grandpa and Hawthorne, who is talking on a cell phone. She stops to say hello as Helen waves, on her way to the Sports Room. Ash signals to Bryant, who reacts quickly and brings him an ice water.

"Whoa! Isn't that a little strong, Ash?"

Ash laughs, "I know, I know. I had to go into the plans archive with Dad, and I always get a dry throat in there. Too dusty!"

"Plans archive?" Pat asks, his interest piqued.

"Yeah, Dad is working on a…"

"No, no, no…it's a surprise, Uncle Ash." Eli says, swearing her Uncle to secrecy.

"What is?" I ask, *my* interests being piqued now.

"Do we not understand the concept of a 'surprise'?" Eli asks. "I think you will all be very happy with it."

"Happy with what, Elizabeth?"

"The surprise that Grandpa is working on."

Zach nods.

"Do you know what it is?" I ask. Zach shakes his head no. "Aren't you in the least bit curious?"

"Don't even go there with him, Sean! *Don't. Even. Go there,*" Patrick says, as he looks to Zach who wears that goofy grin of his.

"Don't worry, Guys. It's good. *Trust me.*"

Eli's words are punctuated by the loud and raucous cheers of the patrons enjoying the Super Bowl in the Sports Room; I take that as a good sign.

Robert

Stepping inside the doors of Circles, I see the band hard at work rebuilding the place from top to bottom. They did a great job making it stable enough to have a full-house for Super Bowl Sunday two weeks ago, but it's gutted now and well on it's way to being bigger and better than before. Waving to Michael, I turn to go and run into an old friend.

"Where the hell have you been?"

"Hello to you, too, Rob. What's going on here?"

"Well, Connie, the place was a little more torn up than we all thought. Michael and the guys were able to make it work for Super Bowl; but after that, well...," I say, motioning to the big fucking mess it is now.

"Where..where is...?"

"Your *friends*? *The team*? Across the street at the office."

"The office?"

"Yeah, *the office*. I'm headed there now. Class starts in fifteen minutes."

"Class? What? Robert, wait!"

"Connie, look, I know how hard it was seeing your folks and knowing how they died. I get it. I do...but there comes a time when you need to pick your own self up and say 'Fuck it' to the things you can't control and then move on. Whatever guilt you're feeling for acting like a brat, same thing."

"Excuse me; you have no idea what I've been going through. Did your grandmother come to you in a nightmare and tell you that she tried to kill your mother? Did your parents' ghosts tell you they knew they were going to die, so they left you behind purposely because there was no one else they knew of to care for you?"

"No," I reply, "They didn't. …but I *was* possessed by the ghost of my incestuous, psycho, half-brother and tried to kill one of my best friends. Then my father told me, after all these years of believing he'd been forcibly raped by that whore in Napa, that he *loved her*. He wanted her…and if it wasn't for me, he would have left with her when she came back with Corson. My mom being pregnant with me is the only thing that kept him here."

Connie's confused but also pissed at me and breathing hard.

"I cried for a week!"

"I was drunk for a week," I say, fully aware of the fucking pity-party she's still harboring and ready to match her shit tit-for-tat. "It's over, all right. If you want to keep your ill will, then so be it. None of your friends are angry at you…"

"No one?"

"Well, maybe one; but Connie, think a minute. You left your goddamn engagement ring in the Ladies' Room and no note. Your phone's been off, and no one knew where you were. Yes, the caveman is hurt. Really hurt, with good reason to be. The rest of us…just really worried."

Connie is staring at me not saying a word, and it gets too fucking old, fast.

"I need to go. I'll be late."

"I'm scared," she says, as I quickly walk away.

"Yeah, I know. There's a lot of that going around. *It's called life,*" I reply, crossing the street.

The giant three-story, mirrored building that Corson used to bring the Vorax army over from was for sale. Asmodeus called in a few favors and bought it. It's vastness allowed us room for a classroom on the top floor, interrogation on the second, and an office for each of us on the bottom. Opening the door, I see my shadow running up from behind. Holding the door open, I wait…and wait…and wait for her to catch up, but she stops just outside.

"Did you become a Vampire in the last two weeks and need to be invited in or what?"

"Actually, that's a myth, you know? Vamps don't need to be invited. They can go where they please," Hawthorne says, giving me today's handout, calendar update, and curriculum. "Ah! Miss Gutierrez, so good to see you. Here is today's information. I've been setting aside everything you've missed. It's all in your office."

"My office?"

"Yes. I can show you after class…or perhaps during the break," Hawthorne says, as he returns to his office in the front of the first floor.

Pressing the button to call the elevator, we ride up together to the third floor. When we arrive, I speed walk down the hall while Connie takes her sweet-ass time looking at the pictures on the walls.

"We decided to put those up. Pictures of fun times at Circles, personal family snap shots. We thought having them up would remind us why we're doing this…you know, during bad times. Peg says they act as a Talisman; it's good energy having them up."

Opening the door to the classroom, Tempus greets me, "Just in time, Mr. Benoit."

"Sorry, I, um…I met a friend outside," I say, once again holding the door for my slow-moving shadow.

Connie walks in shyly; Tempus nods to her; Patrick, Bryant, Sean, and Dave greet her happily. Zach waves as I take the seat next to him.

Marco and Eli ignore her.

The only two seats open are next to both of them. Connie takes the seat next to Eli, farther away from Marco.

Tempus jumps into reviewing the material from yesterday on the difference between Vampires and Succubae, Werewolves and Wendigo and Vampire/Werewolf lore versus the truth. The look on Connie's face is priceless.

"Este bien, Consuelo. Yo te voy a ayudar en lo que has faltado y vas a estar al corriente con los demás."

Relying on only my high school Spanish, I think Tempus told her he'd help her catch up. To which Connie replies, "Gracias, Maestro."

Tempus moves onto today's lesson, and Connie finds she has no pen or pencil. Without looking, Eli reaches inside her binder and takes out a bright pink pencil with a sparkly pom-pom on top and places it in front of her. Keeping her head down, Connie smiles; neither of them looks at each other. Making eye contact right now is difficult for Connie.

Eli knows this. She's smart that way.

I'm sure Connie knows that, and knows Eli would never steer her wrong.

That's why Connie's here.

That's why we're all here.

Tomorrow

Nancy

"We hadn't heard from my nephew, Craig, in weeks, and we were getting worried; it wasn't like him to not call his family. He lives in an older apartment building, just outside the San Jose State campus where he's a student; a Senior next year, Fine Arts major. My older sister, Laura, was frantic, and she asked me to go with her."

"She was jabbering on and on about his new friends and how she didn't like them and that they were scary...Or hairy? I really wasn't sure what she said. She was speaking so rapidly, she sounded like one of those old telegraph machines. Got my car and our dad and then we went to pick her up."

"The drive over was short and quiet. Laura was so pale and her eyes were red and swollen. She was clutching a picture of Craig in her hands. His baby face was smiling up at her with all the promise a newly-graduated high school kid can have. Not a care or worry in the world was on his shoulders. That was meant for his mom to carry now. Tears started to fall from her eyes, and I jammed my foot on the gas peddle."

"The neighborhood Craig lives in is dark; only one street light was alive and glowing: the one directly across the street from his apartment building. The only parking available was under that lamp, so our arrival was obvious and visually announced. Large, dark, two-story building that seemed to breathe us in when we arrived. Someone was at the door before we even closed ours on the car."

"Evenin' folks! To what do we owe this *delightful* visit?" the young, lanky man asked.

"His eyes were glassy like some of the addicts that come in the Emergency Room late at night looking for anything they can pinch, but they weren't red and his face wasn't gaunt like an addict, so I didn't get the impression it was drug induced. He was breathing slowly and deeply;

smelling the air as we walked up. He reminded me of my Rottweiler, Elvis, sniffing the air to see what was coming or what had gone by. Shirtless and shoeless, he was wearing torn blue jeans that were faded six shades lighter than when they started, and his hair needed washing: dark brown, wild, long, with split ends. He reminded me of what a rock star would look like on his day off."

"No track marks were evident on his arms when he welcomed us to the porch; the nurse in me was taking in every physical aspect of the doorman. It's a hard habit to turn off, plus I wanted to help Laura as much as I could."

> "Good evening, Tyson. We came to visit Craig. Is he home?" my sister asked, strangely averting his eyes.

> "Why, yes, he is, Mrs. Marsh. I think Cutter just ordered him a pizza. Welcome to our happy den," Tyson said, opening the etched glass and oak door, welcoming us in with a sweep of his bony arm.

"Dad glanced sideways at me with a warning look I was more than familiar with; he gave it to me once before when I was eight. We were camping; Dad and I went off for a morning hike and came across a bear. Dad gave me *that* look; a look that said do as I do and nothing else. Now, his aged eyes had that same foreboding stare that sent a chill down my back, just like it did then."

"We walked into the old building, announced by the creaking floors and stood collectively with our backs to the oak wall facing Tyson. It was a small, stark lobby to the left of a broad, carpeted stairwell. Straight ahead, down a narrow corridor were three doors; one of which appeared to be a storm door leading to the backyard, a sheer shade covered the glass pane on the top.

"There was an odor. I couldn't put my finger on its exact smell, but at times it reminded me of work: bodily fluids and the weird, sometimes repulsive stink of humans when fatally injured, scared, or near death. Then again, it kind of smelled like Elvis and his bedding when they both needed a good scrub. Tyson closed the door behind us, and the sound echoed through the walls; Laura jumped."

> "Easy girl. Breathe," I told her, hoping to calm her down. She looked at me with eyes wide and face still pale.

> "There's something wrong here, Nanc! That smell?" she started to whisper to me when Dad stopped her and stepped between us.

> "Girls, we're not alone," he said, putting an arm around each of us.

"Mrs. Marsh, how nice! Have you come to join us? For Dinner?"

"No, Cutter, we're just here to see my son," Laura said. *Her voice calm and yet commanding, but her eyes still averting the speaker.*

"If Tyson was the rock star on a day off, then Cutter was five minutes to show time. He strutted down the stairs never taking his eyes off of us."

"His short-cropped, shaggy, black-and-white-streaked hair made his ice-blue eyes cut like daggers through you. His attire matched his hair; black jeans and boots, long, leather jacket with a white shirt that was unbuttoned to his waist. Around his neck he wore a strange charm on a leather cord; it looked like a piece of marble or alabaster."

"Two women followed closely behind him; groupies would be my guess judging by the limited amount of clothing they wore and the putty-knife applied make-up. One blonde, one red head; the latter crossed in front and clung to Cutter's side, glaring at me with black, lifeless eyes while she stroked his exposed abs, laying a more than obvious claim to her property. Quietly bringing up the rear was another male: a hulking mass, three times the size of the others, dressed more like a construction worker. His hair was literally dirty-blonde and long, hiding a majority of his face except for the left eye. It peeked through a split in his greasy mane and inspected each of us closely."

"Oh, I'm so disappointed. I thought perhaps you came to... play. Maybe next time, hmmm?" Cutter said, in an overly patronizing manner.

"The doorbell rang, startling Laura and Dad, but I couldn't take my eyes from the group on the stairwell and their reaction. Their heads snapped to the door's direction in almost rehearsed unison with eyes focused and nostrils flaring, again bringing familiarity of my Elvis when the mailman arrives. Tyson had moved to the redhead's side; and he, too, was at attention."

"Mmmm...Pizza Boy," the blonde female purred.

"Tyson stepped to the door and welcomed the young delivery boy inside the building."

"Delivery for, Craig," the freckle-faced boy said from under the bright red baseball cap, looking from character to character in the confined space and swallowing hard.

"This should cover it young man," Cutter said, leaning over the railing and waving a few bills at the kid. The boy took the cash and started to hand the box to him.

"No, no, give it to those delicious people. They can take it to him," Cutter said, with a devilish grin. The kid turned and handed the box to Dad.

"You should take that to him, door on the right. Now!" Cutter barked, indicating down the hall with his thumb. "GO!" he ordered us.

"Dad, Laura and I quickly moved to the door as a breeze blew in from behind us. I glanced at the door figuring it was the pizza boy leaving, expecting to see the group still watching us from the stairs. But everyone was gone. The door wasn't open; I wondered if it ever was? I wondered what happened to the pizza boy?"

"Laura knocked on the door. Once, twice, but Craig answered before the third. He was thin, frail, and looked like he hadn't slept in days."

"Mom? Grandpa? Aunt Nan...?" Craig said, shaking his head in disbelief as panic took over his sleep-deprived eyes. He grabbed the pizza from Dad.

"You guys shouldn't be here! You have to leave! Please? You have got to get out of here. It isn't...!"

"Craig stopped speaking when the door behind us opened. He looked terrified. We turned to find a faceless being, backlit by a single lamp against the wall of his apartment. He...she...was barefoot, wearing jeans, and a blue hoodie."

"You shouldn't be here. You really need to leave. Please? You...!" Craig said, but stopped again.

"He stopped this time because of the sounds coming from above us; furious movements and scratches at the floor. Muffled voices? Strangled cries? Voices barking orders? We all watched the ceiling, listening carefully. Another sound, strangely familiar, came from above."

"A chill ran down my back when I realized what the sound reminded me of. It was a growl; a territorial growl of an animal claiming its place or its property. Elvis does it all the time when the neighbor's cat comes in the yard."

"Please? I beg you? Go!" Craig cried out as he slammed the door, and we heard several deadbolt locks drop into place.

"You should listen to him. Go," said the voice; a woman's voice; deep and smoky, from behind us.

"I startled at the feel of a hand on my shoulder, but gasped and had to stifle a scream when I saw the condition of the hand: fingers, long and boney with claws where the fingernails used to be. Thick hair covered the top and sides of the discolored epidermis, like fur. The hand began to tremble; then I heard the growl."

"Go...Now!" the woman's voice commanded.

"The hooded being pushed me towards the back and held the creature at bay by holding up her hand. I turned away and pushed my Dad and sister in the direction of the door. Laura opened it as quickly as she could, and we were outside. The being said two words before closing the door, 'left' and 'run'."

"The shadow cast on the frosted pane of the back door was shaking violently as the sounds continued to grow. Growling, snarling, and...howling. Laura gasped and clamped her hand over her mouth when we witnessed what 'it' was becoming. Dad grabbed us each by the arm and dragged us to the left of the apartment building as the girl directed us; and then we ran to my car, locking the doors after we were safely inside. Laura was crying hysterically while Dad was holding her in the backseat, praying as he stroked her hair."

"Starting the engine, I put the car into gear and took one last look at the building and counted five pairs of glowing, yellow-orange eyes watching as we pulled out, made a u-turn, and headed back to the freeway passing the abandoned Pizza Universe delivery car."

Silently, I sit looking at the trio of people listening intently to my story. Through the glass windows of the office, I can see people drawing diagrams on a white board; another cleaning some sort of gun/crossbow combo weapon; and another couple mixing herbs in a pot while others watched and made notes. I had been recommended to them by Edna Blue after I went to the Sheriff's Department to ask what rights we had, and what we could do if we thought someone was being held against their will. My neighbor, Peggilyn, said Edna could help; I hoped she was right. The one introduced to me as Eli spoke first.

"You saw only five pairs of eyes?" she asks, never looking up from her notebook.

"Yes, only five," I confirm.

"A familiar, Sean? Is that possible? It's so out-dated and old school," Eli asks, looking to a man with his nose deep in an old book.

"Could be. In this day and age anything is possible. Bill?"

"If we are dealing with true Were's, yes. But Were's that are *made* are part human, so they use logic and reasoning; but they also have the survival skills of the animal counterpart; the two minds together can devise all sorts of strategies, plus movies and books have them believing lies," Bill says, standing up, getting a pitcher of water and refilling my glass. I didn't realize that I'd emptied it while I was telling my story.

"Ms. Cramer, tell me, when you were in front of your nephew's open door, could you smell or feel anything? Do you remember, maybe a change in temperature?" Bill asks, returning to his chair.

Searching my memory as best I could, I didn't come up with anything. I shake my head, but my thoughts are interrupted by Eli.

"Ms. Cramer, may I?" she asks politely, holding her hand out to me. I hesitate but give in to curiosity and take her hand. A coolness comes flooding over me, relieving the fever in my brain from reliving that night. The brisk feeling gently subsides, and Eli lets go of my hand.

"You smelled rosemary, juniper, acacia, wolf's bane, and thyme coming from his room. There was no way you would have known this, especially with the smell of the garlic in the pizza. You saw books in his room; but again, you'd have no idea what they were. He has an Alchemy Guide and a Grimoire. He's protecting himself as best he can; but to the inexperienced person, using a Grimoire can be tricky. All the herbs he is using are used for protection, but they can also be used for power. He *could* be making the beasts stronger when what he *means* to do is the opposite. And there's one more thing….," Eli says, thumbing through the pages in the front of her notebook. She quickly locates the one she needs, sets the book down by Sean, and indicates something on the page. She holds her hand out to him; he takes it and closes his eyes. Opening them abruptly, he stares at Eli with his mouth open. She looks to Bill and nods with a stern look on her face.

"Ms. Dante, please? What is it?" I ask, feeling my heart race faster with each passing second.

"You left something out of your description of Cutter and his pack, Ms. Cramer. The tattoo on his neck, it was an hour glass. Do you remember it?" Eli asks, touching the right side of her neck.

"My God! How could I forget that? Yes, of course!" I say, nodding to her, feeling that somehow a breakthrough has been reached. Eli smiles.

"Well, Ms. Cramer, that hourglass is the mark of a very dangerous Demon that we've been tracking. The girl who helped you escape is a Shuvani…a Traveler…a Gypsy witch. Her powers are being used by this Demon for all sorts of things. For some reason…he wants your nephew. It seems this Cutter was cursed, and he's sharing it with others. They are…well, guard dogs. Do you want the good news or the bad news first?"

"Six of one, half a dozen of another," I say.

"The bad news is you're correct. Your nephew is indeed being held against his will; and yes, he is in very grave danger of either being eaten, being turned, or giving the Demon what he wants and becoming a slave to him for the rest of his life, or being killed because he's no longer needed," Eli says very seriously.

"And the good news?" I hesitantly ask, watching a smile come to Bill's face. He speaks and the hope returns to my heart.

"You've come to the right place, just in time."

Acknowledgements

To my three, personal "Eternals"; Candy Cota; my sister and partner-in-crime, Sharon Smith; Editor and Grammar Goddess, and Margo Donohue, my best friend and Muse of Hope. Thank you, thank you, thank you, thank you, thank you!

Eric Raleigh; (the real "Tempus" in my life) It's been a long time, my brother. Thank you for your time, patience, friendship and for the opportunity to let you shine like the star you are.

Eren Loza – Gracias por su ayuda, mi hermana.

The Web Administrators at UC Berkeley (http;//www.berkeley.edu/ucbwww@berkeley.edu). You guys rock! Thanks for your endless assistance! Go Bears!

For all the followers on Facebook, Twitter and Goodreads, thank you for your generous support!

Special thanks to Danielle Goddard, Annette Monteriro-Parker, Leesa Paige DeJager, Angel Aguilera, Deanne Rhoton-Hein, Chris Messer, Dan Lopez, Erin Fyfe, Greg Beltran, Anita Bernard, Dawnette Brenner, Sam Reeves, Mark Nelson, Keith Minyard, Greg Frates and Claudia Luce for all your personal support reviews in helping to bring the Dante Chronciles to the public. YOU, are all worthy of "Kindred" status!

As always, many thanks to my family who serve as not only a source of inspiration, but the greatest example of what it takes to be a family. Still dancing, Mom and Dad! Love you all so very, VERY much! Cheerz!

"For all those we have lost, but will forever live on in our hearts, minds, and souls..."

William Leon Goff, Lynn William Hossum, Kathy Kenyon-Crummy, Nate Winston Wood, Buffy Loza, Lucky Loza, Martín Loza, Marilyn Rainey, Felix O. Cruz Jr., Tracey Ann Nelson, and "Zeus", Michael Dowling, Joseph Brian Donohue, John Dpnohue, Rose Marie Donohue, Joseph Brian Fonohue, Derek Torley, Robert "Bobby" Beltran, Ruth Jackson Maziarka (Mimi), Adele Dean, Shaun Alan Fyfe, Terrie Stahl, Wilma Jean Reeves, Samuel H. Reeves, Sr., Lucy Jane Young (Nanny), Mario Bertolotti, Annie Mae (Snow) Myatt, Kevin Allen Rhoton, Darren Allen Scott Brenner, Arnold Monteiro, Rudolf and Nellie Franke, Thelma "Nonnie" Miller, Lidia Aguilera, Leo Minyard, Harold K. Carstensen, Aurelia Camacho, Carlos Zavala, Felipe Zarrate, Frank Moreno, Ida Moreno, Juan Cota, Candido Cota, Marian Cota, Laura Cota-Mele and Jenette Zavala Herring.

...the world is a little less bright without you... Rest.

Made in the USA
Middletown, DE
04 November 2023

41863333R00172